continued . . .

Titles by CJ Lyons

CRITICAL CONDITION
URGENT CARE
WARNING SIGNS
LIFELINES

CRITICAL CONDITION

CJ Lyons

JOVE BOOKS, NEW YORK

THE BERKLEY PUBLISHING GROUP
Published by the Penguin Group
Penguin Group (USA) Inc.
375 Hudson Street, New York, New York 10014, USA
Penguin Group (Canada), 90 Eglinton Avenue East, Suite 700, Toronto, Ontario M4P 2Y3, Canada
(a division of Pearson Penguin Canada Inc.)
Penguin Books Ltd., 80 Strand, London WC2R 0RL, England
Penguin Group Ireland, 25 St. Stephen's Green, Dublin 2, Ireland (a division of Penguin Books Ltd.)
Penguin Group (Australia), 250 Camberwell Road, Camberwell, Victoria 3124, Australia
(a division of Pearson Australia Group Pty. Ltd.)
Penguin Books India Pvt. Ltd., 11 Community Centre, Panchsheel Park, New Delhi—110 017, India
Penguin Group (NZ), 67 Apollo Drive, Rosedale, North Shore 0632, New Zealand
(a division of Pearson New Zealand Ltd.)
Penguin Books (South Africa) (Pty.) Ltd., 24 Sturdee Avenue, Rosebank, Johannesburg 2196,
South Africa

Penguin Books Ltd., Registered Offices: 80 Strand, London WC2R 0RL, England

This is a work of fiction. Names, characters, places, and incidents either are the product of the author's imagination or are used fictitiously, and any resemblance to actual persons, living or dead, business establishments, events, or locales is entirely coincidental. The publisher does not have control over and does not have any responsibility for author or third-party websites or their content.

CRITICAL CONDITION

A Jove Book / published by arrangement with the author

PRINTING HISTORY
Jove mass-market edition / December 2010

Copyright © 2010 by CJ Lyons.
Cover photograph by Claudio Marinesco.
Cover design by Rita Frangie.
Text design by Kristin del Rosario.

ISBN: 978-0-515-14868-8

JOVE®
Jove Books are published by The Berkley Publishing Group,
a division of Penguin Group (USA) Inc.,
375 Hudson Street, New York, New York 10014.
JOVE® is a registered trademark of Penguin Group (USA) Inc.
The "J" design is a trademark of Penguin Group (USA) Inc.

PRINTED IN THE UNITED STATES OF AMERICA

10 9 8 7 6 5 4 3 2 1

This book is dedicated to all of my readers:
Thanks for joining me for the ride!
Hope you had as much fun as I did.
—CJ Lyons

ONE

Friday, December 31, 6:24 P.M.

HIDING BEHIND A SMILE, DR. GINA FREEMAN OPENED the door to her fiancé's hospital room.

She watched from the doorway, juggling a bulging garment bag and a tote, assessing the scene before committing to entry.

It was a typical hospital room, like so many the world over. Until she was forced to spend the last few weeks at Jerry's side, she'd never realized just how much the typical hospital room resembled a jail cell.

There was no privacy. People came and went as they pleased. Except for Jerry, who was expected to be always in the same place until called for. Everything was beige: the walls, the floors, the curtains, the food, the view, the smells of floor wax and body odor, even the smiles of the caretakers—at least the ones who hadn't known Jerry or Gina from before the shooting.

The smiles of the ones who had, those smiles were tentative, fearful of unraveling the delicate shift in power between Gina and Jerry that was so obvious to everyone except Jerry. Suddenly Gina found herself the caretaker, the one making decisions for and about—but seldom with—Jerry.

She dared a step inside. Jerry sat in his bed, on top of the beige blanket, wearing his Steelers sweatshirt. There was no food on the wall or window, no soft restraints on his wrists to keep him from throwing things, and the nurses hadn't confiscated his "real" clothes or slippers, so it must be a good day. As good as days around here got since the shooting, anyway.

Normally it would be Jerry, a detective with the Pittsburgh Bureau of Police and consummate people-reader, who would have picked up on these little details, not Gina. But then nothing had been normal, not since a hired killer had almost killed both of them and ended up shooting Jerry in the head.

Everyone except for Gina seemed to have forgotten that first part, that she'd been targeted too, but she hadn't—how could she?

Snuggled alongside Jerry was Deon, the ten-year-old great-grandson of the hospital librarian, Emma Grey. Deon had adopted Jerry for his own a few months ago after they'd first met. Emma sat beside the bed, in the visitor's chair in front of the window, knitting something bright and colorful and most definitely not beige.

The windows, opaque with frosted snow and fog from their breaths, reflecting the overhead lights, added to the home-for-the-holidays glow. Deon held a picture book open and was reading aloud from *How the Grinch Stole Christmas*.

More like the hit man who stole Christmas, Gina thought. But if Jerry was having a good day, she'd fake some New Year's cheer. Odds were he wouldn't remember or realize her efforts, but it was important to keep the peace.

After working a twelve-hour shift in the ER, she was long past due for some peace. Although the ER had been reasonably quiet for New Year's Eve—except for a deluge of car accidents caused by the arrival of the snow this afternoon. But then things had slowed down for most of her shift as the city waited for the plows to work their magic, slow enough that her boss, Mark Cohen, had let her leave a half hour early. He knew she was dividing her time between the ER and Jerry, but as an emergency medicine resident, Gina didn't have the luxury of being able to take the holiday off.

The overhead fluorescent lights reflected off the fresh scar tissue crossing from ear to ear over the top of Jerry's shaved scalp as he nodded in time with Deon's words, following the little boy's finger as it traced the words, scrutinizing each letter, searching for a key to hidden treasure.

If the shooter's bullet had been a centimeter in any direction . . . Gina shivered away her fear along with the memory of bullets, blood, and her own screams.

She busied herself hanging up the garment bag, removing her shearling coat and shaking the snow from its shoulders before draping it over the door handle while they finished the story. Jerry didn't seem to notice the tears streaming down his own cheeks as Deon closed the book. He didn't notice Gina either.

"Happy New Year's!" Gina called out gaily, placing a bottle of sparkling cider on the bedside table.

"Gina's here!" Jerry shouted.

As if he'd never expected to see her again. He always greeted her with the same startled expression whether she'd been gone fifteen seconds or fifteen hours. She couldn't help but wonder if he totally forgot she existed in between.

His smile was brilliant, piercing her heart. With joy that he was alive. With fear of what could have been. Heartbreak that in many ways, she had indeed lost him anyway.

Then he followed with the same greeting he gave every woman who walked into his room: "Where've ya been, sunshine?"

Emma, one of their many friends who'd been helping out since the shooting, bundled up her knitting. "Happy New Year's, Gina. He's having a good day today, aren't you, Jerry?"

"So I see," Gina said. "Did he have dinner yet?"

"He wasn't hungry and then he took a nap, so no." Emma straightened the stack of books that lay at the foot of the bed. Mostly children's picture books. Before the shooting, Jerry had been the one reading to Deon—he'd been reading the boy *The Lord of the Rings*, censoring out the "gory" bits, although they both knew that Deon was sneaking peeks so as to not miss anything juicy.

"What happened to the hobbits and orcs and that big, slimy spider?" Gina asked Deon.

Deon squirmed, then, to Gina's surprise, hopped down from the bed. He avoided her gaze as if caught in some kind of betrayal.

"No mood," Jerry answered her question, using the clipped shorthand that colored his speech now. He reached for the tumbler of water at his side. He made two attempts, missing both times. Deon expertly snagged the glass, adjusted the straw, and held it up to Jerry's lips in one well-practiced motion.

Jerry frowned and shook his head, refusing to drink. "Headache. Go 'way." His speech was as blunt as a two-by-four. He lay back on his pillows and closed his eyes, dismissing them all.

Deon joined his Gram, taking her hand in his. "He can't read anymore," he whispered to Gina, shuffling his feet as he tattled the awful secret. "I miss the old Jerry. He promised to take me hiking, teach me how to use the compass he gave me, show me how to take pictures of the animals and stuff. When is he coming back?"

Same question Gina had been too terrified to ask herself. She dredged up a new smile, lowered herself to crouch at Deon's eye level, and offered him the same clichés the neurologists had given her. "It takes time, Deon. Healing takes time. And sometimes"—her words snagged and she had to swallow before finishing—"sometimes people change. But he'll get better."

She stopped short of making a promise she couldn't keep. Deon pursed his lips and narrowed his eyes, too smart to blindly believe. Gina would have applauded his skepticism if she didn't need so badly to believe herself. She pulled him into a hug, denying the tears she was desperate to shed. He too-quickly squirmed free.

"Hey, before you go, I found a Christmas present for you." She'd finally had the energy to face Jerry's ransacked apartment and, while sorting through the debris, had stumbled across a bag filled with gifts. She hadn't had the strength to unwrap hers, but no sense not giving Deon his. She handed him the box. Jerry had wrapped it in crime-scene tape—which somehow didn't seem so funny anymore.

Deon eyed it with suspicion, hefting it. "What is it?"

"I don't know. Jerry got it for you." Gina shoved her hands into the pockets of her cardigan and looked over at the bed. Jerry was now asleep. One of his frequent catnaps that had replaced normal sleep. Sometimes he'd fall asleep in the middle of a sentence, only to wake a few minutes later confused and combative, trapped in the memory of fighting for his and Gina's lives. "It's okay, he won't mind if you open it."

"Can I, Gram?"

"Of course. As long as you don't forget to thank Jerry later."

"I won't." Deon eagerly shredded the tape, exposing a pocket-sized digital camera. "Wow!" He turned the box around, already immersed in the directions and list of features. "Zoom! Look, Gram!"

"What do you say?"

Deon threw his arms around Gina. "Thank you, thank you! It's the best ever." His voice dropped into a whisper. "If Jerry doesn't get better, maybe I can teach *him* how to take pictures again."

"I think he'd like that." If any part of Old Jerry had survived, it was his artistic vision. The one activity that seemed to calm him was scribbling with crayons and markers, delighting in combining them to create kaleidoscopes of vibrant color.

"We'd better go before the roads close with the snow," Emma said with a glance out the window.

"I heard they were pretty bad. Be careful." Gina stood, then noticed the Dr. Seuss still clutched in Jerry's hand as he slept. "Don't you want your book?"

Deon didn't even look back. "Jerry can keep it. He *is* still my friend."

Out of the mouths of ten-year-olds. Gina watched the door close behind them, tried not to envision a prison door clanging shut, trapping her with her beige future.

She sighed and turned back to the bed, then started. Jerry lay perfectly still with his eyes now open, watching her warily. How much had he heard?

New Jerry was paranoid when people whispered around him. New Jerry hated being talked about. Hated it more that even when he was a participant in a conversation, half the time he couldn't remember it five minutes later. And New Jerry really, really hated being reminded of his shortcomings.

She freshened her smile for him as she rearranged the get-well-soon trinkets and flowers arrayed along the windowsill, simultaneously sliding them all out of reach of his throwing arm. "I'll get your cane and we can go for a walk."

He grunted at that—he felt self-conscious, stumbling through the hallways leaning on a three-footed cane for balance. "No. Too many people." Jerry flung his hand toward the snow-frosted window. "I want to go out."

"There aren't really that many people. And you don't want to go out in this weather. They say this storm might grow into a real blizzard. The entire city is pretty much shutting down." Gina was prattling, but New Jerry wasn't exactly a sparkling conversationalist.

He said nothing, just kept watching her, a stranger who wore Jerry's face like a Halloween mask that slipped and wrinkled in all the wrong places.

"Want my gun."

New Jerry was only nineteen days old—and had spent the first three of those in a coma. His gag reflex still wasn't working properly, so he couldn't handle anything more solid than oatmeal without triggering a coughing fit. He was easily frustrated, especially when he couldn't ignore his new clumsiness and inability to perform simple tasks that used to be automatic, like adjusting a toothbrush to the right angle while looking in the mirror. He couldn't sleep and alternated between outbursts of tears, laughter, fury—sometimes all three at once.

Words and faces and entire chunks of his life had been lost to him, maybe forever. He remembered Gina but had forgotten their engagement, and seemed to have blacked out most of the shooting, except for when he dreamed. Yet he constantly asked to see Lydia Fiore, the ER doctor who'd been the real target of the hit man.

And his gun, he wanted his gun back; he would retreat into a glowering silence for hours if she didn't let him have it.

Gina blew out a sigh that left a steam cloud floating on the window, obscuring her reflection. Her dark skin was dull and had lost its shine, her braids were haphazard, her eyes appeared bruised. The woman in the window was a stranger. She drew Jerry's Beretta from her sweater pocket—it was unloaded, of course—and handed it to him. He grabbed it greedily, clutching it like a security blanket. For the first time since she'd entered the room, his face relaxed, a glimpse of Old Jerry—*her* Jerry—winking into sight.

Then it was gone once more. "Lydia?"

Never once did he ask how Gina was—ask about her own nightmares and lack of sleep and outbursts of tears, laughter, fury. So totally unlike Old Jerry who had cherished and protected her, solved her problems, vanquished her fears, and wrapped her in Kevlar.

"It's New Year's Eve," she said, forcing a laugh, hoping it disguised her anger. If it weren't for Lydia, he wouldn't be lying here, both their futures in shreds. "I'm sure she and Trey are home celebrating."

"She's okay?" He frowned as if Gina's words made no sense. As if Lydia hadn't come by to visit him every morning since the shooting. "Sure?" He scratched at his scar and the stubble of dark brown hair growing back on his shaved scalp. "I need to—can't remember—"

"She's fine." Her words cracked through the air between them. "Forget about Lydia. Let's work on getting you up and moving." *Getting you back to normal,* she wanted to say but didn't.

She ducked her head to reach for his slippers under the bed, hoping the movement hid her fear: Life would never be normal again.

He ignored her as she knelt before him, guiding his feet into the slippers. Cradling his gun, he rubbed it as if it were Aladdin's lamp, waiting for a genie to emerge. "Don't know," he whispered, clutching her shoulder, his gaze skittering around the empty room, searching for enemies. "Not safe. Out there."

"It's okay," Gina lied. She stood and wrapped her arms around him, gun and all. "I'll keep you safe."

AMANDA MASON LEFT THE HOSPITAL CAFETERIA through the front door, clutching her prize: a large aluminum can clad in a black-and-white generic label. She paused for a moment, looking at the way the snow swirled over the glass walls and ceiling of the spacious atrium to her right. The snow was pretty, but she hoped it didn't get any worse—she had big plans for tonight.

Turning her back on the atrium, she passed the auditorium and went to the rear elevator bank reserved for staff and patients, which usually moved a bit faster than the visitor ones. Although the elevators' idea of "faster" left a lot to be desired. She was debating taking the stairs instead when she saw ER charge nurse Nora Halloran approaching from the hallway behind the auditorium, pulling on a jacket over the top of her scrubs.

"Can you believe how quiet it is?" Amanda asked by way of a greeting.

"The ER got a bit busy when the snow started, but we haven't had a new patient in the past two hours," Nora agreed.

Amanda noticed how her friend avoided the use of the Q-word—ER people were so superstitious. She herself missed the hustle and bustle that usually energized the hospital. This quiet was nothing less than eerie; it made her nervous, like the way the wind held its breath before a squall hit back in her hometown on the South Carolina coast. But Pittsburgh was home now, ever since she'd left the Lowcountry to attend medical school here four years ago.

"With the holiday and no elective surgeries, we only have four patients in the PICU. Rounds went by like lightning," Amanda said. It was the last day of her pediatric ICU rotation but, despite the holiday, the PICU fellow had initially scheduled her to be on call. Which, with so few patients in the unit—and since as a medical student she was low person on the totem pole when it came to any interesting procedures—also meant sitting around doing nothing.

"Any news on when Lydia's coming back to work?" she asked Nora.

"Don't know. Hard to do much in the ER with one arm out of commission." Nora punched the elevator call button again even though it was already lit. "Have you been up to see Jerry yet today?"

"I stopped by around lunch. He's doing good today, only got frustrated once. Said he was tired of everyone treating him like he wasn't normal."

"He might never be back to normal," Nora said in a soft tone.

"Don't talk like that. Lucas says it's a miracle Jerry survived at all, much less came out of the coma as quickly as he did." Lucas Stone, Amanda's fiancé, was Jerry's neurologist.

"Is that what you have there?" Nora nodded to the can Amanda held. "More of your sensory therapy?"

Every day Amanda had brought Jerry something to stimulate one of his senses—lilac water sprinkled on his pillow, a fuzzy koala bear with whiskers that tickled, a Bach CD. Lucas had given her articles on traumatic brain injury, so she was trying her best to help any way she could. "Something must be working. He's making progress."

"What is it today?"

"The cafeteria ladies found me some banana pudding. Isn't that great?"

Nora took the can of pudding and squinted at the label. "You realize that bananas aren't even listed in the ingredients?"

"The gift shop is closed because of the holiday. It's the best I can do."

Nora's cell phone buzzed. She glanced at the display, sighed, and closed it. "Seth. Checking up on me. I called him twenty minutes ago to let him know I'd be late getting home, but—"

"He's worried about you. After the shootings, you can't blame him." Seth was Nora's fiancé, a surgical resident who had also been injured the same night that Jerry was shot and Lydia broke her arm. Amanda hated even thinking about that night—though it could have been so much worse than it was. Both Nora and Seth had almost died on that awful night, along with Lydia, Gina, and Jerry.

"I know. And I'm worried about him—he's been climbing the walls, waiting for the doctors to let him get back to operating."

"Gina said they were letting him go back to work in the clinic next week?"

"Thank God, he can finally stop driving me crazy." Despite Nora's words, Amanda knew she was more concerned about Seth than she wanted to admit. "It's hard, you know." Nora's tone lowered and she stared at the elevator button as if confiding in it instead of Amanda. "We both want—need—to talk about it, but neither of us wants to let the other know how bad . . . how close . . ."

Her words trailed off. Amanda said nothing, instead just wrapped an arm around Nora and hugged her hard. Sometimes she felt guilty that she'd missed it all, taking care of a sick patient in the PICU, but then she'd see a shadow pass over one of her friends' faces and realize how blessed she'd been. She only wished she knew how to help them better. Bringing Jerry pudding and stuffed animals seemed so trivial compared to what he and the others had faced.

The elevator, which always seemed to have a mind of its own and was moving no faster than usual despite the paucity of people in the hospital, finally arrived. They stepped on, Amanda pressing five for the med-surg patient floor and Nora eight.

"Where are you headed?" Amanda asked.

"Summoned up to Tillman's office." Nora nervously patted her hair, as if her auburn strands weren't already meticulously aligned.

"I didn't think the hospital CEO would be working on New Year's Eve."

"He has to decide whether to call a snow emergency now and pay those of us trapped here for overtime, or if he should call the next shift in early and risk paying *them* overtime to sit around and do nothing."

"The snow isn't that bad, is it? No way am I going to get trapped here. Not tonight."

"So you did get tonight off?"

"Yes." Amanda did a little twirl. "It's off to the ball for this Cinderella. Gina is bringing me this killer dress and shoes to go with it. A real-life ball gown! You should see it, it's silk and matches my eyes and—"

"And Lucas agreed? To go to a fancy ball at Gina's folks' country club? That doesn't sound like him." Nora smiled and Amanda knew why: The thought of genius germophobe Lucas Stone trying to blend in with rich folks like Gina's parents was kind of funny. "What's he going to eat?"

Lucas never ate anything touched by someone else's hands. At least he hadn't until he'd met Amanda and she'd won him over with her Southern charms—and cooking.

"Hah! That's my plan. If he can't eat anything, he'll get drunk all the faster."

"Why do you want to get Lucas drunk?"

"Between this PICU rotation and his work we haven't had a night together—and even if we did, ever since he met my folks, he's acting all old-fashioned. Says no sex until after the wedding."

"The wedding's not until May."

"Exactly. I'm sorry, but I have needs. So tonight's the night. We'll go to the ball, I'll get him drunk, and"—she grinned a wicked grin—"I'll have my way with him." Amanda waggled her eyebrows like a silent-movie Dastardly Dan villain.

Nora laughed. It was the first time Amanda had heard her laugh in weeks. "Poor Lucas. He doesn't stand a chance."

LYDIA FIORE CARESSED THE TRIGGER OF THE TAUrus .357. *Bam. Bam.* A double-tap to the head followed by two more quick-fire shots as she nailed the nine-ring near the center of the target's chest.

Each recoil lanced up her left wrist, across her shoulders, and down her right side, the broken bones in her right arm screeching until her pulse twanged in her eardrums. She lowered the revolver, shifting her weight, her cast dragging her sling against the back of her neck.

"Still feels shaky," she said.

Sandy McKenna, the range master, shook his head, laughing as he reeled in her target. "This fellow might disagree. Hate to think that's your weak hand."

Pain and nausea squared off in Lydia's gut, duking it out to see which could flatten her first. Pain, not just from her broken arm, but also from the memory that came with it: Just nineteen days ago she'd been forced to kill a man. Shoot him dead. Brain and blood and bits of skull splattering against her in an unholy ricochet.

It was different from the deaths she'd encountered during her career as an emergency physician. In the ER, she used all her skills to fight death, and won many of those battles. But during the events nineteen days ago, she'd been forced to watch as a man sent to find and kill her targeted her friends. Just as eighteen years ago, she'd been forced to watch as another man killed her mother.

The fact that when Detective Jerry Boyle had reopened the investigation into her mother's murder, he had somehow—for reasons Lydia didn't understand—summoned a killer to Pittsburgh, to her own hospital, made things worse. Not only did she have the blood of the man she'd killed on her conscience, but the blood of her friends haunted her as well.

It wasn't over yet. Whoever had sent the hit man—someone who obviously wasn't worried about how many innocents died during his search for Lydia—was still out there. Somewhere.

And she had no idea why he was hunting her.

The unwanted taste of fear scratched at her throat as Lydia cleared the rounds and reloaded the snub-nosed revolver. It was hard with one hand, but she refused Sandy's help. He'd been kind enough to give her the long-term loan of one of his own weapons—a kindness not taken lightly, not when the man doing the lending was a police officer and former army sniper. He'd chosen the titanium snub-nosed Taurus .357 because it was small enough for her to carry on her person and she wouldn't have to mess with a manual safety or a slide. Still, she missed her Para-9, now safely ensconced in the bowels of the Pittsburgh Police Bureau's evidence lockup.

"Try the laser sights. Your Para doesn't have those. Pretty sweet for such a tiny thing, ain't she? Even if she does only carry five rounds." Sandy activated the sights to demonstrate. "How's Jerry doing? The guys been asking."

An image of Jerry's goofy grin—he smiled more than anyone she knew; so strange for a cop, but then Jerry wasn't like any cop Lydia had ever met before—flashed through her mind. Fast on its heels was the vision of him, covered in blood, one bullet through the head and one in the gut. He was lucky to be alive.

Even if he might never be the same again. All because of her. Because he was her friend and had made the mistake of trying to help her find her mother's killer.

Lydia sucked in her breath and froze. Then she fiddled with the strap on her sling to cover. "I heard they're getting ready to move him to rehab in a few days."

"That's good." Sandy paused, his gaze raking over her, taking in everything she wasn't telling him. Zeroing in on her expression before she could shut it down, block her guilt. "You're taking time off, right? Whenever us cops discharge our weapon, we're benched until the headshrinker clears us. Not a bad idea, I guess."

His way of asking how she was doing.

"I'm fine." Other than the nightmares, pain, nausea, flashbacks, and constant dread of worse yet to come, it was the truth.

Sandy's look said he didn't necessarily agree with her assessment of her well-being. "Never hurts to talk."

Great. Another worried man for her to deal with. Bad enough she had Trey hovering over her in between his shifts as district chief of Pittsburgh's EMS. She'd sneaked out after he'd left for work, knowing he'd freak when she brought another gun into the house. But she felt naked without her Para-9. Like there was a bull's-eye between her shoulder blades and no place to duck and cover.

Shoving her fears aside, she slid the Taurus into the

paddle holster at the small of her back, turned away from the targets, then whirled back, drawing and firing four shots in quick succession. Sandy whistled at the results. "Nice."

Lydia squinted downrange. The bullet holes were so close together they made one not-so-big hole between the eyes and another through the heart. Bingo.

Ignoring the pain whipping her guts into a nauseated frenzy, she said, "Told you I was fine. I'd better get back home before Trey gets off work."

"Happy New Year's, Lydia," Sandy said as she turned to leave.

Lydia stopped and glanced back. The pricking between her shoulder blades intensified. Gauzy blurs of her mother's bloody body, of Jerry in the ICU, of the man she'd shot filled the void between her and Sandy, Technicolor ghosts dancing in the gun smoke.

"Happy New Year's, Sandy." The words emerged like a eulogy.

Lydia walked away, the weight of the Taurus at her back more comforting than any holiday cheer.

TWO

NORA HALLORAN HAD NEVER BEEN CALLED TO THE principal's office during all her years in school, but now she knew what it felt like. Oliver Tillman, the Angels of Mercy Medical Center's CEO, kept her waiting for twenty minutes before he deigned to make an appearance.

The visitors' chairs in front of Tillman's elevated desk were sleek Scandinavian designs that looked stylish but were painful to sit in. Nora would have preferred to stand but didn't want to look nervous. So she sat, her butt falling asleep and a wooden dowel poking into her spine with every movement.

Then the man himself arrived. A few inches shy of six feet, compensated for by a blond toupee puffed up to make him look taller, Oliver Tillman liked to describe himself as Pittsburgh's answer to Donald Trump. As if his overbearing manners and tendency toward misogynism weren't enough for Nora to have to put up with, he arrived accompanied by Jim Lazarov, the emergency medicine intern whose sole goal in life was to make Nora's life hell.

"Have a seat, Jim," Tillman commanded, barely acknowledging Nora's presence.

Jim nodded, smirked, and perched on the edge of the other Scandinavian torture device, appearing ready to spring up at moment's notice to kiss Tillman's butt. He slanted a triumphant glance at Nora, and she had the sinking feeling he already knew what the outcome of this meeting would be, and it had nothing to do with nursing staffing or overtime.

Great. She'd just gotten her life back together and now she was about to be fired.

"Seems like you two have a problem," Tillman started once he'd settled himself into his leather executive chair. "Which means I have a problem." He paused.

Jim kept nodding, a damn bobblehead, his foot tapping in time.

"I could fire Nora or have her transferred out of the ER."

Jim's fingers joined in the rhythm, tapping his knee as he showed his teeth. He scooted forward, ready to leap up and shake Tillman's hand or burst into a victory dance, Nora wasn't sure which.

"But," Tillman continued, "then I'd have to deal with the nursing union. Because of the recent violence here at Angels, we're already short-staffed. And with contracts up for negotiation, I don't want that."

As his words sank in, Jim's fingers stopped their tap dance. They lay limp on his knee. His foot slowed as well, now beating out a dispirited dirge.

"I could suspend Jim."

Nora didn't bother responding to Tillman's words even though she knew he expected her to. She wasn't playing his games.

"But," he went on, "then I'd have to justify it to the Resident Review Committee, and that means paperwork and jumping through hoops and tarnishing our reputation as a teaching hospital."

Jim was perfectly still now. Tillman leaned back in his chair, steepling his fingers—a pose copied from The Donald, no doubt.

"So, we're going to have a little team-building exercise. You two"—he brought his body forward with a dramatic flourish—"are going to work together. I canceled the second shift because of the weather, but I understand the ER patient census is down, so you can start immediately. Jim, Nora's your nurse, the only nurse who will take your orders."

Jim's snaggletoothed grin returned as he clearly envisioned ordering Nora around, his own personal scut-monkey. Nora swallowed her groan, not wanting to reveal any weakness.

"Nora, you'll decide which patients Jim takes. Any nursing procedures he orders will be performed by both of you, together."

Jim sank back, realizing that he'd be the one actually doing the scut work.

"All of the patients you two treat will be interviewed after their care is completed. If I receive any less-than-satisfactory comments, then you're both gone." Tillman stood, bracing his weight on his desktop. "Do I make myself clear?"

Before either Nora or Jim could speak, the door opened and a man in a black suit strode in, followed by Tillman's secretary, who was sputtering, "I'm sorry, sir, he barged right past me."

The man came to an abrupt stop in front of Tillman's desk, effortlessly meeting Tillman's gaze as he snapped open a small black wallet. "Harris, DEA. I need to speak to you about one of your physicians."

"I'm in the middle of—"

The DEA agent rotated his gaze to narrow in on Jim, then Nora. He dismissed them without a blink. "We need the room. Now."

Jim scrambled to his feet and was halfway out the door before Nora even got up. Tillman glowered at the agent but nodded to his secretary. Her phone was ringing, so she scurried back to her desk.

In the anteroom, Nora started to take a chair, then stopped—should she wait, or had Tillman finished with them? Jim seemed to be having the same conundrum, shifting his weight, pacing one way for two steps, then returning to stand beside the door they'd just come through.

"He was just yanking my chain," he said. "No way he was serious about firing me if we can't work together."

"It's my job on the line, too," Nora reminded him.

Jim opened his mouth to say something, then held his hand up. He leaned closer to the door, his ear against the crack between the hinges.

"The DEA guy says he's on the trail of a woman who forged her credentials and is running a prescription drug ring. He's asking Tillman about doctors who came from California." Jim pushed away abruptly, shoving his hands in his pockets and acting nonchalant. The door opened.

"I'll let you know if our records show anything," Tillman was saying, "but I really think you have the wrong hospital."

The DEA agent was stone-faced. "We're checking all the hospitals in the area. If I have to, I'll get a court order for your personnel files."

Tillman flushed. "I already told you we would cooperate to the best of our ability."

The agent narrowed his eyes, then gave a nod. He left without a word. Tillman scowled after him, then turned his wrath on Jim and Nora. "What the hell are you two still doing here? Get back to work!"

Tillman returned to his office, slamming the door. Nora glanced at Jim and saw that the intern's eyes were unfocused; he was undoubtedly thinking of twenty ways to wiggle out of this assignment, leaving her with any blame.

"Guess he was serious," she said. "We'd better get down to the ER."

"Wait here," Jim said. "I want to talk to that DEA guy first."

He rushed through the door. Nora stood there, eyeing Tillman's closed door and then the outer door Jim had gone through. She considered her options—neither were good.

The receptionist looked up from her computer. "Not to worry you or anything," she said, "but Mr. Tillman always says it's easier to find cause to fire a nurse than a doctor."

"Thanks." Nora followed Jim out, saw him standing with the DEA agent at the elevators.

"Her name's Lydia Fiore," Jim was saying when she drew close enough to hear him. "She's an attending physician in the ER. Be careful, though, she killed a man. Shot him."

Agent Harris looked interested at that.

Nora came up behind Jim, nudging him aside. Just because Jim didn't like Lydia was no reason for him to tell the DEA that she was running a prescription scam. Or might have faked credentials.

She leaned forward to tap the elevator button. "We're late, Jim."

"I'm telling you," Jim continued, "check out her credentials. She's been nothing but trouble since she got here from L.A."

"He doesn't know what he's talking about," Nora said,

shoving Jim inside the elevator before the doors fully slid open. As usual the intern was clueless about any repercussions his brash words could have. "I'm an ER charge nurse. I work with Dr. Fiore all the time. She's an excellent physician; there's no way her credentials are faked. And she would never be involved in any kind of drug scam."

Just because a doctor was a magnet for trouble didn't make her suspect. But from the agent's expression, she was pretty sure he disagreed.

He joined them in the elevator, stabbing the button for the first floor. "I think I need to learn more about this Dr. Fiore."

THIS ISN'T MY REAL LIFE, GINA THOUGHT AS SHE steered Jerry through the circle of hallways surrounding the fifth-floor nurses' station. *My real life is going to start again. Soon. Once Jerry gets better.*

Jerry wobbled, misjudging the placement of his three-footed cane, and almost fell. Gina pressed her hands against him, one to each of his hips, realigning and steadying him. Instead of thanking her, he glared at her. "I can do it."

He took off, faster than before, using his unsteadiness instead of the cane to propel himself. A deranged pinball set loose, he careened against a stray drug cart, then ricocheted off in the other direction. But he made it all the way to the end of the hall and turned, hoisting the cane like a trophy, grinning in triumph.

Jerry should be dead. No one had expected him to make it through that first night, much less wake up fairly intact. He was a walking miracle—and it broke Gina's heart. These little triumphs, the greater failures.

But it hadn't broken Jerry. That part of him—the too-stubborn-to-die part—that had survived.

So she couldn't help but clap and cheer as she jogged down the hall to join him.

"Told you. I can."

"You did." She kissed him on his cheek. "You can do anything."

"Except remember." He pulled her close so that she couldn't see his face. "Tell me. I need it, Gina. I need it all."

Suddenly his shoulders shook with sobbing and his tears wet her turtleneck and cardigan. Gina took the cane before it could fall from his hand. She circled her arm around his back, surprised at how bony he felt; he'd lost more than his memories in the weeks since the shooting.

She walked him back to his room. After settling him into bed, she wiped away the tears he'd already forgotten, hoping that he'd also moved past his request, burying it in the crevasses that mauled his memory. Last thing she wanted was to tell him again what had happened that night. Every time she did, she relived the horror, and, unlike Jerry, she wouldn't forget in five minutes.

But this time he hadn't forgotten. He grabbed her hand, not allowing her to escape. "Tell me."

Gina sat with him on the bed. "There was a man. He was looking for Lydia and he knew you could take him to her. But he found me first."

Jerry nodded in time with her words, eyes narrowed as if working hard to commit them to memory. "Why was he looking for Lydia?"

"Something to do with her mother's death. Do you remember calling your friend in L.A.? Having the old case reopened?"

Frustration cascaded through his exhalation. "No. All I remember is Lydia being in danger—and I don't know why."

"I'm sorry. That's all I know."

"But Lydia. She's okay, right?" Fear and confusion filled his face.

She laid a palm against his cheek. Didn't have the heart to remind him that Lydia had been coming to visit him every day. "She's fine, Jerry. Thanks to you."

"Thanks to me?"

"You saved her. You saved us both."

The door popped open and Gina's roommate, Amanda Mason, bounced in, smiling as usual, her blond hair shiny, her eyes as blue as a summer sky. Amanda's perpetual cheerfulness sometimes made Gina wince—like staring at the sun without sunglasses.

The medical student was just entirely too bright, casting darker shadows over Gina. Amanda never had to fake being happy, put on a pretense for the rest of the world. She simply *was* always happy, a natural flaw in her character.

"Got a surprise for you today, Jerry," Amanda sang out, holding a bowl aloft as if it contained diamonds.

"Amanda!" Jerry bounced up in bed, forgetting all about Lydia or the shooting, holding his arms out, palms up, eyes closed, waiting for his daily surprise.

Amanda shared her smile with Gina and winked. Maybe there was something to Amanda's sensory stimuli theory of rehab. Gina did always feel better after the medical student visited, and so did Jerry.

Wafting the bowl below his nose, Amanda sat on the bed beside Jerry. "What's it smell like?"

He sniffed, wrinkled his nose, inhaled again. His face grew puzzled as he strained his memory. "Monkeys."

Amanda laughed and placed the bowl in his waiting hands. "Close. Here, try tasting it." She guided Jerry's finger into the yellow goo. "What does it make you think of?"

Jerry stirred his finger around, then brought it to his face, eyes still shut, smearing most of it before reaching his mouth. He dutifully licked and swallowed. He smiled. "Summer. Yellow. Nilla wafers." His eyes popped open. "Banana!"

"Yeah, Jerry! You're right. Banana pudding." She took the bowl from his hands, pulling a bedside stand close, positioning the bowl on a rubber mat so that it wouldn't slip and then wrapping his hand around the spoon with the Velcro splint that helped his grip. "Go ahead, you can do it."

As Jerry fought to maneuver the spoon successfully to his lips, Amanda turned to Gina. "Did you get some sleep?"

"Yes," Gina lied. "I brought the dress. Did you get the night off?" She nodded to the garment bag, which Amanda gleefully unzipped.

"Yep. I'm officially off duty, finished with my PICU rotation." Amanda grinned as she pulled the exquisite Carolina Herrera from the garment bag and held it up to her body. "It's gorgeous. Gina, thank you so much."

Gina couldn't help but smile in return. A real smile this time. It hurt—as if her muscles had forgotten how to express anything but worry. She'd left Post-it notes for herself all over the house and a voice mail on her cell to remind her not to forget the ball gown, but it was worth it to see Amanda's joy. "You're very welcome. Go try it on. Let's make sure it fits before tonight."

Amanda vanished into Jerry's bathroom, shedding her scrubs and medical student lab coat and reemerging a few minutes later transformed into a beauty queen. She stepped into the stilettos that matched the blue-green of the gown and twirled, the silk swishing and humming.

Jerry clapped, ignoring the too-yellow-to-be-real pudding that flew from his spoon. "Beautiful!"

Amanda blushed. "Thanks. I hope Lucas likes it."

"If he doesn't—" Jerry sounded like his old self, his

normal, wisecracking self. But then he stopped, spoon hanging from his hand, gaze vacant as he forgot what he was going to say.

"If he doesn't, then he's the one who needs his brain checked," Gina finished for him as she took the spoon and wiped his face clean.

Amanda tottered back and forth, practicing walking in the stilettos, more unsteady than Jerry, lurching against the wall, in danger of twisting the heels off.

"Want my cane?" Jerry asked.

Amanda beamed at his attempt at humor. "No. I can do it."

"They're Manolo Blahniks, not running shoes," Gina told her with a laugh.

"Mannilow what?"

Gina shook her head. Her phone rang before she could educate Amanda about designer labels.

"It's Nora. You need to get down here to the ER."

Disturbed by the urgency in Nora's voice, Gina moved into the bathroom for a little privacy. "Why? What's wrong?"

"There's a DEA guy named Harris here. He's asking questions about Lydia—and now he says he wants to talk to Jerry about the shooting."

"Why?" Gina's nerves jangled in alarm. She pressed her palm against the bathroom mirror. Wouldn't it be nice to find one she could escape through, like Alice in Wonderland? Fear choked her for a long moment. Only a handful of people knew that the hit man who'd shot Jerry had been after Lydia. And the only reason he'd been able to find Jerry was by following the trail of law enforcement officers that led from L.A. to Pittsburgh.

What if whoever was after Lydia had sent someone to finish the job? To tie up loose ends as well as potential witnesses?

Like Gina. And Jerry.

Her breath was swept away by a rush of adrenaline. "I'm on my way."

To Lydia's surprise, Jerry's partner, Detective Janet Kwon, was waiting for her and Sandy when they exited the gun range.

"Nice shooting," Janet said. Her face was perpetually devoid of a smile, so Lydia didn't start worrying about Janet's frown until she added, "Sandy, can we use your office?"

"Sure, just close up after you're done. I've already got the range and vault locked up." He looked curious but said nothing as he grabbed his parka and stepped into a pair of snow boots. Sandy opened the outside door; a blast of frigid air and snow fought to tear it from his grip. "Don't dawdle, this is looking like some serious snow."

Janet ignored him, heading into his office, and setting her laptop on his desk. "I think I've found your mother's real identity," she said to Lydia without preamble.

Lydia's brain filled with a roaring louder than the wind pounding against the windowless cement-block walls. "You found her?"

"Maybe. But it all fits. Explains why after eighteen years, a few inquiries from Jerry about your mom's cold case suddenly ended up with someone interested enough to send a shooter."

Lydia collapsed into the scuffed tweed armchair beside Sandy's desk, releasing a cloud of stale cigar smoke to mix with the smells of gun oil and ammo that clung to every surface. "Tell me. All of it."

"When Jerry reopened your mom's case, he repeated the AFIS search—the Automated Fingerprint Identification System. Sent her prints from the medical examiner through the system again. Back when your mom died, not every jurisdiction entered their fingerprints into AFIS, particularly not the smaller places that didn't have the budget. But in 2004 the government began digitalizing those smaller places, starting with the Indian reservations' tribal police."

"My mom lived on an Indian reservation?"

"I don't know if she lived there, but she was arrested on one."

"So you know? You really know who she is?"

"Yes." Janet began typing. A set of fingerprints appeared on the computer. "Here's the arrest record matching your mom's fingerprints. Picked up for shoplifting on a reservation in Nevada."

Lydia looked at the date. "She'd have been six months pregnant with me then, if the birthday she told me was anywhere near the truth."

"Yeah, and I'm guessing she was newly on the run—probably hadn't figured out yet how to get alternative forms of ID, so had to use her own." She scrolled down to the demographic information. "In which case, her real name was Martha Flowers."

"Martha Flowers." Lydia tried it on for size. It didn't feel any more "right" or natural than the other aliases her mother had used during their life on the run. Maria would always be Maria to her. "Are you sure?"

"I called and asked them to scan in her booking photos." Janet clicked out of the screen and logged onto her e-mail. "Okay, here we go."

One click and three black-and-white images filled the screen: a dark-haired teen, eyes wide, lips pursed, in full face and both profiles. The flash glistened from the girl's cheek on the left-hand profile shot. Tears.

Lydia wrapped her arms around herself, hugging her cast to her chest, cold despite the fleece pullover and long underwear she wore beneath. She was still a California girl, trying to dress against Pittsburgh's perpetual chill.

Janet broke the silence. "Is it her?"

Lydia tried to speak but couldn't. All she could do was nod. She traced the image with her finger, the closest she'd been to her mother in eighteen years. She swallowed her tears. "It's her."

"Then it's a start. Let me call them back, see if they've dug up anything else." She dialed out from Sandy's office phone, and after a few minutes on hold she connected with the officer she needed in Nevada. "Yeah, I know it's New Year's Eve. Do you think—? Sorry about the lousy connection, we're in the middle of a big snowstorm here. So did you find out more? Tell me. She left the following day after her hearing. Okay." Janet began scribbling notes that Lydia couldn't read. The detective nodded her head and made a few noises of surprise. "And he ended up in the hospital? Is he still around? I'd love to interview him. Oh, I see. Thanks."

Lydia listened without really hearing, her mind spinning back to the day her mother was murdered. She and Maria had argued. Maria had come to her school, about to go on the run again, but Lydia didn't want to leave her friends. They'd been too late, and ended up being chased by a man Lydia had never seen before; she'd thought he was a cop, after Maria for playing her fake psychic scam, conning people.

She'd been wrong. So very wrong. The man chased them into an empty church. Maria forced Lydia to hide in the confessional and faced the man alone. Maria had struggled, but he'd beaten her to death, stopping only when interrupted by a priest and running off.

Lydia had been only twelve, but that day had changed everything for her. Not only had she lost her mother, she'd lost her one connection to her own past—she didn't even know who her own father was, much less any other family. Maybe today was the first step to regaining that lost history.

Maybe she had a family. Maybe they were still looking for Martha and her baby, even after all these years. . . .

"What happened?" Lydia asked once Janet hung up.

"Looks like your mom was right to run. Storekeeper dropped the charges the next day and she hitched a ride out of town with a local trucker after her hearing. But that same day, a man came to the station saying he was her lawyer and demanding to see her—even though she'd never requested a lawyer and hadn't made any phone calls." Janet paused, eyes squinted at the cement-block wall, thinking.

She shook her head, her frown deepening. "The next day when the trucker got back into town, a gang of guys beat him to a pulp. Wanted to know everything about her—where she went, what they'd talked about. They were interrupted by the trucker's son coming home, otherwise they probably would've killed him, sounds like."

"Are you going to talk to him?" Hope flared through Lydia. Maybe Maria—Martha—had mentioned her home, who her family was.

"Can't. He died in a traffic collision a few years later. Wouldn't matter anyway—we already know where your mom went. What we need to know is where she came from. Why she was running."

Reality dashed Lydia's hopes—she'd been foolish to get so excited anyway. She knew as well as anyone that Maria had been terrified of going home. She'd been running for her—their—lives. "And who she was running from."

THREE

GINA WAITED FOR THE ELEVATOR, FATIGUE BLUR-
ring her vision. As a third-year emergency medicine resident, she was used to being tired, but this was something
different. A weariness that crept into her blood, numbing
her from the inside out. Every move, every decision—
hell, every blink—left her feeling empty.

She twisted the engagement ring hanging from the chain
around her neck. Jerry's ring. Maybe her New Year's reso-
lution would be to finally be honest with herself, that she
wasn't good enough for him, and she should walk away
forever. Lord knew, he'd be better off without her—just
look where loving her had gotten him.

If there was one thing Gina could be brutally honest
about, it was her own shortcomings. She couldn't take
care of Jerry. She didn't have the strength, the patience.
Hell, she couldn't even take care of herself—wasn't that
why she'd stayed with Jerry for so long?

He'd made her feel safer than anyone else ever had. Protected. Cherished.

Even Old Jerry had been putty in Gina's manicured hands, no match for a mind trained in the art of verbal guerrilla tactics by the famous trial lawyer, her father, Moses Freeman.

It had been oh-so-easy to persuade Jerry to race to her rescue in the past, when she was in trouble. What the hell else could she have done when the hit man took her hostage?

She had the feeling that when she finally figured it out, she'd hate the answer.

The elevator arrived and the doors opened. Gina stepped inside and immediately wished she'd taken the stairs.

Ken Rosen stood in the corner, sandwiched between a woman whose arms were filled with balloons and a man on crutches who was clutching a pack of cigarettes.

Ken, an attending in immunology and infectious disease, was dressed in his usual casual hospital uniform: jeans and a polo shirt. No lab coat, so she guessed he wasn't seeing patients today. You never knew with Ken; he was the essence of Bohemian/Zen master/don't-give-a-shit casual. Aside from occasionally also wearing the lab coat, she'd never seen him in anything other than jeans and a polo—except for when they'd first met and he'd been wearing running shorts and dodging bullets during a drive-by shooting.

The fight-or-flight urge raged through her, leaving a cascade of sweat streaming down the back of her neck. But Gina didn't want to fight Ken. Didn't want to run from him either.

She sucked in her breath. Inhaled the scent of cigarettes. God, she would kill for a cigarette. Nineteen days cold turkey—no patches, no gum. Small penance. Or punishment.

Ken broke the silence. "I'll catch the next one."

He pushed past her. The doors banged against his arms, but he didn't seem to notice. His back was rigid, his shoulders tight—as knotted as his expression when he'd seen her. A wince that etched his eyes into two slits, as if merely seeing her was painful.

All because she'd chosen Jerry instead of him—seeing how that was working out, she'd think Ken would be celebrating.

Instead, his pain sucker punched her. Gina turned to face the blank rear wall of the elevator, aware that the other occupants were staring at her. She sniffed. Pinched the bridge of her nose, her eyes suddenly hurting.

Hah. Well, at least she'd finally gotten some emotion out of Mr. Zen Master. . . .

Unlike Jerry, Ken had made it very clear that he wouldn't play nursemaid to her, that he wouldn't coddle her or solve her problems, wouldn't make everything she screwed up right again.

He'd told her the truth about herself even when she didn't want to hear it. And damn him, he'd been right. If she'd listened to him sooner, Jerry might never have been shot.

Gina turned to the man on crutches. "I'll give you fifty bucks for that pack of cigarettes."

"YOU KNOW THE ONLY REASON TILLMAN IS DOING this is so one of us will quit. Just so we have things straight," Jim told Nora after she hung up from calling Gina. "I'm not leaving."

"Yeah, well, that makes two of us." Nora scanned the ER census board. Only two patients, both from an earlier traffic collision. "Are those the guys from the zoo? Why are they still here?" she asked Jason, the desk clerk.

"One's waiting for crutch-walking instructions, and they're both waiting for their ride."

If her staff was going to be working a double shift, she had better start rotating them, send a few to get some rest. And she had to talk to Mark Cohen, the attending on duty and ER department head, to make sure he was on board with that. Even if things stayed slow, it was still going to be a long night. No one was going to be happy about missing their New Year's Eve plans. Including Seth. Damn. Nora dreaded making that phone call.

Her fiancé, Seth, had also been injured during the violence that had swept the hospital almost three weeks ago and he was still off work, recuperating at their home. He'd almost died. Every night Nora woke, fighting nightmares about finding him . . . all that blood.

"Jim, can you go teach a guy how to use crutches? Do you know how to do that?"

"Tillman said we need to work together." Jim's petulant tone sent the message loud and clear: If he was being relegated to performing scut work, then Nora was damn well going to suffer alongside.

She wanted to get rid of him long enough to call Lydia, as well as find out where Harris had wandered off to, so she could keep an eye on him. "You get started. I'll be right there."

Jim stood his ground. Just then Harris appeared down the hall, accompanied by Mark Cohen. The DEA agent appeared frustrated. Good for Mark. Nora knew he'd never betray any of his people, especially not Lydia.

Jim tapped his foot and handed her the patient chart.

"All right. Let's go," Nora conceded. Damn Tillman. He had the worst timing.

Apparently medical school had never covered basics like how to walk with crutches, much less how to measure them or teach a patient how to go up and down steps and overcome other obstacles, so Nora had Jim read the patient education handout while she measured their patient, Mr. Olsen, for his crutches. It didn't help that Mr. Olsen was distracted, more interested in talking with the other patient than learning how to use his crutches.

"What's the status of the *Spheniscus*?" he asked his friend, who was nodding his head, listening to his cell phone.

"They've left the airport, but the roads are awful. The state police are diverting people off the interstates and have closed down the turnpike."

"Damn weather."

"What's a *spheniscus*?" Jim asked, forgetting about the crutch he was supposed to be adjusting.

"*Spheniscus mendiculus*," Mr. Olsen answered. "A very rare and valuable specimen of equatorial penguin."

"We're awaiting a shipment of twelve of them from Galapagos," the other man put in, hanging up his phone. "We were supposed to pick them up at the airport, but—"

Mr. Olsen rolled his eyes. "They'd be in the habitat where they belong, acclimating to their new home right now, if you knew how to drive in snow."

"There was ice. I couldn't help it."

"Now we need to rely on Zimmerman. He doesn't appreciate how delicate they are."

"Calm down, Henry. Zimmerman understands. He's doing his best."

Now Nora was intrigued. "Wait. You're worried about penguins getting cold?"

Both men began speaking at once. "These penguins—"

"*Spheniscus*."

"These *spheniscus* are equatorial."

"Where it can be as warm as thirty-eight degrees Celsius."

Oh. Nora saw how that could definitely be a problem. That was over one hundred degrees Fahrenheit.

"And, to make matters worse," Mr. Olsen continued, "several of them are molting in preparation to mate. Which means they've also been fasting."

"So, they're particularly vulnerable to the elements?" Jim asked. He looked surprisingly interested—unlike his usual haughty, too-bored-to-be-bothered expression. "What kind of transport are they in? Is it climate controlled?"

The zookeeper warmed to Jim's concern. "It would have been if someone hadn't crashed it. Zimmerman has them in the back of his van, so if the trip isn't prolonged they should be okay." He paused, looking morose. "I hope."

"Are Galapagos penguins related to the Magellanic penguins off the coast of Argentina?" Jim asked.

"Yes." Mr. Olsen brightened, obviously excited to find another penguin enthusiast. "The Galapagos penguins traveled the same Humboldt currents up the coast to the equator and settled there. They're a unique population."

"Jim, I didn't know you were so interested in penguins," Nora said, hoping to redirect the conversation back to medicine. Although it was nice to see Jim treating his patients like human beings for a change, rather than nuisances. "At least not the non-NHL ones."

"I did a summer working with an Earthwatch expedition studying Magellanic penguins in Argentina," he murmured. "Came home wanting to be a zoologist, but my dad had different plans."

"Let's get Mr. Olsen up and walking so he can get back to the zoo and take care of his new charges." Nora handed Jim the crutches she'd adjusted to fit their patient.

"Right. Okay, Mr. Olsen. All you need to do is remember that you don't want your weight to rest on your armpits." He tapped the padded top of the crutch. "But rather on your hands. Always move the crutches and your injured leg first, then swing your good leg to catch up. Like this."

Jim demonstrated, taking a few steps, then handed the crutches to Mr. Olsen. Before taking them, Mr. Olsen turned back to his coworker. "Call Zimmerman again. Call the police, get him an escort if you have to. We must protect those penguins."

IT WAS A LOT TO TAKE IN ALL AT ONCE. LYDIA stood beside Janet Kwon, hovering over the laptop. "Do they say anything else about my mother? Where she was from? Any family?"

"Not here. Now that we have a name, though, I can search for more information later. But right now we need to concentrate on the immediate threat."

"The man who almost killed Jerry."

"And who wanted to find you."

Lydia sank back into the chair, thinking hard. "How did the people responsible for my mother's death find out that Jerry had reopened her case?"

Janet's frown corrugated her forehead. "You've always said the man who killed your mom was dressed like a cop."

"Jerry's the first person I told that to. Ever." She'd been too terrified to confide in either the L.A. police officers who'd found her standing over her mother's body or the social workers who'd taken her into custody.

"What if the killer kept looking for you after he killed your mom? Best way for him to keep an eye on anyone looking into Maria's case would be to flag those finger-print records."

"Which means he really was a cop."

Janet seemed to reluctantly agree. "Back then, before a flick of the computer could get you into records, it would have been hard. And even now with all the security clear-ances, virtually no one outside law enforcement could do

it. In fact"—somehow her frown managed to deepen—
"unless he works in the same jurisdiction where your
mom's murder took place, it'd be tough to pull off."

"So he must be LAPD."

"Or maybe L.A. County Sheriff."

"Why didn't he just come after me while I was in foster care? What stopped him?"

"As far as I can tell, since you had no ID or birth cer-
tificate, family services initially labeled you a Jane Doe
until the lab tests confirmed your relationship to your
mom, right? Way back then the records were pretty much
all on paper—so even a police officer wouldn't have had
access without first knowing your name."

"And since Maria was labeled a Jane Doe as well, he'd
have had no idea what name I was using." Lydia never
realized it before, but thanks to the foster care system, for
the past eighteen years, she'd been as good as invisible to
anyone looking for Maria or her. Including Maria's killer.

"Or what name you went by now—after eighteen years,
you could have taken on an adopted family name, or been
married, more than once, even. But he must have flagged
your mom's AFIS file as an early-warning system."

"So when Jerry reran Maria's prints and got a match,
the killer knew someone was looking into her case. Which
meant that Jerry probably knew where *I* was."

"So the hit man was sent here to Pittsburgh, to get
Jerry to tell him where you were." Janet bolted upright,
her feet slamming against the floor. "Eighteen years of
law enforcement. He's gonna be high ranking—or"—she
paused, clicking her nails against the butt of her gun as
she thought—"or maybe he's gone federal. The AFIS system is run by the Department of Justice." She shrugged,
deflating a little. "Or he could just be a clerk in a cubicle
somewhere with access to the database."

"But that still doesn't answer the real question: What does he want from me? It's been eighteen years."

That was the question that had kept Lydia awake for the past two and a half weeks. She'd been just a kid when she witnessed her mother's murder—she doubted that she could identify the man's face. Not that he'd even known she was there; she'd stayed hidden, just as Maria had told her to. The killer haunted her dreams, but by the time she awoke, she never remembered anything but the terror he provoked. Her attention had been focused on her mother's screams, the blood, the need to stay small and quiet and hidden.

"Whatever it is, he didn't think twice about targeting police officers." A glower darkened Janet's face, and Lydia knew she was thinking of Jerry. "That's high stakes."

"I don't have anything worth killing for—and neither did Maria," Lydia protested. "We lived on the streets most of the time, were constantly on the move."

"Maria worked as a con artist, right?"

"I don't know if you'd call it 'con artist.' Some days I think she really believed she was psychic, but she pretty much just told people what they wanted to hear."

"Maybe one of her clients told her something—"

"Something worth killing her over? Seems unlikely. And why then come after *me* after all this time?" Lydia flounced in the chair, frustrated, and immediately regretted the sudden movement when it jarred her sling and pain bellowed from her arm. She took the sling off—she was more comfortable without it anyway, and had worn it only to help with any recoil while she was shooting—and propped her cast on the arm of the chair so it was elevated. The throbbing quieted.

Janet shut down her computer. "I should get back to the station. I'll call you if I learn more."

Lydia remained sitting in the chair beside Sandy's desk.

"You okay to get home by yourself?" Janet asked. Lydia glanced up and realized the detective had already put her coat and gloves on and was standing by the door.

"I'm fine. Just moving slowly." Lydia nodded to her arm, as if that were her excuse. "You go ahead."

Janet hesitated. "Okay," she finally said. "Drive safely." A blast of wind and snow heralded her departure. The office felt ten degrees colder after she left.

And still Lydia sat, thinking of the frightened teenage girl from those booking photos. Martha Flowers had been skinny—much too thin for a pregnant woman. There'd been what looked like track marks visible on her arms, and her eyes had held the sunken look of a junkie wanting a fix. No surprise to Lydia. Maria—Martha—had confessed to her daughter that she'd been a heroin addict once, but told Lydia she'd quit cold turkey when she found out she was pregnant. It was about the only fact she'd ever shared about her life before Lydia.

Young. Her mother had been so very young. And alone. And terrified. Of what?

Of whom?

Lydia's father. They'd been on the run from him since before she was born. Lydia didn't even know his name. To her he was the bogeyman.

When she was older she used to think he was actually a figment of Maria's mind, an imaginary specter who allowed her to justify their nomadic existence, the way her mother dragged them from place to place, living-like pieces of debris swept through the streets of L.A. by the Santa Ana winds.

She'd blamed her mother. Thought Maria was crazy.

The morning of the day Maria died, Lydia had threatened to leave, to turn herself in to children's services, ask them to find her father so she could live with him instead.

All she'd wanted was some normalcy, a taste of security. A bathroom with a real door on it instead of a sheet draped over a curtain rod. A place her friends could visit. A home.

It was the worst fight they'd ever had. A few hours later, Maria was dead.

Nausea twisted through Lydia's gut, an echo of the awful wrenching feeling that had consumed her as she watched Maria die. For eighteen years she'd felt guilty. Even though she hadn't made the call to children's services, she still blamed herself that the bogeyman had found them that day—or the monster he'd sent to do his dirty work.

Now the bogeyman was back. And he was after her.

FOUR

GINA BOLTED OFF THE ELEVATOR, THEN SLOWED her pace to a calm, confident stride—everything she didn't feel. She pushed through the doors to the ER and saw Jason, the ER day-shift desk clerk, sitting at his usual place behind the nurses' station, playing a handheld video game as he lounged in a well-padded office chair.

"Have you seen Nora?" she asked, scanning the patient board. Still slow. Only two patients, both marked as discharged. Gina took a banana nut mini-muffin from the basket in front of Jason and crammed it whole into her mouth, unable to resist. It took everything she had to fight the urge to grab the entire basket and gobble them all down. So much for calm and confident.

"She and Jim Lazarov just headed out to triage. How's Jerry?"

Gina choked on a last swallow of muffin, forcing it down even though it gouged her throat. "A little better. I guess."

"Remember that news guy who got hit in Iraq? They removed like half his skull, but a year later, he's walking and talking and back doing the news."

It was the same kind of miracle story everyone kept sharing with her. But they had the opposite effect on Gina— as if for every other person she heard about who beat the odds, it meant that Jerry's chances at a winning ticket in the traumatic brain injury lotto were diminished. But she nodded her thanks anyway.

Surreptitiously, her hand jammed deep into the pocket of her sweater, Gina slid a cigarette from the pack she'd bought off the patient in the elevator and rolled it between her fingers. Wondered if she could sneak outside for a quick smoke before heading back up to Jerry. Maybe grab some cookies from the lounge on her way back. Her need to binge tasted like burnt caramel—made her salivate with anticipation as she allowed her urges to stampede over her willpower.

Even better would be the pain when she purged. Pleasure and pain, spiraled together in a macabre dance, that was her. A whirling dervish. Out of control. Just like her life.

Gina hadn't given in to her eating disorder since Jerry was shot—weeks of restraint, surely she deserved one little binge? It would feel so good.

The thoughts and emotions sprinted through her mind. She forced them aside, turning a calm façade to Jason. "Was there a guy here, looking for Lydia?"

Jason snorted. "Suit. Flashing a badge and a gun—you'd think after the shootings, they wouldn't let anyone with a gun in here."

Unfortunately the hospital security guards, like the entire hospital, were seriously short-staffed and administration had temporarily forbidden them from carrying any weapons other than pepper spray—which, in Gina's mind, made them more liabilities than assets.

She continued to caress the pack of Marlboros in her pocket as she fought to keep her attention on what Jason was saying. "So the guy with the suit and the gun, where did he go?"

"When I told him he'd have to talk to Mark Cohen if he wanted any info on an attending, he grabbed a copy of the schedule." Jason gestured to a ripped remnant of paper hanging from his well-ordered corkboard. "Too bad it was an old one. From before Lydia broke her arm. It listed her as working today, so he's probably combing the hospital for her."

Gina didn't like the sound of that. "Which way did he go?"

"Mark blew him off the first time around." Jason jerked his head toward the ER department head's office. "But I think the suit headed back for round two."

"Thanks." Gina jogged down the maze of corridors to Mark Cohen's office. The door was closed, which was unusual—if Mark was here, his office door was always open. She pushed it open without knocking and walked in to find a man sitting in Mark's chair, rummaging through his desk. "Can I help you?"

The man jerked his shoulder, but otherwise hid any signs of being startled. "You're not Dr. Cohen."

He stated it as a fact, dismissing her. He was about Jerry's height, just shy of six feet, brown hair, brown eyes, totally unremarkable. Except for the air of command.

"Neither are you." Gina held her ground as she channeled Jason and the other ER clerks—none of them anyone you'd want to mess around with. She was glad she wasn't easily identifiable as a doctor. After her shift, she'd changed into one of her most comfortable "frumpy" outfits: black turtleneck, black jeans, bulky cable-knit cardigan. "Want to explain to me why you're going through Dr. Cohen's desk? And just who the hell you are?"

"Official business." He snapped open a credential case and waved it in front of her. "Harris. DEA."

Gina grabbed the case before he could repocket it and scrutinized it. It said his name was Nathaniel T. Harris, and the picture was him, the seal and identification looked real enough, but the hackles on the back of her neck still screamed that something was wrong here.

He snatched his credentials from her, sliding them into his jacket pocket. "Do you know where I can find a Dr. Lydia Fiore?"

For an instant, Gina was tempted to tell him that *she* was Lydia. It might be the best way to find out what was really going on. She hugged her cardigan tighter, kneading her fingers into the wool as she wrestled up the courage.

But of course, it would never work. Even if Harris didn't know exactly what Lydia looked like, he surely could tell the difference between a five-foot, ten-inch black woman and Lydia's skinny five-five. Besides, too much of Lydia's past was a mystery, even to her closest friends. There was no way Gina could keep up the pretense. Anger flashed over her—Jerry had paid the price, almost with his life, for Lydia's secrets.

"I'm not Dr. Fiore's personal assistant," she said instead, raising herself to her full five-ten, using her anger to bolster her lies. "I work for Dr. Cohen. I suspect they're both busy with patients, so if you'd like to make an appointment—"

Harris frowned at her. Slowly, he unfolded himself from Mark's desk chair, making it clear that Gina's interruption was a mere inconvenience. "No need. I'll find her." He sauntered past her to the door. "I always do."

He left. Gina pushed the door shut, leaning against it as

she caught her breath. God, she needed that cigarette. She rushed to the desk, trying to figure out what Harris had been going through. Mark's computer was turned off, but his Rolodex was open to the *F*s. And where Lydia's card should be, with her address and phone numbers, there was an empty space.

Damn Mark. He refused to get with the twenty-first century and abandon his paper-and-pen record keeping. Gina sat at his desk and tried to call Lydia's home and cell phones. No answer at either. She had no idea what message to leave, so settled for, "It's Gina. Call me right away."

She hung up and called Janet Kwon, Jerry's partner. Janet's cell rang several times, and just before it went to voice mail the detective answered. "Kwon."

"It's Gina."

"What's wrong? Is Jerry okay?"

"Jerry's fine. But there's a guy here who says he's from the DEA, a Nathaniel Harris. He's looking for Lydia. Wants to talk with Jerry as well."

Static-burred silence. Gina could imagine Janet's scowl. The detective wasn't one for smiles, even in the best of circumstances, and the last few weeks had hardly been those.

"What the hell would the DEA want with Lydia?" Janet finally said. "It makes no sense."

"That's what I thought. And why would a DEA agent come all the way from L.A. to investigate?"

"He's from L.A.?" In the background Gina could hear the sounds of men talking, something about the National Guard and the Fort Pitt Tunnel being closed, and she realized the detective was at work. Good, maybe Janet could access one of their police databases to see who this Harris guy was and what he wanted.

"That's what his ID said."

"Remember anything else from it? A middle initial, date of birth, anything that will help me track him down?"

Or maybe it wasn't so easy. Gina concentrated. It was difficult; her mind felt fuzzy after so many days filled with worry and no sleep. "His middle initial was T. He's Caucasian, about six feet tall, brown hair and eyes. Sorry, I can't think of anything else. But Nora said he was asking about Jerry and the shooting."

"I'm going to call L.A., see what I can find out. Until then, try to keep Jerry away from him. At least until we know for certain what he's looking for."

"How long do you think it will take?"

A man in the background called Janet's name, and she snapped at him to give her a moment. "Depends on the guys in L.A. It *is* New Year's Eve—everyone has less staff working. And feds tend to take their time when it comes to us locals asking about their business anytime, holiday or not. Plus, we're in a bit of a crisis here—this storm blindsided us when it grew so fast. But as soon as I hang up, I'm calling L.A."

Finally the crackling nerve endings making Gina's hair stand on end relaxed. Janet was on the case. She'd take care of it. "I have a bad feeling about him. Something just doesn't feel right—and Nora felt the same way."

The sound of several phones ringing interrupted her. "Listen, Gina. I'm going to try to get out there as soon as I can, but the entire city is shut down with this storm. Nothing's moving. So, until I get some answers, just be careful, okay?"

It was so unlike Janet to offer any concern that Gina pulled the receiver from her ear in surprise.

"I won't let anything happen to Jerry," Gina promised, realizing who Janet was really worried about.

*   *   *

BY THE TIME JERRY FINISHED THE PUDDING, HE
was getting the spoon to his mouth mostly on the first try.
All he needed was practice and patience.

Last week, a few times when Jerry was left alone with
his food, Amanda had found him using it as pigment and
the window as a canvas. Given that his fifth-floor room
faced the patient parking garage, as uninspiring a view as
you could get, she thought this actually revealed how resilient and creative he was. The nurses saw it otherwise,
though, and had confined him to his bed.

Which was the last thing Jerry needed. Lying there
brooding. He needed to be moving, having his mind
stimulated by smells and sights and textures. But even
though he'd turned from food to his markers and pens as
his artistic outlet, he still tended to wander off and get
lost, so the nurses tried to keep him in his room as much
as possible, sedating or restraining him when he got too
agitated.

Amanda hid her own frustrations from him as best she
could, but it was infuriating to know what a patient needed,
yet be unable to provide it because of budget and staffing
shortages. Maybe by the time she was a full-fledged attending, after she did her pediatric residency, she could work on
changing that.

"Let me get changed out of this fancy dress and I'll
take these dirty dishes to the kitchen," she told him.

"Don't change," he said. "I like the dress."

"You do?" She felt a blush heat her cheeks. "Do you
think Lucas will?"

"He will." Jerry smiled and for a moment, looked just
like normal. Except for the shaved head, the surgical scar,
and the dab of pudding clinging to his cheek. "Keep it on."

Why not? Now that he was done eating there was
no danger of getting Gina's dress stained. Amanda wiped

the pudding from his cheek, then replaced it with a kiss. "Thanks. When I come back, we'll take a walk."

He nodded eagerly, eyes drifting as he fell asleep. He'd nap for a few minutes at a time, didn't seem able to sleep except in snatches before the nightmares woke him.

Amanda headed to the nurses' station after depositing the dishes on the cafeteria cart in the dirty utility room. There was already a large stack waiting to be returned to the kitchen—the nurses weren't the only ones short-staffed during this long holiday weekend.

"Whoa, Amanda, did you come to sweep me off my feet? Take me away from all this drudgery?" the clerk asked with a wink.

She laughed, unaccustomed to flattery. Who knew a party dress could make a person feel so good?

"When's Jerry due for his next therapy session?" she asked. "I'm going to take him for a walk and I don't want him to miss it."

"No therapy today because of the holiday. And he's scheduled for discharge tomorrow, so none then either."

What? That was the first she'd heard of it—and she was pretty sure Gina didn't know either. "You're sending him home *tomorrow*?" she asked incredulously.

"Not me. Dr. Stone." The clerk jerked his chin, pointing to the dictation room behind him. "He just wrote the orders."

Amanda immediately marched into the dictation room, where her fiancé, Lucas Stone, was thumbing through Jerry's chart as he dictated a discharge summary. "You can't send Jerry home tomorrow!"

Lucas snapped his head up at the interruption but didn't look angry, just frustrated as he paused his dictation. Then he blinked twice, in slow motion. "Wow." The word emerged as an exhalation of amazement. "Amanda. You look fantastic."

"Don't I?" She twirled, almost falling off the high heels, her anger forgotten for a moment. It was worth it to see his rapt expression; he'd totally forgotten his dictation or medicine or the hospital. For hyperfocused Lucas Stone, that was a minor miracle.

Gina was right. Glamour could be powerful. And useful. Amanda leaned forward, kissing Lucas firmly while giving him a glimpse of her décolletage. "Tell me you're not going to send Jerry home."

"I don't have any choice."

She pulled away, the layers of silk flouncing. "Lucas, he can't even feed himself. He needs inpatient rehab."

Technically they shouldn't be discussing a patient who wasn't under both of their care, but she'd convinced him early on that HIPAA rules didn't apply to Jerry. He was almost family, and fiancée privilege applied. Besides, if she didn't hear it from him, she'd just ask Gina, anyway.

"His insurance won't cover it. They're arranging outpatient therapy."

"Who's going to take care of him? Surely they don't expect Gina to quit her job." As always, the paradoxes and illogic of the insurance system perplexed her. They wouldn't pay for inpatient services or home care, but if the family took care of the patient full time, then they'd lose their jobs and with it the insurance . . . it was a lose-lose proposition for everyone except the bean counters.

"I persuaded them to provide four hours a day of respite care. Besides, Gina's got money; she can pay for a private service."

"That's not the point, and you know it. It's about doing what's best for Jerry."

Lucas closed the door, giving them some privacy, and pulled Amanda down onto his lap, the ball gown billowing around them like floating on a silk cloud. "Sure you're not more worried about Gina than Jerry?"

"What's she going to do all day, trapped at home, just her and Jerry? She can't put her life on hold, or give up her career, give up everything—and he might never . . ." Amanda shook her head, letting her hair fall into a veil between them. "No one should ever have to make these choices."

He smoothed her hair, tucking it back behind her ear. "Jerry's made remarkable progress—too good, in fact. That's why the insurance company denied the inpatient rehab. They don't think he needs it."

"Idiots. Don't they know that the more intensive therapy a traumatic brain injury patient gets early on, the better they do?"

"To them it's about doing what's most cost effective."

"Like I said: Idiots."

They sat in silence as Lucas wrapped his arms around her and held her for a long moment. "Sorry I can't do anything about it. Or about tonight."

"What about tonight?" No way was anyone going to take away her one and only chance to go to a real live society ball! It was New Year's Eve, and now that she had the dress and shoes on, Amanda wanted the entire Cinderella experience. "You are *not* canceling. Lucas, don't you dare—"

"Not me. The weather. Have you looked outside recently?"

"No." And she wasn't about to if the view would shatter her fantasy for tonight. She caught herself pouting, something she never did. Maybe that also came along with the dress and heels? Funny how a few scraps of silk could change so many things.

"It's a full-blown blizzard. The state police are asking everyone to stay off the roads, and the governor's already declared a state of emergency. The city is totally shut down. We're stuck here."

Disappointment squeezed at her heart. She knew it was silly—giving up a chance to attend a fancy dress ball was nothing to the people endangered by the weather, but Amanda couldn't help it. For once, she'd thought it was finally her turn to live a fairy tale.

Before she could say anything, her cell phone rang.

"Amanda, are you still with Jerry?" Gina asked.

"Just down the hall, why?"

"Get him out of there. There's a DEA agent in the hospital asking questions about Lydia and he wants to talk to Jerry. I don't trust him. Just hide Jerry until Janet Kwon can find out what's going on, okay?"

"Sure, no problem." Before Amanda could ask for more info, Gina hung up.

"What was that all about?" Lucas asked.

"Gina wants me to hide Jerry from some DEA agent who's asking questions about Lydia."

"You can't do that. It's like harboring a fugitive or obstruction of justice or something." Just like Lucas, always by the book. At least he had been until he'd met Amanda.

"Sure I can. I'm just going to take him for a walk. Not my fault if a federal agent can't find him."

"Amanda—"

"Gina sounded scared. She and Jerry are our friends. We need to protect him and give her time to check this guy out, that's all."

Lucas didn't look convinced.

"Don't worry, I'll take him myself." Amanda slid off his lap and opened the door to return to the nurses' station.

"Oh, no, you don't. I'm done here, I'll come with you."

She'd hoped he'd say that. "See, now it's official therapy, doctor's orders, not obstruction of justice or anything illegal."

He rolled his eyes. "Why do I have a bad feeling about this?"

NORA TOOK JIM OUT TO THE ER'S TRIAGE AREA so that they could relieve Melissa Jendrezejewski, the nurse on duty, and let her get some rest before the storm broke and things picked up again. The waiting room was empty except for a mother chasing after a preschool-aged boy. Melissa, a few years older than Nora and a mother of a toddler herself, smiled knowingly as she watched.

The kid was a bouncy, dark-haired, dark-eyed, olive-skinned handful who was trying to climb on the freestanding video console in the children's area of the waiting room.

Once Nora wrangled the boy into the triage exam room, his mother had to pull him out from under the stretcher as she explained what had happened. "I was baking vasilopita, for the New Year's. And before I could stop him, Nicky snatched the St. Nicholas coin. I think he swallowed it."

"Has he shown any trouble breathing? Choking? Difficulty swallowing?" Nora asked.

"No. None of that." The mother frowned. "But—"

"You need the coin back."

"If he swallowed it, it's going come out the other end," Jim said, examining the boy. "Equal lung sounds, no signs of airway obstruction."

"It's very valuable, been in my husband's family for generations."

"Let's see if he swallowed it first," Nora said. "Shall I order an X ray, Doctor?"

It was a trick question. Before Jim could answer, the head of the ER, Mark Cohen, joined them. "I hear we're having a team-building exercise," he said with a grin. "Thought I'd observe."

Jim shuffled his feet.

"Doctor?" Nora handed him the chart. "Your orders?"

"Wait. First let me complete my history and exam."

Nora gave him an encouraging nod—finally, he was learning. Most of ER diagnosis was best done by listening and paying attention to your patient rather than blindly ordering tests. It was an art that up until now Jim had shown little talent for.

"Did you see him put it in his mouth?" he asked Nicky's mother.

"Well, no. But one second it was there and the next— poof."

"Any choking or trouble breathing or talking after?"

"No, I had to chase him down."

"Then let's not rush to expose him to an X ray if we don't need to. First, let me check the usual suspects." Jim positioned Nicky on his mother's lap and had her wrap her arms around the boy in a bear hug. "Hold him still." He checked the boy's nostrils and ears. "They're clean."

"So do we need an X ray?" the mother asked. She was looking at Mark and Nora more than Jim. There was an uncomfortable silence, and Nora thought she might need to answer.

"No." Jim said. "Give me a minute." He ran out. Nora craned her head out the alcove and saw him rush across the waiting room and through the glass door to the security office. Bingo.

"I think you're good for Lazarov," Mark said to Nora with a wink. "I should assign you two to work together more often."

"Bite your tongue."

Jim returned carrying a black object that resembled a

cricket bat. "This is a metal detector. Do you know what the coin was made of?"

The mother frowned. "It was gold-colored, but I'm sure that was just gold foil or paint. It's very old. Maybe nickel or lead?"

"We should be able to find those. Let's see. Go ahead and take his clothes off."

"Can I leave his Pull-Up on? He's not quite potty-trained yet, and when he gets excited—"

"Sure, no problem." Once Nicky was nearly naked, Jim positioned him standing in front of his mother, arms up in the air. "Okay, Nicky, listen to the machine."

Starting at Nicky's feet, Jim slowly moved the wand up the boy's body. A faint whistle sounded as he crossed the belly button region, then silence. Jim sat back on his haunches and frowned. "That doesn't make sense. If he swallowed it, it can't already be down that low in his intestines, and if he aspirated it, it should be near his sternum."

He tried again, waving the wand over the front of Nicky's body. Same results.

"Is that bad?" the mom asked, worried. "He's going to be okay, isn't he?"

Nicky just laughed.

Nora avoided eye contact with Mark for fear she'd start laughing as well. "Um, Doctor," she said in a meek tone. "Maybe you should try down his back."

Jim nodded and tried once more. This time when he reached the buttocks area the wand began to whistle and buzz. He smiled and looked up at the mom. "I think we'll be needing to take those Pull-Ups off after all."

"Oh dear. He just switched over from diapers and he's fascinated by them," the mother said, her face flushing with embarrassment as she fished the St. Nicholas medal out of the Pull-Up. At least it was clean. "He thinks they're like an extra pocket. I'm so sorry."

Usually Jim would have chewed a parent out for wasting his time, but not today. Nora wasn't sure if it was Tillman's threat, or because Mark was standing there supervising, or if the little urchin had charmed Jim, but today he just smiled and said, "No problem at all."

A loud honking and the squeal of brakes came from outside. Mark moved out into the waiting room and cleaned the fog off one of the picture windows, staring out at the driveway. "What the—"

FIVE

GINA HUNG UP AFTER CALLING AMANDA AND
stared at the closed door to Mark Cohen's office. Now that
Jerry was safe, it was tempting to simply sit here in
Mark's oh-so-comfortably-broken-in chair, soaking in the
peace and quiet like a spa treatment. Her muscles drooped
and her eyelids slid shut as she slumped back. God,
maybe she could finally sleep, even if just for a few moments.

*The sounds of gunfire cracked through the air. She threw
up her hands, as if she could stop the bullets hurtling toward her, her breath snagged by the fear throttling her
throat.*

Gasping, fighting the urge to vomit, Gina collapsed forward, resting her forehead on the desk. She hated how the
flashbacks sneaked under her guard, catching her when she
was most vulnerable.

Ignoring the hospital's rules, Mark's personal space,
and state law, she fumbled a cigarette from the pack in her

pocket and lit up. Inhaling the poison slowed her breathing and steadied her nerves. Exhaling the cloud of toxins
helped banish the bad memories.

Who said smoking was all bad?

She didn't finish the cigarette—there were only three
left in the pack. Instead, she savored two more drags, feeling the nicotine race along her nerves, soothing the adrenaline overload the flashback had caused. Then she tamped it
out against the bottom of her shoe and carefully slid the
remaining half of a cigarette back into the pack.

Suddenly she felt clearheaded, closer to her normal self.
Enough so that she realized that as nice as a vacation here
closeted behind Mark's office door seemed, she really
needed to be out in the hospital keeping an eye on Harris.

Gina left the office and returned to the nurses' station.
The ER was empty except for Jason. It felt unnerving,
eerie. Like the moment in a horror movie right before the
stupid babysitter decides to open the basement door.

Jason looked up and anticipated her request—one of
the many reasons he was so good at his job. "You looking
for Mr. Personality again? Nora caught him barging into
exam rooms and threw him out. He stomped off toward
the cafeteria."

"Thanks." Gina turned away. As she reached to her left
for the silver button to open the double doors leading out
of the ER, the noise of a car horn honking filled the air,
followed by the screech of brakes slipping, the clamor of
breaking glass, and a crash that rocked the building.

It was a car.

Coming right at them.

The car ripped through the outside wall, the waiting room,
the inner wall into the ER, and the wall in front of the nurses'
station, stopping a mere two feet in front of Gina, its snow-
covered headlights winking at her.

Looked like a BMW 6-series. Her mother had one just like it.

Dust filled the air. Then the tinkle of glass as the overhead light bulbs shattered and rained down on them. Then came the whine of metal snapping as the rectangular fluorescent light fixture swung loose, dangling by an electrical cord, followed by a cascade of ceiling tiles.

"Son of a—" Gina was surprised to hear her own voice over the kaleidoscope of noise. She steadied herself as the front of the nurses' station collapsed, leaving Jason sitting on his chair surrounded by chaos and looking stunned.

"Jason, get into triage and clear it of any patients, see if anyone's hurt. I've got the car." She coughed against the dust, heard Jason calling a trauma code. He was standing, the phone to his ear, staring at the car that now occupied the space where the wall once stood—where Gina had been standing not ten seconds earlier. "Jason, go!"

The clerk started and ran past the crumpled car hood and pushed through the door to the waiting room. Gina made her way to the driver's door of the now-totaled car, which was pinned shut by the remnants of the wall.

The driver was hidden behind the front and side air bags. Gina raced around to the other side, her shoes slipping in the puddles of melting snow the car had dragged in. The passenger door was more exposed, though not enough for Gina to open it. But the window was cracked, barely hanging on.

She grabbed a phone receiver from the nurses' station and used it to finish breaking the window. The glass rained down in small pebbles. She cleared as much of it as she could, then pushed the passenger-side air bags out of her way. The car's interior was filled with smoke and powder—residue from the air bags deploying. Still no sound or movement from the driver.

Adrenaline urging her on, Gina copied a move she'd seen the medics do—they made it look easy, but as she climbed in feet first, she caught her ankle, banged it good, then almost fell out again before she managed to leverage her weight into the passenger compartment. Her braids caught on the upper seat belt anchor, and she lost some hair yanking herself free.

Finally she could reach the driver. She shoved an air bag out of her way and got her first look.

It *was* her mother.

"LaRose Freeman, what the *hell* are you doing here?" Gina asked as she stabilized her mother's cervical spine. "Can you hear me? It's Gina, your daughter. Open your eyes!"

Nothing. Gina checked her airway—clear. Breathing was even. Pulse rapid but strong. A small abrasion marred LaRose's smooth, Botoxed brow line, but not enough to explain her lack of response. Head injury? Spinal cord damage?

Gina's adrenaline revved into panic.

She turned to call out behind her, "I need some help over here!"

No one came. The nurses' station was destroyed. Where the hell was everyone?

That was when she saw the flames snaking out from under the hood of the car.

WHEN JIM SAW THE CAR AIMING FOR THE WAIT-ing room windows, he tackled Nicky and his mother, pushing them under the stretcher—the only shelter the alcove provided. At least that was how Nora chose to see it—although, because Nicky and his mom were between Jim and shelter, Jim's actions may have been motivated by something less altruistic.

There was no place for Nora to hide, though, so as the car crashed through the front windows, all she could do was to flatten herself against the wall and pull the alcove's curtain around her to shield herself from flying glass and debris.

The crash had been loud yet strangely muffled, like being under water. Then everything became bigger, brighter, as the howl of the storm joined the carnage inside the waiting room. Thuds of furniture being thrown aside mingled with the cracks of wood breaking, the ripping of drywall, and the screech of metal against metal. The sounds collided so that it was impossible to tell which came first as Nora's brain tried to process them and put them in proper order.

The sounds were accompanied by the smells of winter, brisk and clean, and the stench of burned rubber, charred plastic, and gasoline. When the last hit Nora's nostrils, she thrust the curtain aside, clearing her field of vision.

Dust and broken glass and pink insulation filled the air. Paper was everywhere—magazines, patient charts, lab slips. All now confetti spinning in the wind. It was like being inside a snow globe of destruction. One that also featured a car sitting in the middle of the ER, trapped inside the wall separating the waiting room from the nurses' station.

The car had smashed right through the children's corner of the waiting room. Thank God no kids were playing there when it happened.

But Mark Cohen had been standing there, looking out the window.

"Mark?" Nora called. When she inhaled it tasted like wood pulp and sawdust. She coughed and tried again. "Mark?"

"I'm here," came his answer from the opposite side of the car. "Gonna need a little help."

"I'm coming."

Jason, the ER desk clerk, came running in. "Gina's

taking care of the driver," he gasped, breathless as he took in the carnage. "What can I do?"

Nora turned back to Jim and their patients, the ER's disaster protocol ratcheting through her brain. First, evacuate any non-emergent patients from the scene. "Get them and any patients left in the ER down to the auditorium. Then see if there's anyone hurt in the ER. Grab the nurses, tell them to implement the disaster protocol."

Jason nodded and turned to help Nicky and his mother to their feet. Nora picked her way through the rubble, carefully stepping over broken glass and skirting fallen furniture as she circled around the rear of the vehicle. Snow was blowing inside, already half an inch or more covering the debris. With it came a biting cold, impossible to ignore, even with her mind focused on finding Mark and making contingency plans to evacuate the ER.

"Mark!" she called. "Where are you?"

"Over here." His voice came from beneath the overturned play center that had housed several video screens meant to entertain kids while they waited. "I'm stuck."

Nora assessed the situation. The video components themselves weren't heavy, but they'd been encased in a weighty metal and wooden frame to prevent theft. She found an opening and spotted Mark's face.

"I'm going to need some help moving this. Are you hurt?"

"Yeah. Feels like a tibia fracture. And I think I blew my knee out. Hurts like a son of a bitch, but I'm fine otherwise." Snow blew in between the gaps in the wrecked equipment.

"Let me get you some blankets, then I'll grab some guys to help." She reached through the gap and held his hand for a moment. Good strong pulse, but his fingers were cold and his lips were already blue. "Aren't you glad we didn't get the aquarium you wanted for out here?"

He laughed, then choked it off. "Damn, that hurts."

"I'll be right back," Nora assured him. "Don't go anywhere."

"WHERE SHOULD WE TAKE HIM?" LUCAS ASKED Amanda once they had Jerry and his cane loaded into a wheelchair. Jerry said nothing but seemed alert, concentrating on his surroundings, realizing that something was wrong.

"The clerk said there are no therapists in today; let's take him up to rehab. You can get us in, right?" Amanda asked. Lucas nodded. "Then you can see for yourself that he's in no condition to go home tomorrow."

They rolled Jerry down to the elevator.

"Amanda, I might not be able to delay Jerry's discharge," Lucas said as they waited.

"What's he going to do at our house? He can't manage stairs yet." Amanda shared a house with Gina—well, technically it was Gina's house and Amanda only rented a room, but Gina had made sure that Amanda felt like it was her home as well. "I guess between the two of us—"

"What about his parents?"

"They live in Orbisonia. And Gina said they have Jerry's sister's family living with him while her husband is deployed. He can't go there."

Jerry's cane hit the wall with a bang. "*He* is here." He glared up at them, his eyes clear for the first time that Amanda had seen in weeks. Ever since the shooting. "Want. To. Go. Home."

He punctuated each word with a fist against the arm of his wheelchair. Amanda flushed, ashamed to have been talking about Jerry as if he weren't there—even with her pediatric patients she tried not to ever make that mistake.

She crouched down, the silk ball gown rustling, and

stroked his arm, meeting his gaze. "It's okay, Jerry. We'll work something out. You can come home to our house."

He shook his head vehemently. "No. *My* home."

The elevator arrived and Lucas pushed Jerry's wheelchair onto it. Amanda followed with the cane.

"Do you mean your apartment?" Lucas asked as he pressed the button for the eighth floor, where PT was located.

"Yes. My home."

Lucas and Amanda exchanged glances. Jerry's apartment was a crime scene—at least it had been.

"It's all one floor," Lucas said agreeably. "Small and contained—that should be manageable."

"But, Lucas—"

"Surely the police would have released it by now. And Gina can have it cleaned, clear out any clutter he might trip over."

To ask Gina to go back there—to the place where she could have died? Could she even step foot inside, much less stay there?

Jerry seemed to follow Amanda's thoughts—was that another glimmer of the old Jerry returning? She hoped so. "Gina's strong."

The elevator doors opened onto the eighth-floor lobby. Across from them was a large picture window and to the side the doors leading to the pedestrian skywalk that crossed from the main hospital to the research tower. Amanda stared out the window in amazement.

She could see more of the storm from up here with the lights of the skywalk illuminating the evening. The windows rattled—even worse, the skywalk itself was swaying in the wind, snow so thick it resembled shrouds of white.

"Good thing the research tower is closed today," Lucas said, nodding toward the skywalk that connected the two buildings.

"I thought you were exaggerating about the snow," Amanda murmured as she gazed out into the maw of the storm. When she'd driven to work at five that morning, almost fourteen hours ago, it had been barely flurrying. The weather had been calling for only a few inches, most of it falling later tonight. But this—

"The storm turned a bit. Picked up speed. Plus the lake effect. Like I said before, it's a full-blown blizzard now."

Forget the ball, Amanda realized now. In the four years since she'd left South Carolina to come here to Pittsburgh, she'd never seen snow like this. "We're not even going home tonight, are we?"

"No, maybe not for a few days. Happy New Year's."

Jerry wheeled himself to the window, pressing his nose against the trembling glass. He seemed to be enjoying the chaos outside.

"Lucas, how can you be so calm? Aren't we supposed to be doing something? Is there a disaster plan?" And here she was parading around in a fancy ball gown. How unprofessional. She should run back down to Jerry's room and change back into her scrubs.

"We're at low census. Administration will be taking care of canceling the night shift; the staff already knows they're in it for the long haul. They'll be moving patients, consolidating them. There's nothing for us to do."

"But—" Amanda waved her hands at the snow hurling itself at the window.

"They'll call us if they need us. Until then we wait and stay out of their way." Lucas unlocked the door to the therapy room. "Okay, Jerry, show me what you've got."

LYDIA FINALLY GATHERED ENOUGH ENERGY TO leave the shooting range and trudge out to her SUV. At some point someone—Sandy, no doubt; the ex–SWAT

team leader had the instincts of a Jewish grandmother—
had cleared her Ford Escape of snow. But she'd sat inside
his office long enough that a new coating of snow already
covered it.

This snow was different from the snow they'd had a
few weeks ago. That snow had been friendly, fluffy. Snow
for making snow angels and catching on your tongue.
This snow was wicked, flung about with the force of a nail
gun fired at her face, sharp and biting.

There'd been only wet flurries and a few inches of
slush when she'd arrived at the training center two and a
half hours ago. Now standing in the empty parking lot
was like being in the center of a white tornado. Snow
came up above her boot tops; wind blew her parka hood
back, exposing her face; ice crystals stuck to her eyelids.
She slushed through the accumulation and awkwardly
climbed into the SUV using only her left arm.

Once inside the car, Lydia started the engine and let the
defroster do its work. She'd left her sling off to get into her
coat and was glad to have both hands free, even if she
couldn't move the right one very well. Technically she
shouldn't even be driving with one hand, but she'd been
going crazy trapped at home and couldn't resist. Of course,
that was before she realized this winter storm was far more
serious than AccuWeather had predicted.

She cradled her arm in her lap as the windshield wipers
scraped the snow, smearing it back and forth across her
field of vision. No fair blaming the weather forecast—it
was her own decision to come out here, and she'd have to
live with it.

Just like her mother had lived with her decisions.

Tears shanghaied her. Lydia swiped them, furious at the
way her body betrayed her. This was no time for crying—
and what was there to cry about, anyway? Maria had been
gone eighteen years. Those tears had been shed long ago.

Nevertheless, she laid her head on the steering wheel and stopped fighting the tears. Her cell phone rang. Trey. He'd hear how upset she was, want to know why—and she just wasn't strong enough to tell him. She'd call him back once she had her emotions under control. She turned it off and tossed it into the passenger seat.

She'd told Trey everything about her mother. He'd said he understood. Seemed more angry than frightened by the prospect of someone wanting to hurt her. He refused to accept that he could be in danger because she'd decided to stay with him, that just being with her made him a target, too.

Decisions. Consequences.

Now there was so much more at risk than just her life. Lydia squeezed her left arm tighter against her belly, hating the weakness the tears revealed. More than weakness, an old companion: fear. A fear that had lived inside her ever since Maria's death, curled up in her gut like a serpent waiting to coil itself around her body, stealing her breath, snatching her life.

The fear was back, wide awake, and ready to strike when she was most vulnerable.

Lydia sat up straight, choking down the tears. This was no time for hormones or emotions or whatever was roiling around inside her. She had to get back home, find a way to . . . She faltered. What could she do? She didn't have the resources of the police. She had no idea what her mother had been hiding from or who was after her.

Maybe all that was left was to run and hide. And take Trey with her.

She put the SUV in gear and hunched over the steering wheel to see through the windshield. Being from California, she wasn't used to driving in snow, but wasn't that what SUVs were made for? She wasn't too worried.

The wipers couldn't compete with the storm, giving her only a small squiggle of clear vision to navigate by.

The all-wheel drive handled the snow—a good ten inches by now, she estimated—without trouble as she pulled out of the parking space and began down the long driveway leading to Lexington Avenue.

As she approached the main road she squinted at what appeared to be a white and ash-streaked mountain of snow at the end of the drive. Almost as high as the SUV's hood, it blocked the exit. She stopped and considered her options. Obviously the plows had driven past, leaving behind a wall of snow that extended as far as she could see in either direction.

She backed up, revved the engine, and accelerated forward, hoping to burst the dam of snow and emerge on the other side. The tires fought for traction as she sped up. She rammed the snowbank head on.

But instead of driving through a pile of soft, fluffy snow, it was like hitting a brick wall. The impact roared through her arm; her head jerked forward and back, but the seat belt held her tight. She was glad she'd turned the air bags off. Something near the front of the car screeched, tore, then crunched sickeningly. The engine strained, wheels spinning, the front of the car actually driving up at an impossible angle, leaving the SUV canted at an unnatural angle as it came to a stop. Nowhere near the top and nowhere near through the mountain of snow. In fact, the damn snow pile appeared barely dented by the weight of the vehicle.

A shower of ice and snow rained down on the SUV, laughing at Lydia's foolhardy attempt to conquer it. The headlights reflected off the glistening whiteness, then slowly dimmed as snow buried them.

Then the engine gave a final whimper and died.

SIX

GINA FOUGHT THE PANIC THAT AMBUSHED HER AT the sight of the flames. She focused on her mother. No. Her patient. Who was still unresponsive—which meant she couldn't risk moving her.

The flames grew higher, licking paint from the crumpled hood.

She was going to have to take a chance on LaRose's cervical spine—the definite possibility of being burned alive trumped the remote possibility of an occult spinal injury. She reached over to undo LaRose's seat belt. It was jammed.

Gina tugged, but the latch wasn't budging. The fire was hot enough to make the sweat dripping from her neck crackle.

Smoke blinded her as she fought the seat belt. Every inhalation brought with it the rancid smell of burning oil and plastic, gagging her. She angled her body, bracing herself against the jagged edges of a buckled two-by-four protruding from the wall that sandwiched the car, and pulled on the belt.

Nothing. She'd kill for a good set of trauma shears right now. The flames had gotten greedy, reaching out, trying to set the wall—and Gina with it—on fire.

Her vision blurred with tears. She tried one last time to free LaRose.

A whoosh of white foam and powder blew across the windshield.

"Looks like you could use a hand," Ken Rosen said, hoisting the fire extinguisher and taking another shot at the flames.

Gina sputtered and gagged on the fumes, nodding her thanks as she shifted LaRose's weight, releasing the pressure on the buckle mechanism, and it finally clicked free. "Help me get her out."

Ken disappeared then returned, carrying a cervical collar and a short board used to do CPR. "Closest thing to a backboard I could find," he explained. Then he saw the occupant of the car. "Is that your mother?"

Gina didn't bother answering, she was too busy applying the c-collar. She stabilized her mother's neck and spine as Ken slid the CPR board behind LaRose.

"This isn't going to work," Gina finally decided. "We'll never get her through the window."

Ken left and reappeared with a blanket. "Cover both of you with this." He raised the metal base of an IV stand and hefted it like an ax in front of the windshield.

"Wait," Gina called as she covered LaRose with the blanket. "Shouldn't we wait for fire and rescue?"

"No way they're gonna get here any time soon, if at all. Have you seen the roads? The city's shut down. Now get under the blanket."

She did as she was told and soon heard the crunching

of windshield safety glass buckling as his blows echoed through the car. It took him several swings, but a few minutes later he sounded the all clear. In the meantime, Gina continued to assess LaRose. Her pulse was fast but strong and steady, her skin nice and warm. When she removed the blanket, she saw that LaRose's eyes were fluttering open.

"Wha—happ—" LaRose's mouth drooped to one side and her words were slurred.

"It's okay," Gina tried to reassure her even as her own panic escalated. "You're at Angels. You're going to be fine."

"Had—to—get—you." LaRose was more alert now, frowning as she fumbled her words, straining to make herself clear.

Typical LaRose. She'd never adjust her carefully laid plans to suit a little thing like a winter storm. The world, including the weather, was meant to revolve around her. "It's a blizzard out there. You never should have been on the roads."

"Your—father—sent—me."

Moses. He'd made no effort to hide the fact that he saw Jerry's shooting as the perfect opportunity for Gina to disengage from a "relationship with no future." He assumed that the only reason she'd stayed with Jerry was to spite him.

No doubt he wanted LaRose to fetch their errant daughter back home in time for his big New Year's Eve charity ball tonight. Had to show off Gina, give everyone a chance to ooh and ahh over his daughter and her accomplishments—which then, of course, he'd take full credit for.

Guess his plan backfired this time. "Moses can go stag," Gina told LaRose as she secured her to the makeshift backboard with gauze. "We need to take care of you first."

"Hello, Mrs. Freeman," Ken called to LaRose. He'd spread a sheet over the car's hood and climbed on top of it. "Don't worry, we're going to get you out of there."

"Does anything hurt?" Gina asked her.

"My head."

"Can you squeeze my hands?" Gina grabbed both of LaRose's. Her right hand lay limply in Gina's while the left was able to squeeze tight. "No pain here?" She quickly palpated LaRose's belly.

"No."

"Okay, let's get you out. I'm going to slide you sideways onto this sheet." She reached for the end of the sheet Ken handed her. It was an old nursing trick to move patients by sliding them along a sheet tucked beneath their body. Gina gently rotated LaRose, taking care to keep her spine as straight as possible, and slid her head and torso onto the passenger seat, over the top of the sheet. Her legs came free, the right one dragging behind the left.

"Gina." Ken reached in to help LaRose's right leg up onto the sheet.

"I know. Right-side weakness, facial muscles and speech involved as well." She was avoiding using the word *stroke* out loud in her mother's presence. LaRose wouldn't panic overtly—panic was not in the Freeman family vocabulary—but with her high blood pressure Gina wanted to avoid any further anxiety. "Once we clear her for injuries, we need to rule out a CVA."

Ken awkwardly folded his body over the steering wheel and gathered the sheet around LaRose's legs. "Okay, on three. One, two, three."

Together they lifted LaRose over the dash and through the windshield's opening onto the hood of the car.

"Thank God she never lets her weight get over one-ten," Gina joked. She hauled herself through the window she came in by and joined LaRose again, holding her hand as Ken ran for a stretcher.

"Moses—won't—appreci—like it." LaRose said with an effort at a smile that made her face appear ancient as her facial muscles drooped.

"Moses can learn to do his own dirty work instead of sending you." Gina shocked herself with the words, but one look at her mother reinforced her anger.

"Regina!" No surprise that even a stroke couldn't stop her mother from defending her father.

"Don't 'Regina' me, LaRose. Moses can go to hell."

AFTER NORA REASSURED MARK THAT THEY WERE going to get him out, she retraced her steps past the triage desk to the ER. It would normally have been faster to go the other way, through the door leading to the security office, but it was blocked by debris.

The nurses' station—the communication heart of the ER—was in shambles. Smoke stank up the air, the patient tracking board had been impaled by a fallen light fixture, ceiling tiles and debris covered the counters, and the computer monitors were black. Jason's desk had collapsed under the debris, leaving the area looking like a boat with a gaping hole below the waterline, sinking fast.

Cold air and snow gusted through the hole in the wall around the car. She made a note to call maintenance, get some plywood up ASAP. Ken Rosen was working with Gina inside the wrecked car.

"Do you need help?" she called.

"I think we're good. Anyone else hurt?"

"Mark Cohen hurt his leg. I'm going to go for more help."

Ken nodded and turned back to his work extricating the

driver. The path in front of the nurses' station was unnavigable, so Nora jogged around the back of the station and crossed the hall to the trauma rooms. There she grabbed some blankets from the warmer.

As she was leaving, Jim Lazarov came through the doors on the opposite side of the nurses' station, the ones leading from the main hospital.

"Jason is with Nicky and his mom and the guys from the zoo," he reported in a rush. He definitely wasn't bored anymore; his expression was that of a little boy who'd just been told there was a snow day at school and it was time to play. "The nurses are stocking carts with supplies in case we need to move operations."

Nora shivered and draped one of the warm blankets around her own shoulders. "Good. I need help getting Mark out."

They headed to the security office. Only one guard was there, talking on the phone. Nora didn't recognize him; he was one of the new hires, and he seemed both young and enthusiastic, excited about being in on the action. She thought about the shootings that had happened before Christmas and hoped this was the most action they would see tonight.

A shiver shook her as she remembered the panicked feeling of finding Seth almost dead, facing death herself. She tried hard not to dwell on what had happened—everyone had gotten out alive, Seth was going to be okay, she was going to be okay. It was better to focus on work . . . and on building her new life with Seth.

She still had to call him, break the news that she wasn't coming home anytime soon.

"The fire department says they can't send a truck," the guard said, covering the phone receiver with one hand. "They're fighting two major fires, one on the Hill and one on the North Side. They asked if a rescue vehicle would be okay? They have one nearby, but with the roads, it will take them a while to get here."

"I think we're fine," Nora said. "Tell them we'll call them back if we need them. And let them know our ER is out of commission. They'll have to divert any patient traffic and EMS to other hospitals."

He relayed her message and hung up the phone. "Anything I can do to help?"

"Yeah, we could use another pair of hands. Come with me."

They circled back past the wrecked car. Jim stopped and stared.

"Are you coming?" Nora asked.

Jim nodded, his gaze fixated on the activity around the car. Ken had just maneuvered the driver onto the hood of the car. "Is that Gina's mother in there?"

Nora looked more closely. It was. Jeez, like Gina needed any more family drama in her life right now.

Ken Rosen crossed their path, pushing a stretcher. "Looks like she had a stroke," he said, indicating LaRose. "Go take care of Mark; we've got this covered."

Nora led her small band of rescuers back down the hall, stopping at the trauma bay to grab another stretcher, a backboard, a c-collar, and splinting supplies. By the time they arrived back in the waiting room, they found that Mark had managed to clear most of the smaller debris away from his head and torso, leaving just his leg pinned under the supporting wall of the activity station.

"Maybe it's only my knee," he said, teeth chattering. Nora draped a blanket around his head and shoulders. The wind had swept a lot of the paper debris out the gaping hole in the window, replacing it with several inches of snow, drifting around their feet.

"We'll have you out in a second," the guard said, squatting to lift the piece of metal and particle board while Jim and Nora slid Mark free.

Together they splinted his leg and got him on the backboard, then lifted him onto the stretcher. "Let's get you someplace warm."

As they pushed him out into the main ER, Mark gasped, pushing himself up on his elbows to get a good look at the debris. "What the hell happened to my ER?"

SHADOW-ETCHED SNOW FILLED LYDIA'S VISION IN every direction. She sure as hell had something to cry about now. Her seat belt dug into her shoulder, holding her into the seat as the Escape sat tilted to the right and rear. Like a kicking bronco frozen halfway through bucking its rider off.

She tried the ignition again. The battery still worked—the radio came on—but the engine wouldn't catch. She turned off everything that might drain the battery and tried again. No joy.

Should she walk back to the training center? Shelter there until the storm passed? No, the door had locked behind her and she didn't have a key. As much as she hated to do it, she had no choice but to call Trey and ask for help.

She flicked on the interior light and searched for her cell. She had to unstrap herself from her seat belt and crawl downhill to the passenger seat until she found it wedged in the space between the seat and the door. Tugging her glove off with her teeth, she hit the buttons.

"Trey Garrison." His voice was distant and she knew he must be out in a vehicle, using the hands-free.

"It's me. I need a favor."

"Hang on a second." She heard the grating sound of a

truck pulling off the side of a road. "Sure, what do you need?"

"Do you have any trucks out near Lexington? Or even a snowplow I could hitch a ride with?"

"What happened?"

She quickly explained about her mishap with the snowbank. To her relief he didn't laugh—at least not too loudly. "Surfer girl, aren't you supposed to be home resting your broken arm? What are you doing out there anyway?"

Here came the bad part. "Sandy loaned me one of his guns and we met out here to practice, so I'd feel comfortable with it."

There was silence for a long moment and she was afraid the connection had gone dead. "Trey?"

"I'm on my way." He didn't break the connection even though he usually never drove and talked on the phone at the same time—especially not if he was in one of the city vehicles. Trey always played it safe. "You know you're not even supposed to be driving—I should have taken the car keys, should have known you'd—"

"I'd what? Make a decision to protect myself? Seems like a good idea, given that a hit man came looking for me and that there may be more on the way." She didn't understand Trey's hatred of guns. After all, his father and brothers and a sister were all law enforcement officers; he'd grown up surrounded by guns. "I can't sit around and do nothing."

"No. You can't. Instead you have to go blundering around in the middle of a blizzard with one arm out of commission."

"The weather said—"

"The weather was wrong. And you don't have any experience driving in snow—"

"This was when Sandy had the time—" Their words were overlapping so that anyone else would hear only gibberish, but they understood each other. As well as the anger that underlay their words.

"Why can't you let the police do their jobs? We could get out of town for a few weeks—"

"Because I want it over! I can't stand this. Waiting and worrying. Afraid every time you leave the house that I'll never see you again. It's killing me, Trey."

Her words knifed through the silence in the SUV. Even the wind howling outside held its breath, waiting for Trey's response.

The past few weeks, it felt like all they did was argue. He'd tried to coddle her, and she'd bitten his head off, protesting that she wasn't an invalid. He'd tried to comfort her, invited her to join him and his family for Christmas Eve services, and she'd ranted on about the meaninglessness of a holiday based on promises of peace and goodwill that would be broken and forgotten by the time the Mass let out.

He'd tried to make love to her, and all she'd felt was terror that she'd made a terrible, awful mistake staying, that because of her, he would get hurt.

"If you can't talk to me about it, maybe you should talk to someone," he finally replied, his words quiet, his tone carefully neutral. As if she were a strung-out meth-head or the like. "Someone professional. Like a counselor."

Since he couldn't see her, Lydia indulged herself and rolled her eyes. Why was it that Trey thought talking could solve everything? "I'm fine. I don't need to talk to anyone."

"No. You're not fine. You're angry all the time—angry at me, angry at my folks, angry at Gina and Nora when they call, even angry at God. It's poisoning you, Lydia."

"God? Maria died in a *church*, for chrissake! Of course I'm furious with God. Where was he when she needed him? Why wasn't he around to answer her prayers that day?" Her voice was a thunderclap inside the SUV, shaking snow free from the windows, competing with the wind outside. Venting should have made her feel better, but instead it made her feel small and vulnerable. Alone.

If they'd been face-to-face, he'd be holding her hands in his, sharing his warmth. She'd also never be able to say half these things, show such vulnerability, not in person, not even to Trey. But now she was shivering and all alone. Just like she'd been eighteen years ago, hiding in a church confessional, watching her mother get beaten to death.

"God was there, Lydia. Don't you see? He's always been there. He was answering Maria's prayers to keep you safe. It was a miracle you weren't also killed."

"Right." She couldn't erase the bitterness from her tone. "Just like it was a miracle that the hit man found Gina and shot Jerry when he was looking for me? I doubt either of them would see it that way."

"I do. You could have been killed that night. I thank God every day that you weren't."

Trey talked as if he and God were on a first-name basis, could order for each other at Starbucks, carpooled together. Until Lydia had moved to Pittsburgh and met Trey, she'd given up on God, considering him just a wistful idea conjured by humans tired of feeling alone and powerless in the universe. Now Trey had her thinking there might be something—someone—out there.

The thought of a God gave Trey comfort, kept him calm when things got bad. Where was her comfort? Why was it that all she felt when she thought of God was anger? Anger and fear that if he was out there, then he might not keep the people she loved safe—just like he'd failed Maria.

A short burst from a siren jolted her from her thoughts.

"I'm here," Trey said over the phone. "Just give me a minute to clear a path."

She hung up and waited to be rescued—the first time she'd ever in her life let someone else save her.

Don't count on it ever happening again, she decided as she sat in the dark and the cold, her teeth chattering and pain throbbing through her arm. Trey might trust in God, but Lydia trusted in herself.

SEVEN

AMANDA WATCHED LUCAS PUT JERRY THROUGH A grueling set of testing—both physical and cognitive—that left Jerry sweating, exhausted, straining to keep his eyes open. Finally Lucas let him return to his wheelchair, and Amanda helped him from the parallel bars into the chair. Jerry didn't even protest, his body trembling with the strain of remaining upright. She got him settled, made sure he had his cane and his gun.

"It'll be okay," she reassured him. Jerry said nothing, just looked at her as if he knew she was lying. She hoped she wasn't. "Let me talk with Lucas for a minute. You rest here."

She joined Lucas at the desk in the opposite corner where he was writing notes. "You see what I mean now, right? He did awful—his balance is off, his hand-eye coordination is gone, and his memory and language skills—"

Lucas nodded, finishing his note before turning to her. "This is the difference between pediatrics and neurology,

I think. I see progress—remarkable progress, in fact. You see possibilities—you see what he was and want him to get back there, become the same person he was. That's not going to happen, Amanda."

She felt her entire face wrinkle with a frown. Not one of petulance; one of anger. She hated it when Lucas went all I'm-a-genius-and-you're-not superior, but the fact that he was doing it now when they were talking about the future of one of their best friends? If he wasn't careful, she'd be giving him more than a frown. She'd be giving him a fight that he'd never forget, fiancé or no fiancé.

"You're not going to contest the insurance company? Get him into rehab?"

He didn't seem to notice either her scowl or her tone. "How can I? From a neurologic point of view, he's doing fantastic. How can I justify taking up a bed in a rehab facility that could be better used for someone who needs intensive intervention—someone like a soldier returning home after a traumatic brain injury?"

Low blow. He knew darn well that half of Amanda's family had served with the Marines. "But Jerry would get better faster in rehab. You can't deny that."

"Of course not. But it's a question of degrees—"

"I don't care!" Her shout rattled her—and him.

Lucas faced her head-on, arms crossed over his chest, and stared at her. In any other man, she'd take the silence and posture for anger or arrogance, but she knew better with Lucas. He had his hands hidden inside the sleeves of his lab jacket to keep himself from touching her—from touching anything that could potentially contaminate him or hurt him; his face had become an expressionless mask and his foot was tapping a strange cadence, counting out one of the obscure mathematical progressions he used to calm himself when his anxieties were suddenly flushed out into the open.

What in other men would be a show of arrogance, in Lucas was a sign that he was deeply conflicted, torn so much that he'd retreated, a turtle in his shell, unable to speak until he mastered his emotions.

Amanda took in a deep breath, working hard to control her own emotions. "It's not your fault," she conceded. "I understand. It's just that—" She had to look away, couldn't face Lucas—not after he'd worked so hard to save Jerry, worked miracles, in fact. "I want everything back the way it was."

Lucas slowly thawed. He nodded and wrapped his arms around her—an extraordinarily rare display of public affection considering that Jerry sat watching across the room. He said nothing at first, just held her tight. Then he whispered, "I know."

They parted as Jerry approached in his wheelchair. "Can we talk?" he asked, nodding to Amanda.

Lucas sat back down and returned to his paperwork while Amanda and Jerry moved across the room to the chairs so that she could sit and face him at eye level.

"He can't send you to rehab," Amanda said, thinking that was what he wanted to talk about.

But Jerry merely shrugged. "Don't want to go." Then he further surprised her by reaching across the space between them to touch her arm. "Thanks."

She stared at him. What was wrong with everyone today? "What do you mean, you don't want to go? Don't you want to get better?"

As soon as the words were out, she regretted them. They were so harsh—and they unveiled a truth that she didn't want to see. That Jerry might never gain back what he'd lost.

"I want to go home." He was pounding his fist against his thigh in rhythm with his words but Amanda doubted he even knew it, he was concentrating so hard on getting the words out the right way. His eyes squinted with effort. "I *am* better."

Amanda knew that many patients with traumatic brain injuries had no perception of their limitations—their damaged brains couldn't acknowledge the reality of what had been lost; they would delude themselves that they were fine, able to care for themselves, return to their old life. The ultimate power of denial.

She was so frustrated and angry that she wanted to cry—it was the same feeling that overwhelmed her whenever she was faced with a seriously ill pediatric patient, this need to defend and protect and fight.

But how could she fight Jerry's own delusions without hurting him as well?

Shoulders slumped with the weight of her emotions, she rested her forehead in her palm.

Jerry patted her shoulder. "It's okay," he said in a singsong voice as if she were the patient, the one facing the devastation of life as she knew it. "Everything's gonna be okay."

Amanda didn't have the heart to tell him how very wrong he was.

TOGETHER, GINA AND KEN WHEELED LaROSE INTO an exam room at the far end of the hall where the temperature hadn't yet dropped into the arctic realms. Still damn cold, though. Melissa, one of the nurses, came in to help.

They quickly cleared LaRose, ruling out any injuries from the car accident, got her on a monitor, started an IV, and began to bring down her blood pressure, which was an alarming 210/144. Then, just as Ken was on the phone arranging for a head CT, the lights went out.

Gina couldn't even find the energy to curse as they sat

in darkness for three seconds before the emergency generator kicked in.

"What's wrong?" LaRose asked, clutching Gina's hand.

"Nothing. Just relax."

"Did the car accident cause that?"

"I'll go check," Melissa said.

Ken was redialing radiology, who seemed to be giving him grief about the CT. "I know you're short-staffed for the holiday, everyone is. . . . What do you mean, the radiologist doesn't have time to read it? He's not even here. He works from home reading everything on his computer. . . . I don't care. I'm coming down with my patient in ten minutes—did I mention she's the wife of Moses Freeman, the state's largest malpractice attorney? . . . Oh, you'll be ready and waiting for us? Thanks, I thought so."

He hung up with a bang. "Never thought I'd be using your father's name like that."

Gina would have laughed if LaRose hadn't been there watching. Ken Rosen and her father Moses were the modern equivalent of mortal enemies. Moses had once sued a group of doctors that included Ken, which had meant that Ken had to stay in Pittsburgh dealing with the suit while his wife and daughter went on vacation to Disney World. Unfortunately, both of them had died in a car crash while in Orlando and Ken blamed himself for not being there— blamed Moses, too, but not as much as Gina had once she learned the truth: that Moses had known all along that Ken was innocent, and had included him in the suit only as part of a gambit to force a settlement.

"It's the least Moses can do for you," she said. As soon as she knew for sure what was going on with LaRose, she'd call her father. She was dreading it; conversations with Moses had a way of erupting into ballistic warfare.

LaRose began to shiver, and Gina got another blanket for her. Just as she was tucking the blanket around her mother's model-thin frame, Melissa returned.

"The power's out all over the city," she announced. "They're closing down the ER and diverting all EMS calls. Everyone's moving to the auditorium."

"Then I guess we'd better get over to radiology before they go AWOL," Ken said. He and Melissa steered the stretcher through the door, Gina following behind.

She really wanted to get back to Jerry, make sure he was okay, but she needed to take care of LaRose first. At least she could check to see if Janet had any news about Harris.

"I'll catch up," she told Ken as she pulled her cell phone out and dialed Janet.

This time it was the third ring before Janet picked up. "What?"

"Just wondering what the guys in L.A. said about Harris."

"I'm waiting for them to get back to me. In case you haven't noticed, we just lost power, so things are a bit nuts around here."

"It's crazy here, too."

"I'll call L.A. back, see if I can talk to a supervisor. Unfortunately, the DEA doesn't really answer to me, and they won't give me any info on one of their agents or a case without going through channels."

"Did you warn Lydia, just in case?"

"I tried; she's not answering. I can't get anyone out to Angels until the weather clears—even our SUVs have been grounded. I'm going to keep trying, but I can't stop Harris from asking questions. Who knows, maybe he's got a lead on who sent the hit man and needs Lydia to help him piece things together."

"But what if he's not legit? He's got a gun, Janet." Panic filtered into Gina's words as she remembered the damage one man with a gun had done three weeks ago.

"If you're that worried, have your security guys detain him until I can verify his credentials. You can invoke privacy concerns or some other legal bullshit to keep him from wandering around the premises."

Better than nothing. "Call me as soon as you hear anything?"

"I will. Gina, I have to go now."

Janet hung up and Gina slid her phone into her pocket. The ER was now completely empty, as dark and cold as the *Titanic* going under.

She turned away from the corridor leading to radiology and headed back toward the nurses' station. The security office adjoined the waiting room across from the nurses' station and beside the ambulance entrance. It occurred to Gina that maybe she could use the hospital security cameras to find where Harris was.

Okay, then. A plan. She stepped through the debris littering what was left of the nurses' station and jogged down the hall to the security office. Inside, she found hospital CEO Oliver Tillman and three guards behind the counter at the monitors, thick binders of emergency procedures open before them.

"We have three days of fuel for the emergency generator," one guard was saying. "If we minimize consumption."

"I've ordered all ambulatory patients and nonessential personnel to the auditorium," Tillman said. "We'll consolidate all other patients and staff to the ICU floor. Make it easier for staff to rotate care."

"Good. We can cut back on electrical output and heat to the unoccupied parts of the hospital."

Another guard hung up a phone. "Pittsburgh EMS is diverting all ambulance traffic away from us. The police already have most of the roads closed."

"We've got more problems than just the weather and a power outage," Gina told them.

Tillman glanced up at her, scowling. "Dr. Freeman. I thought you would be tending to your mother."

"I would be. Except that I just spoke with Detective Kwon, and she suggested that the DEA agent named Harris be detained until she can verify his credentials. She's concerned for patient safety. The ER staff reported that he was interfering with patient care." It was stretching the truth, but Gina figured better safe than sorry. Especially when it involved Jerry's safety.

"Think he's another hit man?" The security guard's tone was one of excitement. He too was young, obviously new. Where was Tillman finding these guys? Gina wondered.

"If he is, then he's after Lydia Fiore and Jerry. He was asking about both of them."

Tillman's scowl deepened. He reached for the phone. "Thank you, Dr. Freeman. We'll deal with Harris once I've verified it. Please join the others in the auditorium."

"But—"

"Dr. Freeman." Tillman's expression turned glacial. "I have enough on my hands. Now, please go to the auditorium. I'm sure they need your help." He turned his back on her and pointed to the security monitors. "Find me that man, Harris. We can't let him go wandering the hospital until we double-check his credentials."

At least Tillman was working on the problem, even if he had summarily dismissed Gina. He was right, anyway; she would be more help in the auditorium with the others.

Gina left the security office and went down to the ER locker room. There she grabbed her lab coat, pulling it on top of her sweater, and stuffed its pockets with supplies: two penlights, a pen and note cards, calculator, disposable scalpel, hemostats, gloves, trauma radio. The nurses would have pulled supply carts with other essentials like gauze, bandages, and medications.

As the familiar weight of the jacket settled on her shoulders, for the first time since the shooting, she felt close to normal. If not for her worry about LaRose and concern about Harris roaming the hospital, the idea of practicing meatball medicine would be fun.

On her way toward radiology, where LaRose was getting her CT scan, Gina took a route that led her back past the security office. She reached the devastated nurses' station, picking her way through the debris littering the floor—no easy feat, since someone had turned all the lights off—when she spotted Harris talking to Tillman in the security office.

Good. At least they knew where Harris was. They could verify his credentials, make sure he was no threat to Jerry.

Then she froze, pressing her body deeper into the shadows. Harris was holding a gun to Tillman's head.

EIGHT

A KNOCK SOUNDED ON LYDIA'S DRIVER'S DOOR, and then it opened, wind and snow blowing in at her. Trey Garrison was six feet tall, but his head was currently level with hers because of the way the SUV was elevated.

"You're jammed in good." He grinned at her like she'd earned a gold star for her driving skills. That was Trey. Didn't matter that they'd been arguing about the existence of God a few minutes earlier. Didn't matter that they'd been arguing—well, *she'd* been arguing—all week. "Let's get you out of there and I'll take you home."

"Don't you have to work?"

"I was headed over to Angels when you called—seems a car drove through the ER."

"What? Everyone all right?" she asked as he pushed the door into the snowbank, giving her more room to maneuver out of the SUV.

"Said they had it under control when they canceled the rescue call. But they're closing the ER, went on diversion.

With the power out, I thought I'd check to see if they needed an extra pair of hands."

"The power's out?"

"Whole city."

Lydia twisted sideways, sheltering her arm in the cast by holding it against her chest, and slid out the door and into Trey's arms. He held her steady, balancing on the uneven snow and ice as he walked backward to level ground and set her on her feet again. "You're freezing. Can you walk okay?"

She stomped the feeling back into her feet, her toes squishing the snow melted inside her boots, while Trey locked the SUV. He'd broken a path through the mound of snow leading out to the street, but his tracks were already filling in.

The sky pressed down in a smothering, unrelenting blanket, feeling so close that Lydia thought she might be able to stretch up and touch the heavy steel-gray clouds. An eerie silence surrounded them and with the snowbank blocking the street and the falling snow blocking the sight of the training center buildings, it was as if they were marooned alone on a deserted polar ice cap.

Despite her down parka—a Christmas gift from Trey— Lydia shivered. She'd be the first to admit that she had the personality of a hermit, wasn't always suited for human company or socializing, but she was glad Trey was there. This isolation, this feeling of being stranded, cut off in every direction, was enough to make her yearn for the hustle and bustle of the ER.

Trey took her hand and held it tightly, one arm wrapped around her shoulders to keep her balanced as they followed his trail back out.

"What the hell is that?" she asked when she saw the vehicle he'd arrived in. It was a puke-yellow box on wheels with a short snout attached to a small snowplow blade.

"Hey, don't make fun of Bessie. You'll hurt her feelings." Trey patted the ugly truck like it was Old Yeller. "She was one of the city's first rescue vehicles. Doesn't have all the bells and whistles of the new ones and she's been retired for years, but on days like today she still comes in handy. Don't ya, girl?"

Trey helped Lydia climb into Bessie's passenger seat. When his hand brushed against the Taurus holstered at her waistband he flinched as if she were contaminated, but without a word he closed her door for her, trudged through the snow to the driver's side, and climbed in.

"Do you need help with your seat belt?"

"I got it." Suddenly Lydia felt as isolated and alone as she had outside in the storm. Used to be that wouldn't bother her—but now she hated it. Hated his disapproval.

Trey stayed silent. The road was treacherous enough to demand all his attention, but Lydia caught him continuously glancing in her direction. Waiting for her to speak first.

To say what? That she was sorry? Lydia couldn't help it if she didn't feel that his presence alone was enough to guarantee their safety—that was a simple fact. Her choice to protect herself should have nothing to do with his pride or manliness or whatever macho crap was fueling his anger.

In fact, *he* should apologize to *her*. For treating her like she didn't have a brain or a clue about what danger lay out there waiting for them.

Lydia's fury built, going from simmer to full boil, and she opened her mouth to vent it—but Trey spoke first.

"You know how you read about kids playing with guns and someone ends up dead? Ever wonder what happens to the other kid—the one who lived?"

Trey's voice was level, but when she turned to look at him, any hint of his usual good humor had vanished.

"That was me."

His words immediately shamed her. She sucked her

breath back in, swallowing her anger with it. She should never have underestimated him, assuming it was simple wounded male pride that had caused his anger about her carrying a gun. Lydia lay her hand on his thigh, unable to do more as he huddled forward over the steering wheel.

"Tell me." Then she added a word she knew she should use more often, especially with him. "Please."

The only sounds were the slush of the windshield wipers and the grind of the tires against the snow. The street was empty as far as she could see and unnaturally dark. She knew there was a streetlight ahead but couldn't see anything through the blur of white that filled the view.

"I was only eight," he finally started. "School was out for the summer—" He yanked the wheel as a blur of green appeared from the side. "What the hell?"

Bessie shuddered, then rolled to a stop, angled across the road. Brake lights flashed ahead of them from a green cargo van. It slid out of control, first going sideways, then headed toward them, then away but going the wrong direction down the street, and finally, in a gut-wrenching slow motion, careening further and further off its axles until it hit a utility pole, spun around it, and came to a rest driver's side down facing away from them, wheels spinning in the air.

The rear doors had sprung open somewhere midskid, momentum flinging small objects to scatter across the road behind the van. Trey slowly crept forward, keeping a light touch on the accelerator, as both he and Lydia craned to see through the windshield.

There was no movement from the driver's compartment. Trey halted Bessie about ten feet from the rear of the van and opened his door, hopping onto the running board to get a better look.

"I don't see any downed power lines," he said. "Wait here while I check on the driver."

Lydia didn't bother arguing with him. Instead she grabbed a flashlight from the dashboard charger and jumped out of the rescue truck, teeth smacking together as the impact rocked her arm in a less than gentle fashion. She'd taken two steps toward the van when a dark smudge in the corner of her eye caught her attention.

She glanced that way only to see a black blur skid over the snowbank on the side of the road. Then a strange honking sound filled the air—no, not honking . . . quacking?

JIM AND NORA HAD JUST WHEELED MARK BACK from X ray when the power went out. Mark had been only half right: He'd broken both bones of his lower leg. Nothing that he'd need surgery for, thank goodness, but still painful. Despite that, when the power went out and the emergency generator kicked in, he pushed himself up on his elbows and began barking orders.

"Make sure everything is transferred to the red outlets," he said, as if Nora didn't already know the emergency protocols inside and out. "The backup power won't go to the white ones. And charge everything with batteries— defibrillators, IV pumps, instruments."

"Already done," she reassured him. "While you were in radiology we began preparations to evacuate the ER."

He shivered despite the three blankets Nora had draped over him. "They can't fix the window?"

"No. All the maintenance man could do was staple a plastic tarp over the hole. It's fairly useless, already has tears ripped in it from the wind."

"Turn off everything electric and unplug everything," he ordered. "If snow gets into any outlets or lights and melts—"

"Exactly. I've got the lights off, we've moved all portable electronics to a back room, and everything else is shut down. In fact, you're the last patient we need to evacuate. But I didn't want to do it without your permission."

"I feel like the captain of the *Titanic*," he muttered. "Let's do it. Let's bug out."

"Don't you want me to splint your leg first?" Jim asked. He had all the splinting materials ready to go on a small cart. "It will help the pain once we immobilize your leg."

"Everyone else is already in the auditorium?"

"Yes," Nora said.

Mark gritted his teeth. "I'll wait until we're there. Let's go."

Jim and Nora pushed the stretcher out. The ER was dark, only emergency lighting, and the hallway acted as a wind tunnel, amplifying the sounds of the storm. They went down the back hallway, through the double doors, and into the corridor leading to the auditorium. With some help from the rest of the staff waiting there, they got Mark situated on the stage.

"I thought we'd have nonambulatory patients up here where the lighting is better," Nora told him. "I know the original plans called for using the cafeteria and its tables, but there are too many windows. It will get too cold in there if we lose the backup generator."

"We should have enough fuel for a few days."

"That's without a big hole in the front of the hospital sucking heat out. Tillman said to consolidate patients as much as possible." As they spoke, nurses ushered in a group of patients from pediatrics and the med-surg floors. Most had family with them.

"Ambulatory patients," she told Mark, nodding to the new group, "will be in the seating area, each group with a team of staff members assigned to them. And we'll move more cots up here for sleeping shifts for staff and patients—we can close the curtains for privacy."

"Lavatory facilities?"

"There are two large ones across the lobby, but I'm afraid it will be either sponge baths or taking people back to the ER staff locker rooms for showers. We may need to improvise some there if we're stuck here for any length of time."

"Could use the big sprayers from the kitchen sinks."

"Good idea. And the kitchen will stay warm enough since they'll continue providing food for everyone."

"What about the nonambulatory and critical patients? OB, for example?"

"Obstetrics patients are staying on their floor—they have their own OR staffed in case anyone needs an emergency c-section. The other nonambulatory patients are being moved to the ICU floor. If anyone takes a turn for the worse, they'll be in an area with dedicated staffing, the ORs, and all the supplies they'll need. The nurses, ancillary staff, residents, and surgeons are staying up there in the call rooms. I can rotate additional staff up to help if we stay quiet down here—most of our patients here are people who were discharged but unable to leave because of the snow."

"What kind of numbers we talking about?"

"Patients and staff down here? Looks like around seventy. Plus family members and visitors trapped by the storm. I'll get a final head count once everyone's here."

"And what if someone tries to come to the ER?"

"We're on diversion. Security placed a roadblock at the entrance, but it doesn't matter—the entire city is shut down, nothing's moving out there."

"Sounds like you have it all in hand."

Nora grimaced. "Don't jinx us now. Hopefully you'll remain our sickest patient. How about some morphine and we'll let Jim splint your leg?"

"I left the splinting stuff back in the ER," Jim said.

Nora resisted the urge to lash out at the intern—he could have gone back and gotten it while she and Mark were talking. Instead he had just stood there listening, no doubt waiting for an opportunity to curry favor with his boss.

"I'll go back and get it," she said. "I can double-check that we've everything else we need. And that will give the morphine time to work," she assured Mark.

"Good." He lay back on the stretcher. "Wouldn't want to make a fool of myself in front of all these people."

GINA HUDDLED IN THE SHADOWS AT THE CORNER of the nurses' station, trying to blend into the darkness, watching through the window in the security office's door. Harris lined up the three security guards, kneeling against the far wall. The closed door did little to muffle the sounds of the gunshots that followed.

She jerked with each shot. Three men dead in less than three seconds.

Tillman was shouting, but Gina couldn't distinguish his words through the terror screeching through her brain.

The ambulance bay doors down the hallway alongside the security office slid open, groaning against the weight of wind and snow. The sound of more men's voices came from outside.

Hide, she had to hide. Gina felt hopelessly exposed; there was no time to make it across the debris and out the doors to the elevator lobby or back down the open hallway to an exam room or the rear corridor. The destruction of the nurses' station had eliminated any dark corners beneath desks or countertops that she could use for cover. She got down on her hands and knees and crawled, hugging the shadows.

Her mother's destroyed car—no one would look there. It was her only hope.

Ignoring the broken glass scattered around her feet,

Gina shimmied through the BMW's passenger window again. She flung herself facedown across the driver's seat just as she heard the men's footsteps reach the former nurses' station. Inhaling the grainy scent of high-end car leather, she fought not to move, not to cry, not to breathe.

"What the hell, Harris?" a man with a South African accent said. There was the sound of stomping feet, more men following him in. "Thought this was meant to be a soft extraction. Now suddenly, we've a trail of bodies?"

"Couldn't be helped. My cover was blown. This idiot somehow got through to the DEA."

"Actually, it was my secretary," Tillman said, his tone distant. In shock. "Her son works—"

"Shut it." Harris didn't sound upset; he sounded revved up, as if killing three men in cold blood had given him a rush. "You three, get in there and change into the guard uniforms. There's a group of staff and patients being sent to the auditorium; I want them contained there."

"What about the rest of the hospital? We can't have people wandering around while we search for Fiore." The South African seemed as interested in thwarting Harris's plans as helping him—a rival, perhaps?

"Your team will start from the top and seal all the exits, lock down the elevators. Then once we have all the civilians contained, we'll start our search."

"And what about our escape?" the South African persisted. "There's snow drifts four, six feet high already. Only way we're going anywhere is in a snowplow."

"Don't suppose you have one, Mr. Tillman?" Harris's voice sounded jocular.

"No," Tillman replied. "We contract out—"

"No matter. Bring the rest of the gear in from the trucks, then move them into the ambulance bay. Yarborough, you get sentry duty. No one gets in or out. Station yourself where you have a view of the road—when a plow comes along, grab it. In the meantime, if we're not going anywhere, then neither is anyone coming here. This storm is the best thing that could have happened to us. Now we've all the time in the world to hunt for Fiore."

Gina risked edging a glance out from between the steering wheel and the dash. She counted six men plus Tillman and Harris. Who knew how many more there might be?

Even more frightening were the machine guns the men carried. They obviously had no intention of trying to continue any kind of subterfuge. They were dressed for war.

"Let's get this place locked down," Harris said. He was pacing and turned abruptly toward the car. Gina ducked back down, biting her lip. "Begin with killing the cell phones and Internet. Then we start hunting Fiore. Remember, no one touches her until we find out where she's hidden the evidence."

"Yeah, yeah, we know," a third man's voice came, sounding young and cocky.

The smack of flesh against flesh cracked through the air. Gina flinched and buried her face deeper into the seat cushion.

"Don't give me lip. If Mr. Black goes down, it's the needle for all of us. Which means you need to consider this your life's work. As in life or death. You understand me?"

"Yes, sir." Same man, much less cocky now.

"Okay, get started." Harris paced close to the BMW, close enough that Gina could see him raise a cell phone to his ear. "You made it to Fiore's? Has she shown yet?"

Trying to blend into the car's interior, Gina froze as Harris leaned against the driver's-side fender, idly observing the damage done to the wall. All he had to do was turn his head the slightest bit and he'd have a direct view inside the car.

Gina's pulse pounded louder than the bass beat at a rave. Sweat soaked her turtleneck, leaving her shivering as the cold air lapped it up. Her vision blackened from holding her breath for too long. She risked an inhalation, working hard to breathe in deep but silently.

Harris rapped his knuckles against the car hood as he listened. Finally, he nodded and pulled the phone away as he addressed the men. "What are you waiting for? You know the plan. Anyone gives you any trouble, kill them."

He took a step away from the car and Gina relaxed.

Then he returned to his phone conversation, spinning around to lean his elbows on the car hood, idly tracing patterns in the shattered glass. Gina squeezed her eyes shut, certain that if she even blinked too loud he'd find her.

"She's on the ER work schedule and I've been told she's with a patient, but we haven't found her yet," he said. "I've been forced to implement Plan B. I don't know, maybe a hundred or so patients and staff. The CEO said they've got a low census because of New Year's. No problem, we can handle them. Don't worry. No evidence will be left behind. When we're done, this place will be ashes and dust."

NINE

NORA WAS ON HER WAY BACK TO THE AUDITO-
rium with the cart of splinting supplies when her cell
rang. It was Seth. A thrill of anxiety shot through her—
was he okay? She'd been meaning to call him, hated
breaking the news that she was trapped here for the dura-
tion of the storm.

"Are you okay?" he said when she answered, his voice
tight with worry. "Where are you?"

"I'm fine. Sorry I didn't call sooner. You wouldn't believe the night we've had. The power's out so we're on
backup, a car plowed through the ER, I'm moving all the
patients to the auditorium and that means moving supplies
and equipment—"

"I was worried you were stuck somewhere in a snowbank."

"No. But I'm stuck here—probably at least for the
night. Tillman canceled the second shift because of the
storm."

"Yeah, they declared a state of emergency, said no one was allowed on the roads." He sighed. "They've even closed all the bars and restaurants, canceled the New Year's Eve celebrations."

"Well, you know my bad luck with New Year's." Nora tried to make a joke of it. "They'll probably name the blizzard after me."

"I was planning on changing your bad impression of New Year's." Seth's voice dropped into the ruggedly sexy range. "I have French champagne, strawberries, caviar, French chocolate—"

"And no doubt, that French maid outfit you're always fantasizing about," she said with a laugh, loving the idea that despite recuperating from surgery, Seth had made the effort to romance her. Nora wasn't used to anyone working so hard to make her feel good—usually she was the one taking care of everyone else.

It felt nice. Very nice.

"Hmm . . . French maid outfit, that's an idea—"

"Seriously, you're not doing anything dumb like trying to shovel snow? Your doctor said no heavy lifting—"

"Hey, he cleared me for light duty, I'm back in the clinic next week." Thank God. Seth at home, unable to get his adrenaline fix through surgery, was driving her batty. "But no, I'm just sitting on the couch with DeBakey, not shoveling snow. The neighbor's kid is—but we're gonna owe him some serious dough by the time this storm is over." Then his tone brightened. "Think they need another surgeon? I could come in."

"Give DeBakey some puppy loving from me. But no, don't come in. Not only shouldn't anyone be out driving in these conditions, you're not cleared to operate yet. Changing bandages in the clinic isn't the same as working in the OR all day." Then Nora realized why he'd chosen now to call. "Was the game on when the power went out?"

Seth's sigh sounded as sorrowful as a kid sent to bed early without his dinner. "First quarter and Penn State was getting ready to blow smoke up those Trojans' skirts." Seth had gone to college on a football scholarship from Penn State. Even here, in the heart of Pitt Panther territory, he proudly wore his Nittany Lion regalia. "You guys have backup power, so you're still online, right?"

"I guess. I've been too busy to get near a computer, much less surf the Web."

"I don't suppose—"

She was way ahead of him. Parking her cart in the hallway, Nora slipped into Mark Cohen's office and turned his computer on. "Give me a second. Yeah, we still have Internet."

"Great. Just go to ESPN.com, give me a score. Please." He drew out the last word as she typed. "I'll make it up to you when you get home. Caviar and champagne. I'll even put on the French maid outfit if you want."

Yeah, that wasn't exactly a picture she wanted in her head while here at work. "Who knows when I'll be home. You have the fire going?"

"Toasty warm. Don't worry about me, how are my Lions doing?"

She clicked on the bowl update icon. "Cool—they have a little video of the highlights."

"Don't torture me. What's the—"

The phone died. So did the Internet—the screen was replaced with an error message when Nora refreshed it. Had the storm taken down a cell tower? And at the same time the hospital's Internet—but wasn't that satellite? She hung up her cell and tried Mark's landline, but there was no dial tone. Must be the storm.

She pocketed her cell phone. Poor Seth, he'd just have to wait to hear that his Lions were winning. She had more important things to worry about, like an auditorium full of patients.

As she left Mark's office and began pushing the cart once more, the lights flickered, then went dead. That wasn't supposed to happen. Had the backup generator died? That would be *very* bad news.

The battery-operated emergency lighting came on—leaving the hall more in shadows than light, but enough so she wouldn't roll the cart into anything. She went a few more steps when the main lights returned.

Tillman's voice came over the intercom. "Attention. Attention. This is a Code White emergency. Our backup power is failing. All ambulatory patients, family, and staff need to move to the auditorium on the first floor immediately. This is not a drill. We estimate that we have twelve minutes of power remaining. I repeat, this is not a drill."

Good thing the nursing staff had already begun implementing Code White procedures when the main power went out, Nora thought as she hustled the cart through the back hallway leading from the ER to the cafeteria and auditorium. It might've helped matters if Tillman hadn't sounded so damn panicked.

She hoped he took refuge up in his plush offices rather than down in the auditorium, where he'd try to run things and interfere with patient care.

Two security guards waited at the auditorium doors, holding them open for her.

"Thank you," she said as she pushed the cart through. Then she noticed that they both had guns holstered at their hips. Tillman must be scared if he was allowing the guards to carry firearms again. What did he think was going to happen? A revolt? Patients and their families turning on the staff?

Shaking her head at the CEO's idiocy, Nora joined the controlled chaos in the auditorium.

ASHES AND DUST? GINA DID NOT LIKE THE SOUND of that. Who were these guys? And what did they want from Lydia that was worth killing more than a hundred people over? Not including the three guards Harris had already shot?

She clenched her fingers on the leather upholstery, trying to make herself smaller and less likely to be seen. She couldn't risk moving enough to get her phone from her pocket, much less the noise it would make to text Janet. Whoever these guys were, they were deadly serious. Gina had to warn Jerry and Lydia. She had to save the patients and other staff.

A thousand action-hero scenarios collided in her brain as she lay there. Maybe if she had Rambo and John McClane and Indiana Jones with her, she might have a chance, but short of that no option was viable. Right. What the hell was she going to do against a half-dozen armed men? There was no place to go—not with a blizzard raging outside. They were all trapped here. Together.

There was nowhere to run, nowhere to escape to—in fact, the only choice she had was to hide.

She listened as Harris made Tillman call Lydia on the phone and over the loudspeaker. "Dr. Lydia Fiore, report to the ER immediately." He repeated the message over and over, his voice starting to squeak by the end.

She risked another glance over the dashboard. Harris was holding a gun to Tillman's head again. The CEO was sweating so profusely that his toupee had slipped askew.

"No good. She's not answering." Tillman's hand shook as he lowered the phone. "What now?"

"Now you join your people in the auditorium while we tear this place apart."

"You only want Dr. Fiore, right? You're n-not going to hurt anyone else? After all, I've been cooperating."

Harris didn't answer, but merely prodded Tillman down the hall and through the ER's doors.

The ER went quiet. Except for the wind whistling through the hole in the waiting room wall. And the fallen light fixture banging against the nurses' station. And Gina's breathing, heaving, hyperventilating, and out of control.

If she tried anything, she'd get herself killed. Maybe get everyone killed.

Or she could lie here and do nothing. Freeze to death. Peaceful way to go.

She closed her eyes, tried to slow her breathing. Her chattering teeth and shivering didn't help. Although they did remind her that there was warmth just a few feet away. Only she'd have to leave the safety of the car to get to it.

Decisions, decisions. The cold numbed her brain. Couldn't she just lie here and go to sleep? She hadn't slept in weeks. It would feel so good. Not worrying about Jerry. Or her parents—LaRose!

How could she have forgotten about LaRose? Ken would have taken her to the auditorium with the other patients. Unless they were still in CT. Given how slow radiology moved, it was a possibility. Maybe there was still time to save them.

Nothing to do except risk moving. Holding her breath, she raised her head and peered over the dash. The ER was empty, lights out. Nobody left behind on guard duty—at least not that she could see or hear.

Gina sat up and slid over to the passenger side she'd come in through. One more time she climbed out the window, only this time she went inch by inch, trying hard not to make a sound. Then she landed, the crunch of broken glass cracking through the air like machine-gun fire.

No response. Using her penlight to guide her, she crept through the debris that surrounded the nurses' station and ducked into the trauma room, closing the door behind her. She risked using her cell phone, keeping her voice low.

Janet's cell rang and rang and finally went to voice mail. Shit. "Janet, you've got to get over to Angels. We need help. Harris killed the security guards and he's got men with him, six at least, and they've got machine guns. I'm serious. Send SWAT, send everyone. Right away."

And what if Janet was too busy to check her voice mail? Gina hung up, tried calling 911. And got a message that all circuits were busy. No opportunity to even leave a message. What the hell?

Jerry. Harris would be looking for him. She dialed Amanda. "It's Gina. Where are you guys?"

"We brought Jerry up to the eighth-floor rehab. What's going on?"

"That DEA agent isn't a DEA agent. I just saw him kill three security guards."

"Slow down. What did you say?!"

"Harris. He's taking over the damn hospital. Herding everyone into the auditorium while he and his men search for Lydia. They said they'd burn the hospital down, kill everyone in it to cover their tracks."

"Oh my God. What do they want with Lydia?"

"They said something about some evidence they think she's hidden."

"And they've got guns?"

"Lots of guns, big guns, machine guns like you see in the movies. I tried calling the police, but I couldn't get through." Panic edged her words.

Gina could almost hear Amanda blink in the short pause that followed. But having grown up an only daughter with three older brothers, her roommate was nothing if not resilient and fast on her toes. Her mind never slowed down for anything. "Okay. What are we going to do?"

"I'm not sure that there is anything we can do. Except hide. You need to take Jerry and hide him, keep him safe until help arrives."

"What about—" The phone went dead.

Gina glanced at the screen. No signal. Harris had said something about blocking cell phones. Damn. She tried calling out again on the landline from the trauma room but couldn't even get a dial tone. She stood there, the dark punctuated only by the red exit sign above the door, and hugged herself against the cold.

Her fingers brushed against the pack of cigarettes as she returned the useless phone to her pocket. Every cell in her body craved nicotine, sung with a need that transcended chemical dependency, a need translated into the primal fight-or-flight instinct . . . but Gina's mind and body hopscotched over the idea of fight and screamed for flight.

Her lips tingled as she hyperventilated, and she held her hands over her mouth and nose for a moment, slowing her breathing, stilling her panic. Her fingers tangled in the chain around her neck. She pulled Jerry's ring free, clutching it so tight the diamond threatened to break skin. What would Jerry do?

Send her to take cover and arm himself so that he could protect her.

Sounded good in theory, if you were a trained law enforcement officer who'd logged time on the SWAT team. But Jerry wasn't here and neither was the SWAT team—she had to take care of herself. And LaRose. At least until help arrived.

Abandoning the relative safe haven of the trauma room, Gina walked down to the security office. It was empty. The guards' bodies had been shoved under the counter and stripped of their uniform shirts. There wasn't as much blood as she expected, just almost-neat bullet holes at the base of each of their skulls.

She searched for any weapons. Everything was locked away—or Harris's men had taken them, she couldn't be sure. The only thing she found was a Maglite about six inches long but heavy. Better than nothing, so she grabbed it and headed toward radiology.

First, LaRose. Then she'd save Jerry.

AMANDA TRIED CALLING GINA BACK. NO SIGNAL. She grabbed the landline phone from the therapist's desk. "The phones are dead."

The men had obviously overheard enough of her conversation to be worried: Jerry was holding his Beretta, looking anxious, and Lucas now stood beside her, one arm wrapped around her waist protectively.

"Where's Lydia?" Jerry asked—shouted in fact. "She's not safe."

"Lydia's fine," Amanda said, using her most soothing voice. "She's not here. She's safe, Jerry. But we're not." She quickly told them what little Gina had told her.

"Gina's okay?" Jerry wanted to know, surprising her by not asking questions about the armed men or other tactical details. Usually he'd be three steps ahead of everyone else, making a plan.

"She sounded fine. She's safe in the ER."

"Good," he said, blowing his breath out in a sigh of frustration.

"Why are there armed men looking for Lydia?" Lucas asked. "Storming the hospital? Are they nuts? They can't kill us all. They'll be caught for sure."

"On a normal day, maybe. But today? In this?" Amanda gestured out the window at the storm—except it didn't look like a window anymore. The darkness beyond felt heavy, unnatural, and had turned the window into a mirror. All she saw were the three of them: a man in a wheelchair cradling a gun, a silly girl in a silly ball gown, and Lucas, whose distorted reflection appeared scrawny, his white lab coat making him look more nutty professor than dashing hero.

The three of them made for the most unlikely team of rescuers anyone could imagine.

"If they're searching the hospital, first thing we need to do is to arm ourselves and escape," Amanda said.

"Where to?" Lucas asked.

Amanda thought. "Across the skyway to the research tower. They won't go over there."

"They won't need to. They can just lock the doors."

"Still, it's our best place to hide, buy some time until we figure out what to do."

Jerry nodded in approval. "We're going to get Gina?"

Teaming up with Gina sounded good—in theory. But without communications, what were the chances of their meeting up?

"We need weapons," she responded instead.

"This is crazy," Lucas said. "We can't go up against armed men. It's suicide."

His words stunned her—Lucas had many faults, but she'd never thought being a coward was one of them. "Lucas, we can't abandon them! Those are our friends, our patients. We have to do something."

He shocked her by grabbing her by her arms and stepping in, so close that she had to look up at him. He lowered his forehead to touch hers, his voice low and urgent. "I can't risk you, Amanda. If anything happened to you—" His Adam's apple jumped as he swallowed hard. "And Jerry is in no shape. We need to find someplace safe, where I can protect you both."

He wasn't a coward.

She stood on her tiptoes and kissed him. He resisted at first, but she persisted, until his lips opened beneath hers and he surrendered. His arms wrapped around her, pulling her so tightly against him it was like he wanted her inside him, a part of him forever. At least that was how she felt, what she wanted.

Finally they parted—it seemed like a kiss that broke records for the world's longest, but the clock across from them said it only lasted a few seconds. Maybe time had stopped, Amanda thought with a smile.

"Okay," Lucas said, defeated. "We'll do it your way."

"Weapons." They split up and scoured the therapy area.

"Hot paraffin, no good, it'll cool without its heat source," Lucas said as he cataloged everything. Thinking out loud was a nervous habit of his, so Amanda let him talk while she did her own inventory. Jerry immediately threw his aluminum three-legged cane down and wheeled over to the wall to grab a hefty wooden cane in exchange.

"You won't be able to balance as well on that one," Amanda told him.

"No. But it hits better." Jerry clutched the cane across his lap along with his gun, looking fierce. She didn't argue. Instead she grabbed a roll of packing tape from the receptionist's desk, along with a box cutter and a pair of shears. She pulled the cord from the back of the phone— could be used as a garrote or a restraint. She looped her prizes into the sash of her dress.

"Did you find anything, Lucas?"

"Casting supplies, medicine balls, splints. Useless. But what about these?" He held up a set of Velcro wrist weights. "Wrapped around your fist they'd be like brass knuckles, or you could use them as a sap and knock someone out."

"Do you know how to do that?" Amanda couldn't imagine Lucas hitting anything—least of all a person.

"I'm a neurologist. I've seen enough head injuries. I

can do it." His voice was stronger, as if he had some sliver of hope that they wouldn't all be gunned down before they had the chance to do anything.

Jerry rolled past Amanda toward the doors just as the lights began to flicker.

"Hurry," Lucas said. "We need to get to the skywalk doors while the power's off."

They rushed across the hall to the doors. The lights came back on.

"Damn," Lucas muttered, rattling the locked doors.

"Can't we just break the glass, open the door?" Amanda asked.

"The locks are electronic. But when the power goes out they all open so that no one gets trapped inside."

"How do you know that?"

"I'm on the safety committee. We talk about things like that. And bed rails—lots of talk about bed rails."

"I never knew life as an attending was so exciting."

"Hurry," Jerry said. "Gina needs us."

Then the lights went out again. A metallic click sounded as the locks disengaged. They pushed through the doors and entered the skywalk.

The floor rocked beneath their feet as the gale-force winds blasted the skywalk. The storm was merciless, whipping around the glass-and-metal structure in a frenzy, hitting the windows, sending the floor bucking in every direction. Not just the floor; the walls vibrated as well, emitting an unnerving hum that made Amanda's skin pucker with goose bumps. With the doors at both ends shut, it was like being in an echo chamber, every rattle of glass, every shriek of metal amplified until it drilled into their bones.

Jerry didn't even have to push the wheels; his chair glided forward under its own volition. Then it stopped in the center. Amanda and Lucas rushed after him, but the farther they traveled across the skywalk, the more the floor shook.

"I think it might come apart," Lucas shouted over the howl of the wind.

"We need to get out of here," Amanda called back— even though they were holding hands, she could barely hear him. She'd been on her father's boat in the middle of squalls that had been less noisy than this. "Hurry!"

TEN

LYDIA SLIP-SLIDED HER WAY TO THE OVERTURNED van. The slushy-icy-half-packed snow wore a dingy gray topcoat thanks to a mix of salt and ashes. Whenever her feet broke through an area not packed down by earlier traffic, snow spilled over her boot tops, so she tried to stay in the tracks left behind by car tires. But from the amount of snow filling the tracks, the green van and Trey's Bessie were the only vehicles that had come this way in quite some time.

The van lay on its side, back doors sprung open. Trey was already inside, checking on the driver. Lydia goose-stepped her way between tire tracks to join him. It was dark inside except for Trey's flashlight and the murky half-light that filtered in through the open doors and the windshield.

"He's fine," Trey called back to her as she entered the van. Using its side panel as a floor made for treacherous footing. The metal pinged and bounced beneath her feet, threatening to tumble her, so she finally sidled along with her back against the wall—well, actually the ceiling—and her good hand braced above her head against the other wall. "Just stuck. The seat slid forward and jammed."

The cargo van stank of fish and something musty that tickled her nose. Wet feathers? A few brown cardboard boxes resembling the ones Giant Eagle used for their take-out chicken had slid out the doors.

Trey knelt behind the sideways-facing driver's seat, trying to ratchet it back to free the driver, but gravity and the driver's weight worked against him. All Lydia could see of the man were his legs trapped beneath the dash and his belly squeezed up against the steering wheel.

"Forget me," the driver protested, his voice muffled, since his head was lying to the side. "I'm fine."

Trey ignored him and spoke to Lydia. "Can you call it in so the utility guys can check this light pole and the wreckers can add it to their list?"

"Sure." She positioned her flashlight to help Trey see better and reached for her phone. It wasn't there—wasn't in any of her pockets. Must have dropped it when Trey carried her out of her SUV. "Damn. I lost my phone."

"Mine's in Bessie, on the charger. That's okay, cell coverage has been spotty. I'll radio it in. I need to get some tools anyway. Keep him calm, will you?" He crawled past her and out the van door.

Lydia took Trey's spot, kneeling between the seats, angling her body through the narrow space. Now she could make out the driver's features. He looked to be in his mid-forties, his face flushed with exertion and the effects of gravity—it had to be uncomfortable, hanging halfway upside down, squeezed in place by the steering wheel and his shoulder harness.

"I'm Lydia," she said. "I'm a doctor. Are you sure nothing hurts?"

He raised his head with an effort. "I'm Zimmerman.

I'm fine. But you need to find them. They'll die in the cold." His head slumped back against the door frame. "Damn Olsen. I wasn't even supposed to be here—all I do is muck out the habitats."

Lydia wondered if the man had a head injury. He seemed confused and agitated. "Mr. Zimmerman, was there someone else in here with you?"

"It's just Zimmerman. No *Mister*. And there were twelve of them."

She looked around. There were only the two front seats in the cargo van and the passenger seat was empty, the only signs of life a overturned coffee mug and a clipboard with papers that had gotten wedged between the seats. She grabbed the clipboard. On top was a receipt from a cargo transportation company. "What is *Spheniscus*?"

"That's what I'm trying to tell you."

Trey returned and crawled under the seat with his tools. "How are you guys doing?"

"I keep telling you, I'm fine." The driver yelped as Trey rocked the seat abruptly. "But I need you to rescue my *Spheniscus*. The penguins."

Trey stopped at that and exchanged a glance with Lydia. "Penguins?"

"I'm not joking. I wasn't even supposed to be the one transporting them—Olsen is going to kill me if anything happens to them. They're very rare, an endangered species."

"But"—Lydia gestured to the snow all around them—"they're penguins. They'll be okay. We can call animal control to come collect them."

Zimmerman shook his head so hard the seat belt dug into his flesh. "No, you don't understand. They're Galapagos penguins."

"So?"

"As in they live at the equator, where it's really hot all

the time?" Zimmerman grabbed Lydia's hand, almost pulling her off balance and sideways into the seat with him. "Please don't let anything happen to them. It's my job on the line."

Trey looked up from his work. "Go on, look for his penguins."

Ugh. Last thing she wanted to do. Lydia was not a big fan of birds.

"How am I supposed to catch them?" she asked, waving her cast, using her arm as an excuse for the first time since she'd broken it. Trey did a double take, raising one eyebrow.

"What's wrong? You're not afraid of a little penguin, are you?"

No. It was their big beaks she was afraid of. Not to mention their flapping wings and sharp little claws. Did penguins have claws? They definitely had beaks—maybe teeth as well. And who knew what kind of diseases they carried?

Her face twisted with revulsion. Trey's laughter filled the van. "You *are*. Dr. Lydia Fiore who isn't afraid of anything—fire, guns, hit men—is frightened of cute, cuddly little birds."

"I'm not afraid. Just"—she fumbled for an excuse—"inexperienced. I've never been around birds." By choice. Not after the viewing of Alfred Hitchcock's *The Birds* that she and Maria had sneaked in out of a rainstorm for and stayed all day, watching the movie three times before leaving. She'd been six or seven at the time and still had nightmares, would even cross the street if she spotted a crow or starling in her path.

"You can't let them die," Zimmerman said. "I'll lose my job!" He sounded more concerned about his job than his wayward birds.

"We'll come help you as soon as we're done," Trey

assured her. "But this seat jumped its track. It's going to take me a while to saw through the supports." Lydia stood there, not really liking her options. "C'mon, you don't want to be responsible for them freezing out there."

Lydia sighed. "Okay, I'll go look for your penguins."

"They're in carrier boxes, but those are only for convenience, not very sturdy. You need to keep them warm," Zimmerman said.

"Right." She edged past Trey, bracing against the overhead wall of the van as she made her way back to the door. She grabbed the first of the brown cartons she'd noticed before. It was just cardboard folded together. The inside was empty except for the stench of bird poop.

But as soon as she touched the second box, she knew she'd found something, though it wasn't very heavy, maybe five or six pounds. She thought penguins were big fat things, waddling around on ice. "Here's one."

"Is it okay?" Zimmerman called.

She risked a peek inside. The bird was curled up, filling the entire container.

"It's not dead, is it?"

"I don't know," she said. If it was hurt, what the hell was she supposed to do about it? She knew nothing about bird anatomy except which bits of a fried chicken tasted best. "It's not moving."

"You're a doctor," he shouted. "Do something!"

GINA RAN THROUGH THE DARK, EMPTY HALLWAYS of the ER, her pulse beating so hard that it made her vision throb. She could only focus on a small area in front of her, had to whip her head around every time she heard a sound, imagining one of Harris's men lunging out of hiding to tackle her. This wasn't fear, fight, or flight. This was outright terror.

The lights went out for a few moments and she froze, certain it was a trap. Then Tillman's voice whinnied through the overhead speakers. Something about losing power. Liar. They should have plenty of power.

"They're just herding everyone into the auditorium," she said aloud. Her voice sounded loud in the empty corridor. Too loud. She forced herself not to run—that had been a mistake, galloping through the hallways like that. She had to be smarter, more careful. Guerrilla warfare. Sneaky, silent.

Hard to do when your heart was about to scramble right up and out of your throat. She slowed her breathing. After a few deep breaths her vision returned to normal. She stuck to the little-known back hallways and entered radiology from the employee entrance. The door shut behind her with a squeak that made her jump although there was no one else to hear it. The place felt even more cold and deserted than the ER.

Even in the best of times radiology was a maze. The lights were still on here, but that didn't do much to ease the whole spooky-mansion-with-Freddy-Krueger-ready-to-jump-out atmosphere.

ER docs hated radiology—patients got lost there, both physically and medically. Not that radiology and its denizens didn't feel the same about the ER, a place that seemed to exist solely to thwart their carefully arranged schedules and pull their techs for stat portable films. The Hatfields and McCoys played out in the so-called civilization of an urban medical center.

Despite that, right now, Gina would love to stumble across a surly radiology tech. She'd never find an actual radiologist—they were an obscure race of creatures, rarely seen in the daylight, and never on a weekend or holiday, especially not since new technology allowed them to do most of their work from home. One of the ER staff's greatest joys was to pull a radiologist out of bed at three A.M. to perform an intervention like an angiogram that they couldn't turf to the poor tech working nights.

But now it was just Gina wandering empty hallways, head twisted so that she could look over her shoulder, back pressed against the wall, and feeling like a gothic heroine entering Bluebeard's forbidden chambers. She'd come into radiology from the back, the X ray area, which meant weaving through a myriad of changing rooms, waiting areas, viewing rooms, and procedure areas before she'd reach the CT suite where she hoped to find her mother. Maybe she'd feel less nervous if she had any idea about what to do after that, but she'd settle for finding LaRose first and figuring out the rest after she knew her mother was safe.

Footsteps sounded behind her. Gina froze, pressing her body against the wall—as if beige paint could conceal a five-ten black woman in a bright white lab coat. Holding her breath, she listened. Nothing. Maybe she'd imagined it.

There was a fluoroscopy suite across the hall. Looking both ways, seeing no one, she flung herself across the empty space and through the door. She grabbed it before it could click shut and closed it herself, slowly, slowly, without a sound.

The room was dark. She didn't dare turn on a light. The Maglite seemed too bright, too risky, so she used her penlight. The patient bed with the c-ring was in the center of the room, carts of supplies pushed against the walls surrounding it.

On the opposite wall was the revolving door leading to the darkroom and film-developing area. To the left of it was another exit leading to yet another hallway—one that would get her closer to CT.

Using her tiny beam of light to guide her, she skirted

the equipment and edged along the wall toward the exit. Her breathing was so loud, it sounded like she was using a megaphone, but it wasn't as bad as the pounding in her ears echoing her pulse. She wasn't tiptoeing, but each step felt as treacherous as stepping off an abyss.

She'd almost reached the black plastic revolving door when she heard footsteps again. She wasn't imagining them. They were close—and getting closer.

A shadow passed beneath the slit of light below the exit she'd been aiming for. Was he coming here? She skipped her penlight's beam around the room. There was nowhere to hide. The footsteps stopped and she heard a man's voice, although she couldn't make out his words. There were two of them!

Panic seized her and she rushed into the open revolving door of the darkroom entrance. She stopped it halfway, not wanting to reveal herself if one of the men had gone into the darkroom next door. It was pitch-black in the narrow cylinder—it was designed that way, so that no light would accidentally contaminate the darkroom or expose any film. But she'd never realized how tiny the chamber was. It was like being trapped inside a torpedo. Or a coffin.

She wished she hadn't thought of that particular metaphor. Visions of being buried alive flooded over her.

Her breath reverberated against the plastic walls and she was disoriented—if she hadn't been standing on her feet, she'd have no idea which direction was up. She was about to risk entering the darkroom—anything to escape this claustrophobic sensory deprivation chamber—when she heard a man's voice.

If one man was in the darkroom, was the other behind her, in the fluoro room? If so, then she was trapped between them, nothing more than a plastic wall separating her from them.

She covered her mouth and nose with her hands, hoping to muffle her breathing. Because there was no way in hell the plastic wall of the revolving door would stop a bullet.

AMANDA SWAYED AS A NASTY BLAST OF WIND shook the skywalk. She would have fallen if not for Lucas. Damn, she'd never had trouble finding her sea legs before, not even in the worst storms back home on her father's boat. Then she looked down and realized what the problem was: Gina's damned stilettos.

"Keep going with Jerry," she told Lucas.

She stopped and leaned against the glass wall, tugging off one high heel and then the other. That was much better. She caught up to the two men just as Lucas was opening the door at the opposite end of the skywalk. Together they pushed Jerry through, let the door clang shut behind them, and stopped to catch their breath.

The research tower was brand-new, and it showed. On the Angels side, where they had just come from, the lobby was painted a dingy gray and featured peeling linoleum. Here the walls were covered in mauve wallpaper and hung with tasteful photographs of famous Pittsburgh scientists, and the floors were done in a nice industrial pile carpet. Even the emergency lighting seemed brighter than it had on the Angels side.

"We're not going back that way," Lucas said as he pressed his nose against the glass door and measured the arc of the bridge's movement with his finger. "If it oscillates at a certain frequency—"

"It will collapse," Amanda said. "Like that movie they show in science class, that bridge."

"The Tacoma Narrows Bridge." Of course Lucas would know—he knew everything. It was really annoying at times.

He turned away from the view and leaned against the wall. "What's your plan?"

Jerry spun his wheelchair around and looked up at her with expectation. She'd gotten them this far—was she now supposed to come up with a plan to save everyone in the hospital?

"Gina said they were gathering people in the auditorium. We'll sneak down to the ground floor, cross over, and surprise them."

Lucas frowned. "She also said they were planning to burn the hospital down. So where do we take the hostages once we've rescued them?"

Good point. "We can't take them outside."

Jerry drummed his cane against the arm of his wheelchair. "Bring them here."

"To the tower?" Lucas looked up at that, his gaze searching, then glanced out across the distance separating the tower from the main hospital building.

"Do you think it's far enough away?" Amanda asked him.

He thought for a moment longer. "Maybe. If they're really planning to start a fire—and there are countless ways to do that, given all the flammables the hospital uses every day—then probably. We could move everyone to the fire stairs farthest away from the hospital building. But if it's some kind of explosive device—"

Amanda blew her breath out. "We'll have to take our chances. Jerry, can you manage the stairs? The last announcement said the power would be cut in a few more minutes and I don't want to risk being on an elevator when that happens."

"The elevators have a backup battery that's designed to lower them to the bottom of the shaft," Lucas said. More exciting tidbits from the safety committee, no doubt.

"But they might know that and be waiting."

He nodded. "Or they could just grab the fire key from the security office, and that would lock them all down on the basement level as well."

"Either way, we should avoid them. Jerry?"

Jerry didn't hesitate; instead he climbed out of his chair and headed to the fire door, pushing it open. "Let's go."

ELEVEN

GINA STOOD FROZEN, TRAPPED IN THE UTTER BLACK-
ness of the darkroom's revolving door. Her breathing co-
cooned her, smothering her hearing. The men could be
right outside the door on either side and she wouldn't be
able to hear them. They could be raising their guns, taking
aim, right now, right now, right now. . . .

Panic clawed up her nerve endings. She forced herself
to stand still, not move a muscle. It took all her willpower
not to run screaming from her hiding place, just to end the
awful anticipation.

Crazy, that was crazy. She'd get herself killed.

She had to find a way to calm down. Breathe in, breathe
out. She'd been in danger before.

There was another time she'd felt powerless like this.
Out of control. Her sophomore year of college when she'd
realized she wouldn't be making the dean's list. The thought
of facing Moses's wrath and LaRose's disappointment was
crushing, too much for her to bear. Her eating disorder,

always barely manageable—a tightrope of pleasure and pain—had flared, turned into a wildfire single-mindedly bent on her destruction.

Suicidal fantasies had combined with depression and despair to leave her feeling helpless, unable to even fight for her life. If it hadn't been for a resident advisor who refused to put up with Gina's excuses, denial, and bullshit, she wouldn't have survived.

That RA reminded her a lot of Lydia, Gina thought, an unbidden smile curling her lips. What would Lydia do now?

She wouldn't give up, that was for damn sure. She'd go out fighting.

Gina took another deep breath. Unlike back during her sophomore year, now she was in control of her actions. She couldn't stay here forever—she had to find her mother.

She patted her pockets, taking inventory. Jerry had often told her of the power of a well-aimed bright light and the element of surprise. She gripped the Maglite in her left hand.

Her only other weapon was a disposable scalpel—useless except at extremely close range. Who was she fooling? She'd be mowed down by bullets long before she got close enough to use it. Still, it made her feel better having it, so she slipped the handle into her sleeve and hid the blade against her palm.

Before she could retreat into fear, she twisted her feet against the floor, activating its swivel mechanism. The floor rotated silently, bringing her closer to the darkroom entrance.

She pressed herself against the far wall, watching as the red light the techs used when developing film edged through the opening. The opening enlarged from a slit to a few inches to a foot and she sprang out, aiming her flashlight beam and ready to do battle with her plastic disposable scalpel.

The light zigzagged around the room before hitting a target. A man standing at the rack that held freshly developed films. He shielded his eyes against her light.

"Gina, is that you?"

"Ken, what are you doing here?"

He flicked on the main lights. "I wanted to get your mom's CT scan transferred onto hard copies before the power goes out for good. I thought you were the tech. What were you doing in there?"

"We need to leave." She pocketed the Maglite but kept the scalpel at hand as she ran to the door and opened it a crack, looking out. The hallway was silent.

"Why?" Ken asked, joining her, a sheaf of films in his hand.

"The power isn't going out because of the weather. There are armed men taking over the hospital."

Her dramatic statement thudded against the silence that followed. She could sense Ken staring at the back of her head. Sifting through her words and actions, his uncanny mind would skip past inane questions like was she joking and arrive at a conclusion—either what she said was true or that she was mentally unstable.

She didn't have long to wait for his decision.

"They picked a silly time to do it—they're as trapped as we are by the weather." His tone was mild, disapproving of the gunmen's lack of forethought.

As always, Ken's Zen-like calmness infuriated her, though she knew that he had good reason to protect himself behind his Panglossian façade of acceptance—it was a hard-won defense mechanism he'd built after his wife and daughter had been killed.

"They don't care about the weather—or about anyone

else. I saw them shoot three men. And they're planning to kill us all to cover their tracks."

"What do they want?"

"Lydia—apparently she has some kind of evidence they want." Gina cracked the door and peeked out. No one in the corridor. "We have to find LaRose. Where is she?"

"Everyone left when Tillman made the announcement about the power. Surely they took her with them?"

Gina didn't trust radiologists—they spent too much time in the virtual world of their computer scans and dark-rooms to remember that the images they peered at belonged to real, live people. "We'd better make sure. Which scanner was she in? We'll start there."

"Scanner two." He followed her into the deserted hallway. "Her scan showed an ischemic stroke."

Gina slowed to check both corridors as they came to an intersection. A stroke. Exactly what she'd feared.

"We need to get her started on TPA," Ken said. There was a narrow window to successfully treat strokes with the "clot-buster" drug, and the sooner LaRose began therapy, the better her response would be. "If these men are only looking for Lydia, your mother should be safe with everyone else in the auditorium and she can get the TPA there."

"No. These men are crazy. They were talking about burning down the hospital to cover their tracks. And they aren't going to find Lydia because she's not here. Which is really going to piss them off. So we may not have much time."

"They can't burn down anything until the weather clears enough for them to escape."

Typical logical Ken. But logic had nothing to do with their situation. "I'm not risking my mother to the whims of Mother Nature and a bunch of psychopaths." She thought hard. There weren't many options to weigh. "Lucas Stone is with Jerry and Amanda on the eighth floor. We'll take LaRose there."

"It would be good to have a neurologist check her before we begin the TPA," Ken conceded. "But maybe we should just stay here and hide."

Gina shook her head. "No. If we can get to the eighth floor, we can get the others and cross over to the research tower; it would be safer there."

Ken was silent. She knew he realized that as much as she liked Lucas and Amanda, part of her motivation in getting to them was also to get to Jerry, make sure he was safe. She didn't want to hurt Ken more by coming flat out and saying it, but he was smart, he'd figure out where her priorities lay.

They halted at another intersection. Ken rocked back on his heels, thinking hard, but as always his train of thought veered away from her expectations. "This place, Angels, was the closest thing I had to a home after I lost my family. But now I think it's got bad karma."

"Nothing bad ever happened around here until Lydia came along. If it weren't for her, Jerry would never have been shot." Bitterness colored Gina's tone but she was too frazzled to care.

"Just answer me this, Gina. If Jerry hadn't been shot, do you think you—I mean, could we have ever—" Ken's words stuttered into silence.

Ahhh . . . the question they'd been dancing around for weeks. Gina touched his arm. He flinched and she shoved her hand into her pocket.

"Sorry, Ken, but no. I like you; I love the way your mind works and how you make me think about things and you see me for who I really am and that doesn't frighten or disgust you or anything. But I can't help it. Jerry loves me; he takes care of me and puts up with me and, I don't know, I feel safe with him."

"You still haven't said that you love him." He turned to her, his gaze holding hers steady. He wasn't flinching now. Or backing down. As always, Ken was forcing her to take a good hard look at the one place she preferred to leave alone in the dark: her own heart.

"I'm not sure I know how to love or what love really is. But what I feel for Jerry is the closest I've ever come."

She turned away before he could respond and crossed the corridor to the CT scanner. Empty, as was the control room. She pushed through the door to the small patient waiting area.

There, huddled in a wheelchair backed up behind the door and almost hidden from sight, looking frail and frightened and utterly unlike the Queen Mother Gina was accustomed to, sat LaRose.

NORA STOOD AT THE SIDE AISLE BELOW THE STAGE and looked around the auditorium. There were now eighty-six people gathered, with hospital staff—nurses, nursing assistants, ward clerks, dietary workers, housekeepers, lab and radiology techs—far outnumbering the handful of patients and their families. Which wasn't necessarily a bad thing because it meant that the dormitory area on the stage had gotten sorted out quickly as well as a patient care area for dressing changes and medication infusions. The medication carts were arranged around the stretchers so that if they suddenly became inundated with ER patients once the storm let up, they'd be ready.

The cafeteria workers had even brought in food, including milk and cookies to keep the nine kids and their families occupied. In fact, it seemed as if boredom would be their chief enemy once the night wore on. People were already joking about the stories they would tell about their unusual New Year's Eve, spent trapped in a hospital by a blizzard.

Even Jim Lazarov had made himself useful, splinting Mark's leg and having the men from the zoo give an impromptu presentation on penguins to the kids to keep them entertained. Nora hated to think what they'd do once the sugar high from the cookies set in.

Emma Grey approached her. She and her great-grandson, Deon, had also gotten trapped in the hospital by the storm. "I could help," Emma said. "How about some reading material?"

Nora smiled at the older woman. Emma was the hospital librarian and always provided a soothing presence to patients and their families. "Great minds think alike."

"Just one problem. The security guards won't let me go to the library. Maybe you could talk to them? The one with the accent seems to be in charge."

"He must also be new. I don't know him." Nora didn't recognize the other two guards who stood inside the doors either. "Tillman must have hired them after the shooting."

As if she'd conjured him by using his name, the doors opened and Oliver Tillman appeared, flanked by the DEA agent, Harris, and one of the guards. Tillman appeared frazzled, his hair mussed, plastered to his forehead with sweat. No one else seemed to notice his arrival—the hum of conversations continued unabated.

"Something's wrong," Nora said. Emma nodded.

"I need your attention," Tillman said. He couldn't raise his voice loud enough to be heard over the crowd. In fact, it came out as a thin squeak. "Please. Listen to me."

Harris nodded to the guard, who jerked the doors open again. Two more men entered, wearing black combat suits and carrying machine guns slung across their chests, holding them sideways like bad guys in a movie.

Before anyone could react, both men fired their weapons into the ceiling. Nora pushed Emma down between the nearest row of seats, covering her with her body. The sound was like hail on a tin roof, not as dramatic as Hollywood portrayed it, but when added to the ghastly smiles on the men's faces and the shower of shredded acoustical material, it effectively inspired terror.

When Nora dared to look up again, she saw people gaping heavenward, some ducking beneath the seats, mothers shielding their children, husbands and wives clinging to each other. Screams echoed from every corner of the auditorium.

The storm of bullets lasted only a few seconds, but the shouts and cries took longer to die down. Several people actually started forward, faces flushed with anger and fear, but the men in black pointed their guns at them and they froze where they were.

"Quiet!" Harris shouted. He shoved Tillman forward, adding him to the crowd. Slowly everyone hushed except for a few sobs. "I need your attention. Now!"

All eyes were on him. Nora clutched at Emma's arm to prevent the older woman from running to find Deon.

"No sudden movement," she whispered as she helped Emma to her feet. Emma's eyes were narrowed in fury; she looked ready to take on Harris and his men single-handedly, but she nodded and stayed put.

"What do you want?" Nora stepped forward so that she was in front of Emma. Her heart was thudding as fast as the machine-gun bullets and she couldn't swallow—her mouth was too dry—but she was damned if she was going to let him see any of that. "I take it you're not from the DEA, Mr. Harris. Or whatever your name is."

"Harris will do just fine," he said with a benevolent smile. "And I want the same thing I did before: Lydia Fiore." He turned his head to address the entire auditorium, his words carrying effortlessly thanks to the acoustics. "Dr. Lydia Fiore. It's urgent that I find her—life and death, in fact. *Your* lives. Once we find her, we'll leave."

He paused, letting that sink in. Then he unholstered his own weapon and raised it, aiming at Nora. "Anyone who gets in our way dies."

EVEN THOUGH THE MAIN HOSPITAL STILL HAD backup power from the generator, the research tower was low priority and had only battery-operated emergency lighting, which meant that the stairwell was a mass of shadows punctuated by a few halfhearted lightbulbs.

All Amanda could hope was that the bad guys hadn't sent anyone over to the tower because all the noise they were making, sounds bouncing back and forth and up and down the concrete-walled stairwell, reminded her of the herd of cannibal hippos she'd seen on a nature show. A stealth operation, this was not.

Jerry and Lucas went down the stairs together—Lucas leading, pretending he wasn't there to catch Jerry if Jerry fell. After a few failed attempts to use his cane, Jerry finally hooked it over his shoulder, pocketed his gun, and faced the stairwell wall, using both hands on the railing as he side-stepped down.

Amanda was the one who kept stumbling, tripping on the hem of the ball gown, now inches too long since she'd abandoned the stilettos. By the time they reached the second-floor landing, she'd ripped the hem in several places, soiled the beautiful silk, and bruised herself too many times to count.

"Let's take a break," Lucas said, holding the landing door open for them.

Jerry stole a glance at Amanda, nodded, and said, "Recon."

By the time Amanda crossed through the door and out into the elevator lobby, Jerry was leaning against the picture window, peering down into the atrium that separated them and the auditorium. The snow had slowed—or the wind had, it was hard for Amanda to tell. She gazed out at the landscape transformed into an alien world by the storm.

The only lights were the ones from Angels; everywhere else it was dark, as far as she could see. But there was enough light to reveal the snowy swirls and dunes and drifts shaped by the frenzied wind. Small mountains heaped one against the other, stacked against the nineteen-foot-high glass walls of the atrium, almost to the roof. No one could get through that. Not without some serious earthmoving equipment.

The atrium's glass roof was steeply angled and clear of snow, giving Jerry a good line of sight to the space in front of the auditorium's doors.

"Nobody moving," he reported.

Amanda slumped to the floor, kneading her eyes with the heels of her palms. They really were trapped. It was hopeless—there was no way help could reach them, not for hours, maybe not for days. Which meant all those people's lives depended on them.

She sniffed, tried to muffle it without success. She was not going to cry. She absolutely, positively was not. She was too tired, too scared for tears—but then again, tears might be the perfect response to parading around an abandoned hospital actually searching for men with guns. It made as much sense as anything else that had happened today.

"Lucas, do we have money left in the wedding budget?"

He chuckled in response.

She jerked her hands down from her face. It wasn't a funny question, not at all. Suddenly there was no room in her for tears. She scrambled back onto her feet. "Don't you laugh at me, Lucas Stone. This is serious."

Lucas grinned, as if he actually thought this was some kind of game, but one glance at her and he sobered up, fast. "Money? A little. Why?"

"Because we're going to have to buy Gina a new dress."

Now he looked concerned, worried that she'd lost it. "Amanda, don't you think that's the least of our worries?"

"No. It's not." Her voice took a right turn into soprano range, spiced with a little shrill panic.

Jerry turned to look at them, opened his mouth to say something, caught the expression on Amanda's face, and turned back, concentrating on the view. He might not be as quick thinking as he'd been before getting shot, but there was nothing wrong with his instincts for survival.

Amanda stood, considering her options and her less-than-helpful fiancé. Then she grabbed the shears from her sash, raised her skirt, and slashed at the underskirt and crinoline. The only sound was the fabric ripping apart, a piece of art mutilated, vandalized.

She wobbled a bit, her aim blurring at the thought. But it also felt good, releasing her anger and fear into destructive action.

"Gina won't mind," Lucas said as he steadied her with one hand. The layers of silk and taffeta fell to the floor.

"But I do." She was shaking so hard she thought her tears would shake loose. When Lucas's head was turned away, she swiped her eyes with the back of her hand.

"Amanda—"

She brandished the shears on him. "I'm not going into our marriage with a debt to a friend hanging over our heads, do you understand?"

It had nothing to do with Gina or the dress or the money, not really. It was about believing that despite everything happening tonight that their wedding would happen. It was about finding the faith that they would all make it through this night alive.

Lucas was wise enough to understand that. He swept the scissors to one side and bundled her into his arms. This time Amanda couldn't hold back the tears. God, she'd never felt so terrified in all her life. Not even a few months ago when she'd been sick and had been afraid she might die. She'd been scared, sure, but it was a different kind of fear than this.

This was sheer terror. Terror that she was making all the wrong choices, that she'd get Jerry and Lucas killed because of her choices, that if they failed, then so many other people might die as well—all because of her.

Lucas made no empty promises, simply held her tight until her panic subsided. She wiped her runny nose against the shoulder of his lab coat and he didn't even flinch— that was how much he loved her. And she loved him, every germophobic, anal-retentive inch of him. That was one thing she could believe in, no matter what else happened.

Reluctantly she pushed him back. "Help me cut the overskirt."

He knelt at her feet and, with a swift and sure hand, snipped a good foot off the ball gown, leaving it hanging just below her knees. God, she must look like Daisy from *Li'l Abner*. Some kind of hillbilly prom queen.

"Okay. Let's go."

Lucas stood, leaving the shreds of the ball gown behind. "Where?"

Jerry pointed through the window. They joined him there. He was pointing to the left of the atrium, to a row of windows. "There."

"The cafeteria?" Lucas asked.

"The kitchen," Amanda said. "It shares a wall with the auditorium. They cater events in the auditorium and atrium. They might have access."

"So we're just going to waltz through the atrium? And do what, take cover behind the ferns? They'll spot us for sure."

"No choice," Jerry said grimly. "I'll go first."

As a diversion, Amanda realized. Jerry expected to get caught. And killed.

TWELVE

GINA RAN TO HER MOTHER. "LAROSE! I CAN'T BE-
lieve the radiology tech left you here."

LaRose shook her head vehemently. "Man took the tech.
Guard. Didn't see me."

"A guard?" Gina exchanged glances with Ken. "Where
to?"

"We need to get her the TPA. But what about the"—
he glanced at LaRose, choosing his next word with
care—"guards?"

"I only saw six of them," Gina said. "That's not enough
to cover all the floors of the hospital and watch over the
people in the auditorium. The eighth floor is mainly rehab,
closed for the holiday, so they might just give it a cursory
look. Or we could beat them to it, if they're working their
way up from the ground floor."

There were several flaws in her reasoning—but what
choice did they have? She had to get LaRose the TPA, had

to find Jerry, had to protect them both, and getting to the eighth floor seemed the best way to do that.

"What's going on?" LaRose asked, tugging at Gina's sleeve with her good hand. Her voice was clearer now that her blood pressure was back to normal. Gina didn't want to agitate her, risk raising her blood pressure again. But she had to tell her something and her mother deserved the truth.

"Some men have taken over the hospital. They're holding a bunch of people hostage in the auditorium."

LaRose somehow managed to look contemptuous and unimpressed at the same time—a hard feat with only half of her facial muscles working. She gave a one-shouldered shrug, divorcing herself from the ugly situation. "Call the police."

"I did. Hopefully they're on their way, but with the storm—" Gina looked to Ken for guidance. "If Janet got my message there might already be a SWAT team on the way." It was a big *if*, but a more palatable scenario than its alternative.

"Maybe we should stay here, try to hide," Ken suggested.

"No." Even thinking that made her feel guilty—as if she were abandoning Jerry and the others. "Anything we do is a gamble, but I say we go up."

"It would help if we knew where the bad guys were." Ken thought for a moment. "If they've jammed the cell phones, they must be using radios to communicate."

"They are—I saw them. They're just like our trauma radios." She unclipped her own radio from her belt. "Maybe we can hear them?"

The small radio had a knob that accessed several channels—Gina had only ever used the first one, had no idea what the others were or how easy it could be to access other radios. But it was worth a try.

"Can I see that?" Ken asked. She handed him the radio. "UHF, sixteen channels. There's a good chance we can pick them up with this." He began trying the other channels. Silence or static greeted him until he hit channel eight. Then a man's voice came through.

"That's him," Gina said. "That's Harris, the guy pretending to be a DEA agent."

Ken adjusted the volume and held the radio for them to listen. "Auditorium is secure," Harris was saying. "Team One, deploy to block the stairwells and exits, then we'll start floor by floor, ground up."

"Roger that. Team One Oscar Mike." There was a short squelch, then silence.

"Sounds like you're right." Ken handed the radio back to her. Gina turned it off so that it wouldn't give them away while they were on the move. "We should be safest up on the eighth floor. And from there, we can cross over to the research tower, hide out there." He looked both ways down the hall. "No signs of anyone."

Gina pushed LaRose's wheelchair out into the corridor and followed Ken.

They made it through radiology to the doors that opened onto the main hospital lobby without seeing anyone. Ken edged up to the window of one of the swinging double doors and scouted the lobby. He waved them back.

"It's no good," he whispered. "There's a guy with a machine gun out there. From where he's standing he has both the main elevators and the patient elevators in view as well as the hallway to the auditorium."

Gina wheeled LaRose into the nearest procedure room. It was one of the interventional suites, kept sterile and as well stocked as an OR. Ken closed the door behind them.

"What should we do?"

"We could try to draw his attention using the radio," he suggested.

"But that might backfire—bring more of them to us."
She left LaRose in the chair and began to pace the room,
taking inventory. "There has to be another way."

"We can't go back, we'll just end up in the ER. They're
sure to find us."

LaRose beat her good fist against the arm of the wheelchair, getting their attention. "Leave me. You go hide."

Gina stopped midstride, frozen in place by her mother's
words. That wasn't the LaRose she knew—could the stroke
have done more damage than she'd thought? She turned
and saw that her mother's face was streaked with tears.
For the first time in Gina's life, LaRose actually looked
her real age—no, she looked even older than her fifty-eight
years.

"No." The word was out before she could consider the
ramifications. She crouched down to LaRose's eye level
and took her left hand, squeezing it firmly. Her mother's
wrist felt like skin and bones, in danger of being crushed
by Gina.

"I'm not leaving you, LaRose." Gina arched her head to
meet Ken's gaze. "But you can, Ken. I understand—you
don't owe either of us anything."

Understatement of the year. Ken said nothing, just shook
his head and returned to his post at the door, edging it open
far enough to watch the corridor.

LaRose also was silent, her gaze fixed on their joined
hands. Gina could have sworn that she was trying to find
words, but even before the stroke any sentiment of mother-
daughter bonding or approval would have been beyond
LaRose. Now wasn't the time to start.

Gina turned away, not wanting to embarrass LaRose
and ruin the moment. Her gaze caught on the oxygen tank
that sat under the head of the examination table. Maybe
there was a way.

She disengaged her hand from LaRose's and retrieved

the tank from under the table. "Ken, can you find me some tubing?"

He left the door and began to rummage through the supply cart. "What do you have in mind?"

"A diversion. One that hopefully won't blow up in my face."

LYDIA TUGGED HER GLOVE OFF WITH HER TEETH. She held her body away from the box as she dared to lower her hand into it. The penguin's feathers were thick, layered together, soft like fur. She stroked it; it felt warm to the touch and she could feel its heartbeat skittering.

She jumped back as its body quivered. Then it turned its head. Its neck was white with a black streak and its beak was layered black, white, and tan. It blinked at her, then nuzzled its head against her hand. "I think it's okay."

The bird made the honky-quacky noise she'd heard earlier outside.

"Good. There should be eleven more."

"I'll go put this one inside Bessie, crank up the heat." She closed the container, put her glove back on, and carried it outside. The temperature had dropped, creating a slick coating of ice over the top of the snow and ice that already lay on the road. The absence of any lights except Bessie's headlights was startling and unexpected for someone who was used to measuring the city's pulse by its lightscape. And quiet—it was as if they were on the moon with no one else near.

Squonk, squonk. Make that no one else except some runaway penguins.

The noise had come from very close, near her feet. Lydia stood still, scared that she might step on one of the creatures, and looked around, her eyes adapting to the darkness. There, only a yard away, was something moving, jerking its way through a tire track like a Mexican jumping bean.

Lydia approached slowly, afraid of startling the bird as much as she was afraid of what it might do to her if it was startled. The bird in the box she carried must have realized another one was close by, because it began to squawk and move around, making the sides of the container bow out and threatening to burst the flimsy cardboard box wide open.

"Hold still," Lydia muttered, wishing she spoke penguin. Another step and she was right beside the second bird. Carefully, she lowered the box down in front of the bird, blocking its path.

It stopped, cocking its head, its beak bobbing like a conductor's baton, quizzically tapping the box. Now both birds were chattering away. With the second bird immersed in exchanging pleasantries with the first, Lydia lunged forward and scooped it up with her good hand, pulling it tight up against her chest.

To her surprise it didn't resist. She tensed, waiting for it to turn and attack her. Instead, a ripple shuddered over it from head to tail, its feathers rustling, then settling into place. It stroked her parka with its beak—probably liked the smell of the down insulation, she thought. She held her right arm close to her body and the bird settled into the crook of her elbow, resting its weight on her cast. Good thing it didn't weigh more than five or six pounds.

It appeared she had a new career as a penguin nest. Lydia glanced at her left hand, the one that had caught the bird. Her glove was coated with tiny, fuzzy feathers. She grabbed the box and resumed her skating routine across the slick, irregular road surface. The smell was incredible— fermented fish oil. She'd never be able to wear these clothes again.

As she approached Bessie, a wave of laughter overcame

her. The bird nestled in her arm glanced up, then tucked its head back down as if a woman shaking with laughter and stinking of fish were normal in its world. But it was too funny to ignore—the universe was such a crazy, insane place that sometimes you just had to stop and laugh with it.

Despite the stench, she felt calm for the first time all day. The wind and snow slapped at her cheeks and they felt ready to crack with the cold, but she couldn't stop grinning. The only thing needed to make this moment perfect was . . .

"You're a sight," Trey's voice came from behind her. He steadied her, one hand on her hip, as he yanked open the passenger-side door to Bessie with the other. "Hey, you caught another one, good for you."

"Hey, yourself," she said, turning to face him. "Come closer, I want to show you why Eskimos rub noses."

He took the box from her hand and set it down inside Bessie. She grabbed his sleeve and pulled him to her, the second bird nestled between them.

"You smell," he said, his eyes crinkled with mischief. He rubbed his nose against hers, then kissed her.

"Now you do, too." They parted and she released the second bird into the front of the rescue vehicle. Trey carefully shut the door. "Two down, ten to go."

Zimmerman came running up, waving his arms. "I found them. They're all huddled together over here in this snowbank."

Trey chuckled as they followed Zimmerman. "Wait till I write this run report up."

"You mean thirteen reports—one for Zimmerman and one for each penguin. Hmmm"—she bumped his hip with hers—"you might just have to stay home writing reports for the rest of the night."

He took her hand in his, ignoring the sticky feathers covering her palm. "Wouldn't that be nice?"

* * *

NORA STARED AT THE GUN AIMED BETWEEN HER eyes. She was certain she was supposed to feel something: terror, panic, bravado, regret, sorrow, hope . . . something. Instead, her body felt absolutely frozen, unable to think, breathe, move, feel.

Her vision collapsed to take in the very large, very black gun and Harris's finger on the trigger. The rest of the world faded into a distant blur of color. The auditorium had gone silent, so silent that Nora's ears felt like they were trying to pop.

The clatter of something metal hitting the floor broke the spell. Nora's hearing returned with a thunderclap. Harris's hand jerked, his aim jumping up over Nora's head, although he never squeezed the trigger.

"Leave her alone!" It was Mark Cohen's voice. Nora dared to look over her shoulder. Mark had gotten off his bed and was leaning heavily on Jason as he hobbled across the stage. "If you want something, talk to me. I'm in charge here."

Harris simply smiled and nodded to the guard next to him. The burly man leaped onto the stage with grace that defied gravity given his bulk, and with a swift flick of his foot he swept Mark's leg out from under him, toppling both him and Jason to the ground. Mark cried out in pain.

"I think you'll find that I'm in charge here," Harris said calmly, bringing his gun to bear on Nora again. "Now, Ms. Halloran, you're the ER head nurse. Where's Dr. Fiore?"

Ignoring the sudden chill that had settled in her bones, Nora edged forward. It was amazing how much effort it took to shuffle her feet; they felt encased in cement. She angled herself to block Harris's view of the others. Shielding them from his sight—and aim—was the only way she could protect them.

"I don't know where Dr. Fiore is," she said, her voice as loud and clear as it was during the chaos of a trauma code. And as certain. She hoped.

Harris narrowed his eyes, lips pinched in disbelief. Nora counted to five, holding her breath, watching his finger on the trigger. He slowly released the trigger, gave her a nod as if they were equals coming to terms, and lowered the gun.

"I believe you. But"—he waved the gun toward the rest of the auditorium—"she's somewhere in this hospital and I'm going to find her. And if that doesn't happen quickly, we may need to take alternative and more drastic"—he holstered the gun with a dramatic flourish—"methods."

GINA LAID THE OXYGEN TANK ON THE EXAM TA-
ble and connected the plastic tubing Ken had found to its nozzle. "Thanksgiving, we had this lady come into the ER," she said as she checked the gauge. Nearly full; good. "Her cigarette had burned through the plastic tubing of her home oxygen tank and started a fire."

"Too dangerous—if you use an open flame to light it, it could flash over you."

"Ah, but I have a time-delayed fuse." She took her cigarettes and matches from her sweater pocket. "Saw it in a movie once."

Ken frowned. "That's the movies. It might not work in real life."

"You got a better idea?"

"Yeah. I'll do it. That way even if it fails, you can still get LaRose out of here."

He tried to grab the cigarettes from her, but she yanked them out of his reach. "No way. It's my plan and if anything goes wrong, you can protect LaRose better than I can."

Gina wished she felt half as brave as she sounded. One look at Ken's face and she knew he knew she was full of shit. She hefted the oxygen tank and held it under her arm like a football. Tried to ignore the fluttering in her stomach. She'd spent most of her life faking being smart, being confident, being brave. Time to see if she really had what it took.

To her relief Ken said nothing, just gave her a nod. If he had said something, she might have surrendered to her fear, so she was glad for once that he was living up to his taciturn man-of-mystery reputation.

She carried the oxygen and tubing out to the main doors and glanced through the windows. The guard was pacing a pattern at the far end of the lobby, the side that faced the auditorium and elevator banks. The wall with the elevators blocked his view of the radiology entrance for a few seconds on each leg of his journey. That would be her window of opportunity.

"You'll need something to catch fire to make a big enough flame to pull him away," Ken whispered as he wheeled LaRose into position beside her.

"The gift shop?"

"It's closed today."

Gina craned her neck, trying to spot a likely spot to hide her IED. "The rack of pamphlets between the gift shop and the main doors. I can hide the tank under it and once the fire starts they should go fast—they're just bus schedules and Pennysavers and stuff."

"Should work." Ken pressed his face beside hers, their breath steaming the glass. "Once you cross the lobby, you'll be out of his sight."

"I think we'll have around three minutes from the time I light the cigarette until the fire starts. That should give me time to get back here, and once the guard moves out of the way, we'll go to the rear elevator bank, out of sight from the lobby." She hoisted the tank, watching the guard, waiting for the right moment to make her move. "If I'm not back in time—".

"Don't worry. I'll take care of LaRose. You just worry about yourself."

"Okay, here goes."

The guard pivoted and stepped out of sight. Ken pulled the door open for her and Gina dashed through it. Some instinct made her crouch low as if under fire, probably the result of watching too many movies when she was a kid. Funny, the thoughts that raced through your mind when you may have only seconds to live. Her gaze was zeroed in on the corner of the gift shop—once she made it there, she'd be safely out of the guard's line of sight.

It felt that no matter how fast her feet pounded the lobby's slate floor, her goal didn't get any closer. The back of her neck prickled, and she was tempted to stop and look over her shoulder, see where the guard was, even though the countdown in her head told her she had a few seconds yet. Gina didn't look—maybe something good had come of all that movie watching, because she knew it was always the guy who turned to look who got shot.

Instead she drove onward and suddenly found herself skidding around the corner. She had to pull up fast; she couldn't risk getting too close to the automatic eye that opened the entrance's sliding glass doors—that would alert the guard for sure.

Clutching her O_2 tank to her chest as if it were a newborn baby, she leaned against the wall and caught her breath. Then she risked a peek around the corner and saw Ken watching her from the radiology doors across the lobby. He gave her a thumbs-up and she mirrored a response, hoping he couldn't see her hand shaking.

Okay, time to make a flamethrower. She crouched down and gently set the oxygen tank on the floor. Turning the valve on to release the gas—two liters should be about right, she thought—she slid it beneath the wire rack brimming with brochures and pamphlets. She checked the end of the tubing. The oxygen was flowing nicely.

Not wanting to risk any flames—at least not yet—she pinched the tubing, cutting off the flow of O_2, and pinned it beneath the leg of the display rack before striking a match and lighting a cigarette. She took only one puff, although as soon as her lips touched the cigarette she was consumed with the desire to sit back and inhale the entire thing. She folded the book of matches around the filter of the cigarette and carefully placed the matchbook under the end of the tubing.

Now the countdown began. She edged a glance around the corner, then pulled back immediately. The guard was coming her way, varying his pattern by circling out into the lobby. Shit.

Her head rocked against the wall. She glanced at the cigarette—about a quarter of the way burned. Should she pull it out, wait?

The guard's radio squawked. Gina jumped, both arms jerking up as if in surrender. The sound was louder than a flock of seagulls at feeding time. And it was close—the guard must already be right around the corner at the gift shop window.

Did he smell the cigarette burning? Had he heard her? Her breath came in short, quick gasps as her gaze jumped from the cigarette—a third gone—to the corner she huddled against.

"What's your twenty? I don't see you," the radio voice said.

"I'm coming, I'm coming." The guard moved away at a rush. "You guys got food in there? I'm starving."

"Nelson's bringing it."

Gina dared a look. The guard disappeared as he returned to the auditorium entrance. Now or never. She pushed off and dashed across the lobby to the door where Ken waited. Ken's face was smashed against the glass as he watched, his eyes wide.

She was still ten feet shy of the door when flames burst out behind her.

THIRTEEN

THERE WAS NO WAY AMANDA WAS GOING TO allow Jerry to sacrifice himself as a diversion. Apparently Lucas felt the same, springing ahead as they made their way down the stairs to the ground floor. By the time Jerry and Amanda pushed through the door to the lobby, Lucas was crouched against the wall below the picture window, waving them down.

He pointed toward the auditorium and held up two fingers. Jerry and Amanda crawled over to join him.

"There're two guards there now," Lucas whispered. "With machine guns. What do we do?"

The obvious choice was to run away and hide in the farthest corner of the tower, praying the storm died down and they could make their escape before the gunmen took drastic action, like burning down the hospital. Amanda still found it hard to believe that anyone would go to such lengths, but she'd encountered enough cases of abuse and other horrible, unbelievable things that she knew it could happen.

She duckwalked past Lucas and craned her head around the corner, getting a look for herself. One man stood at the doors, his gun aimed in their direction, while the other paced back and forth, focused in the other direction, toward the elevators and main hospital lobby.

The atrium was usually Amanda's second-favorite place in the hospital, after the pediatric floor's playroom. It was designed as a sanctuary of peace and nature, so there were no straight paths through it. People had no choice but to slow down, listen to the fountains burble, sit on the benches or tall rocks, or look at the planters with their miniature trees, evergreens, ferns, and flowering plants.

But now, despite the continued merry bubbling of the solar-powered water fountains, the atrium was shrouded in shadows and had a potential of becoming a killing ground.

"Run and hide?" she asked the men. "Or try to rescue the people trapped in the auditorium?"

Both men stared at her, neither making a move toward the stairwell and safety. Answer enough for her.

Scrutinizing the atrium, she tried to mentally devise a path through it that would give them maximum cover, but there was no way they could reach the cafeteria without crossing space where they'd be hopelessly exposed. Jerry was right. They needed a diversion.

The guard covering the lobby moved out of sight. Amanda watched, motioning to the men to get ready. But then the second guard spoke into his walkie-talkie and the first man returned.

Her attention was still riveted on the guards when Jerry suddenly broke past her, crawling, cane in hand, to the shelter of the first planter.

"Jerry, wait," she whispered, but he waved her back.

His head injury may have left him with no patience and little impulse control, but this was suicide.

Just as Jerry was about to cross into open ground, the first guard suddenly yelled and ran for the lobby. There was shouting back and forth between the guards. The second pulled a fire extinguisher from the wall and raced after the first.

Amanda grabbed Lucas and they sprinted across the atrium. Jerry struggled to his feet and followed behind. Lucas stopped at the sound of Jerry's cane hitting the ground and ran back to help him. Amanda risked a glance over her shoulder; Jerry had slipped on the slate floor and was struggling to get back up.

Holding her shears at the ready, Amanda plunged through the swinging door to the cafeteria.

Only to run headlong into another guard.

THERE WAS A COMMOTION OUTSIDE THE AUDITO-rium doors. Harris and the blond guard rushed out, the guard returning a few minutes later and sending another gunman out in his stead.

"What's happening?" Nora asked. Information was the best way to stave off panic.

"None of your concern," the guard said. His accent was thick—not quite English or Australian—South African, maybe? "But you should know that the power will be cut off in a few minutes. Prepare your people."

"Why cut off the power? You're not going to find Lydia any easier in the dark, and there are patients in the ICU depending on equipment."

He looked at her placidly. No expression, no remorse, not even a shrug of indifference.

Nora sighed in frustration. She couldn't help the people

up in the ICU, but she could help the patients and staff down here. She gathered everyone in the front of the auditorium. "I've just been informed that the power will be cut off in a few minutes."

A babble of voices rose up at her announcement. She gestured for silence and got it a few moments later. "Melissa, you take three people and gather all the flashlights we have. Bring them up front here."

"We also have a few battery-operated work lights," Melissa said.

"Great, set them up." Nora considered. Only a minute or two left. What else? Food, they had. Water, they were good there. The IV pumps had their batteries charged. "Jason, please gather all the blankets and distribute them. You all will need to share; patients take priority." Another murmur of protest. "No arguments. We're all in this together and we'll all get through this together."

She wished she were half as confident as she sounded.

Mark Cohen beckoned to her from where he lay on a stretcher. She joined him, bending low, and he whispered, "It's all my fault."

"What is?"

"I knew Harris thought Lydia was working today and I wanted to buy time to find out what he wanted, so I told him she was with a patient, had taken them for a procedure, and couldn't be disturbed. And now—" He gestured helplessly to the people huddled in the seats in front of the stage. "Nora, whatever happens, we need to protect them."

"I'm doing the best I can."

"Do you think it would help if I told Harris I lied before?"

Nora stared at the guards with their machine guns. They looked like they wouldn't hesitate to kill anyone who crossed them. "No. They'll never believe you. Besides, we've seen their faces—"

Pain flashed across his features. They both knew the implications of that: These men weren't planning to leave any witnesses left behind.

"I'm so sorry."

Nora wished she had words to comfort him. Wished she had a way out of this nightmare for all of them. Leaving Mark with Melissa, she made her way back down off the stage, trying to ignore the dread fear plummeting like a rock in her stomach.

Harris returned, this time with Tillman. He was scowling. He nodded to the South African, who pulled Nora and Jim Lazarov from the crowd and marched them to the front of the auditorium where they joined Tillman. "I'm tired of these games. One of you knows where Lydia Fiore is, I'm sure of it."

He held his wrist up, watch facing him, counting the seconds, staring at each of them in turn. "Where is she?"

Nora couldn't speak, even if she'd known the answer to his question. She stood, her gaze fixed on the gun and the man holding it so nonchalantly on them, and shook her head.

Harris appeared disappointed and shifted his attention to Jim. "Where is Dr. Fiore?"

Jim made a small, choking sound, sucked in his breath, and said, "I don't know."

His voice emerged as broken and high-pitched as a teenager's, but Nora could have hugged him for protecting Lydia. Maybe there was hope for Jim after all. If they made it through tonight alive.

This time Harris clucked his tongue. He aimed the gun at Tillman. "Where is she?"

Tillman didn't even pretend to be brave. He held up his hands, pleading. "I've told you, I don't know where she is."

*   *   *

Gina threw herself forward through the door Ken held open. Behind her she could hear the shouts of the guard, the sound of running footsteps, followed by voices of other men.

She tripped over LaRose's feet stretched out in the wheelchair and slammed against the opposite wall. She felt ready to heave her guts out, grabbed her belly as she caught her breath.

"Get ready," Ken said, keeping watch at the window. He moved behind LaRose's chair, in position to push. Gina hauled in a breath and took his spot at the door.

"I used the radio to make contact with one of the surgical residents up in the ICU," Ken whispered. "They're trapped up there. The exits are all blocked."

Which meant using the elevators might only draw attention from the bad guys. Or they might sneak past, make it to the eighth floor and across to the tower before anyone noticed. Either way, it was risky. But now that the bad guys knew someone was running free on the main floor, they had to leave. No choice but to stick to the original plan.

She glanced through the window in the door. The first guard had been joined by two others, who were trying without success to conquer the fire with a handheld extinguisher. Apparently the wall covering behind the brochure rack had been flammable, because flames crawled up the wall, bright orange ribbons taunting them from above. Every squirt of the extinguisher seemed to create more smoke and reveal a new area of fire. Soon it was difficult to see the men, consumed by billowing clouds of chemicals and smoke.

"Now," Gina said, opening the door. Ken crouched low behind the wheelchair handles, putting his entire body into propelling the chair. LaRose hugged her arms to her chest, her eyes wide, lips sucked in, jaws clenched. Her usually meticulously coiffed hair had succumbed to events—

Medusa's would appear more tame—and her expression was one of anticipation and . . . exhilaration?

Surely she was mistaken? Gina had no time to think about it as she ran after them, keeping one eye on the men in the lobby while also searching for anyone coming from the direction of the auditorium. They made it to the elevator bank, where all three cars were waiting with their doors open.

Ken pushed LaRose across the threshold of the nearest one. Gina ran past to the other two elevators. These elevators had a door hold button to help with patient transport. She disengaged the hold and pushed random floor buttons on both elevators, hoping to further confuse the situation, then returned and squeezed past LaRose to man the controls of their elevator. She jammed the door close button, but nothing happened. Then she hit the button for the eighth floor. Still nothing.

The men in the lobby were shouting now—they must have found the oxygen tank and realized it was a diversion. Any second and they'd be pouring bullets into the elevators. Sweat streamed down Gina's back, her turtleneck stuck to her like a second skin. She stabbed the buttons repeatedly, trying to force the doors closed with her will if nothing else. No way some damn button was going to get them killed.

Finally the doors surrendered and slid shut. The car began to climb upward. Gina craned her head up, hurling silent expletives, trying to make it move faster. The elevator moved as slowly as ever—maybe even slower. Gina bounced on her heels, urging it to speed up. That didn't work either. Ken pivoted LaRose's chair so that she faced forward. She tugged at Gina's lab jacket until Gina tore her attention from the indicator lights and glanced down.

"Good work." It was hard to tell, but LaRose seemed to

be smiling—her lips had moved to bare half of her teeth, but the other half of her face still slumped as if overdosed on Botox. LaRose never smiled. It was undignified.

Gina didn't know what to say—she wasn't used to responding to praise from her parents. Ken jerked his chin at her, insisting that she say something, and she muttered, "Thanks."

The elevator indicator showed that they were at the fourth floor. Gina's nails dug into her palms, and she couldn't stop her bouncing. Jerry had to be okay, he just had to be. And Lucas Stone would take care of LaRose, get her started on the TPA, and Amanda would be there, smiling just like always, and they could wait out the storm, and . . . her thoughts hit a dead end. What to do about Harris? And his threat to burn down the hospital—maybe he'd been bluffing?

Gina's stomach dropped as if the elevator had gone into freefall. She had the awful feeling that Harris wasn't the kind of guy who made idle threats. The indicator light for the fourth floor died. A new one came to life. Fifth floor. Almost there.

Harris's voice came over the elevator's intercom. "I'm tired of playing games, Dr. Fiore. If you don't respond in the next ten seconds, someone dies. And I will begin to shoot hostages, one every five minutes until you give me what I want."

"That's crazy," Ken said. "Surely he's not serious?"

"He seemed serious enough to me when he shot those guards."

"But you said Lydia isn't even here—"

"Doesn't matter. He thinks she is."

The intercom buzzed again. "Time's up."

The sound of a loud crack followed by the sound of screams filled the elevator car.

FOURTEEN

AFTER SECURING THE FIRST TWO PENGUINS IN THE front of Bessie, Trey grabbed a blanket from one of the rear equipment compartments, and he and Lydia joined Zimmerman over where the other ten penguins had burrowed partway into a snow pile and were huddled together. From a distance the birds looked kind of cute—even Lydia had to admit that. And the first two she'd encountered hadn't gone Hitchcock-crazy-mad on her. Still, she was happy to let Trey take charge of this rescue.

"Zimmerman, you get on the other side," Trey directed, handing the truck driver two corners of the blanket. "Lydia, you stand back, watch out for any escapees."

"Great, let the lady with one working arm chase after the rabid penguins once you get them all riled up."

"Penguins don't have rabies," Zimmerman said.

"How would you know? I thought you only cleaned their cages."

"Habitats, not cages. And it's a known fact." He seemed

to feel better about his long-term job prospects now that they'd located the wayward birds.

"Just throw the blanket and get ready to scoop them up," Trey said, unfolding his end of the blanket and holding it like a fishing net. "Ready? Go!"

The men flung the blanket over the birds and rushed to pin down the sides. "Be careful," Zimmerman shouted. "Don't hurt them."

"They'll be fine," Trey assured him. "Just roll the blanket under them and we'll bundle them in it."

Lydia watched, unable to restrain her laughter. What she wouldn't give for a camera—better yet, a TV crew from one of those nature reality shows. The two men were down on their knees, butts aimed up in the air as they reached their arms out, trying to corral the penguins. The penguins obviously weren't too thrilled with the idea—disapproving honking filled the air as they hopped around under the blanket. One bird got his head out and flapped his beak as if affronted by Trey's lack of civilized manners.

As Trey scrambled to push the bird back under the blanket, two more escaped. Lydia followed them, slipping and sliding across the snow in a mad scramble to keep them in sight.

She cornered the two wayward birds against the snowbank on the opposite side of the road. "I've got them," she called to the men, who were hoisting the blanket and hauling its squirming contents toward Bessie.

One of the birds was larger than the other and decided to attack. It stopped squawking and instead opened its beak and bit her on the shin. She didn't feel anything puncture her skin; it was more like getting her leg caught in a vise—but the damn thing wouldn't let go.

She shook her leg gently, trying to dislodge the penguin without hurting it. No good. The two birds had obviously been plotting their escape together because while the first kept her busy, the second made a run for it.

Lydia lunged for it, but it was too fast and it skidded right past her outstretched hand. She concentrated on the big one—the one clamped onto her leg—instead. As soon as its mate escaped, it let go and tried to waddle off as well. She caught it from behind, scooping it up with her good arm and trapping it against her chest, beak pointing out. It banged its beak against her arm in the cast, which hurt a bit, but not half as much as her leg did.

Trey joined her. "I got the little one. You okay?"

"I'm fine," she muttered. "The zoo owes me a new parka." The bird in her arms had succeeded in tearing her sleeve, releasing down feathers into the wind. "Told you I don't like birds."

Trey just laughed as he opened Bessie's driver's door. Zimmerman had the other birds trapped in the passenger-side wheel well. Lydia handed him her bird, as did Trey, and then she climbed up and slid across the bench seat. She had to pull her legs up to her chest because the center console was filled with equipment charging and the radio.

"Can you turn the heat up?" Zimmerman asked as Trey steered the rescue truck past his overturned van. "I don't want them to catch cold."

It was a good thing the cab was dark enough that Zimmerman couldn't see the glare Lydia aimed at him.

Trey knew without looking. He chuckled and squeezed her leg. "What do you think of our winters now?"

"I think we need to talk about a trip to California," she muttered, bracing herself against the dash as the truck bounced over a mound of ice and snow. "Soon. Real soon."

NORA LISTENED WITH HORROR TO HARRIS'S THREATS over the intercom. He was speaking into his radio, but one of his men outside must have been broadcasting his words all over the hospital. Even more horrifying was that he never lost the neutral expression he aimed at each of them—her, Tillman, and Jim, in turn—playing eeny-meeny-minie-moe with their lives.

The crowd behind them became more agitated, but the South African held his machine gun on the rest of them, keeping the others at bay.

Harris eyed his watch. A wry smile tugged at his lips. "Time's up."

He pivoted and shot Jim in the chest at point-blank range.

Screams echoed through the cavernous room.

Then the lights went out.

AMANDA REALIZED HER ONLY HOPE WAS MOMEN-tum, so instead of trying to slow down, she sped up into the path of the guard she'd surprised in the cafeteria. The bad guy was dressed like a hospital security guard, his arms full of snack food, gun in a holster at his hip, and obviously stunned by the sight of a woman wearing a tattered designer gown and brandishing a large pair of scissors appearing from nowhere.

He arched back, weight on his heels, coming to a stop just as Amanda rammed him, using her shoulder and left arm to clothes-hook him, just like her big brothers used to do when they were fighting dirty.

His feet skidded out from under him. Packages of muffins and doughnuts flew around them. Before he could catch his breath or reach for his gun, Amanda jumped on him, straddling his chest, and pressed the point of her shears against his throat, tight enough to feel his heartbeat vibrate through the blades.

"Don't say a word," she whispered. "Don't make a move."

Lucas and Jerry came up on either side of her, Jerry

fumbling for the man's gun, while Lucas knelt beside Amanda. "Are you all right?"

"Fine. Tie him up and find something to gag him with."

Lucas might not have looked like a typical action hero, but he made quick work of binding the man's hands and feet with the strapping tape they'd taken from rehab. He taped the man's mouth as well while Jerry held the gun on him. Once the man was restrained, Amanda climbed off him and returned her shears to her sash.

"Where should we put him?" Lucas asked, rocking back on his heels and admiring his handiwork.

"The pantry—its walls are so thick that even if he gets loose, no one will be able to hear him. Plus it has a door that locks."

The man's radio sounded. "Marcus is ready to shut the power off. Two minutes."

Amanda grabbed the radio and added it to the items hanging from her sash. "Why do they want to turn off the backup power?"

"Ask him," Jerry said.

"After we get him secure. I don't want to be carrying him around in the dark."

Lucas and Amanda dragged the man into the pantry while Jerry stood guard at the kitchen door. When they finished, Jerry handed Amanda the man's gun. The semi-automatic was a Smith & Wesson 910S. Her brother had the same model, along with about a dozen others. Amanda removed the magazine, ten bullets total. She replaced the magazine, then racked one into the chamber, ready to go.

"Shouldn't Jerry have the gun?" Lucas protested.

"No," both Jerry and Amanda said together.

"After all, he's the policeman."

"Not today," Jerry said.

"But—" Lucas said, his dismay evident as he stared at Amanda holding the nine-millimeter.

"You're just going to have to trust me, Lucas. I can out-shoot any of my brothers, even my father on a good day."

Jerry smiled the quirky new smile of his that seemed to find humor in the most ghastly of circumstances. The same smile he'd given Amanda when he'd woken from his coma and she'd let him look in a mirror, to see for the first time his shaved scalp and the ugly scar that ran across it.

"No good days for me," he said.

As if punctuating his words, the sound of a shot rang out followed by screams.

Then the lights went out.

GINA ALMOST DROPPED THE RADIO WHEN SHE HEARD the sound of the shot as Harris carried out his threat. Ken supported it, circling her hand with his, as they both stared at the radio in horror.

She wanted to scream or shout herself, but she couldn't find any words big enough to express her anger and fear and frustration. Someone had just died. Probably someone she knew.

The lights flickered and went out. The elevator lurched to a halt. A small red light came on—the only light.

"What the hell?" Gina slammed the control buttons, but none of them lit up. The elevator reversed course, moving even more slowly than normal, away from the eighth floor, away from Jerry.

"It's on emergency override," Ken said. "It will go down to the basement. Safety procedure to keep any patients from getting trapped if the power goes out."

"They're really doing it. Harris said something about turning off the emergency generator." Gina thought furiously. Her thoughts raced in every direction, but what she really wanted to do was to stop thinking and just curl up and cry. This wasn't happening, it just wasn't. But it was. She'd just heard someone being executed.

Their slow descent continued despite her using every ounce of willpower to make the car change course.

She had to do something—even if she couldn't save Jerry, there had to be a way to save the others.

What did she have to bargain with? What did Harris want? How could she stop his deadly countdown?

"I'm going to tell them I know where the evidence is. Bargain with them, tell them that once the storm dies down, I'll take them to it if they stop killing people." She couldn't use the word *hostages*—those were her friends trapped in there.

The red emergency light made Ken look like a man on fire, his dark hair rippling, his exposed arms sinewy streams of flame. "No. I'll do it."

"You can't. I know Lydia. I can pretend to be her, over the radio at least. I can stall Harris, give the police time to get here. You can't do that."

As long as they never found her, got a good look at her, Gina could use the radio to lead them on a wild-goose chase. At least until the weather cleared and they called her bluff.

Ken frowned, but nodded. "You'll need a safe place to hide for a while. Up through the emergency hatch."

"I need you to look after my mother."

"I will," he promised. "We'll be fine. They'll put us with the other hostages and I can get her the TPA—you know Nora will have moved the meds to the auditorium when they evacuated the ER."

Still, she hesitated. She hated this plan, hated leaving him and LaRose. But she was the only hope the others had. If she could just keep Harris from shooting anyone else, just until help arrived . . .

"Come on, there's not much time." Ken knelt and gestured for Gina to climb onto his shoulders.

LaRose made the decision for her. She clawed at Gina's lab coat, pulling her daughter's face down level with hers. If Ken had looked more alive, aglow, in the red light, LaRose appeared ghastly. The whites of her eyes shone red and the tears quivering on her cheeks reflected like rubies. "Go. Regina, go."

Ken took that as an answer, hauling her past LaRose and effortlessly lifting Gina up, so fast that she banged her head against the ceiling. A cloud of dust made her sneeze—she braced her palms against the ceiling so she wouldn't fall.

"Hurry," Ken urged.

"A little to the left." She reached for the trapdoor in the roof of the elevator, a shadowy outline against the crimson shadows cast by the light.

The hatch wasn't like in the movies, where it simply pushed up. Gina fumbled her fingers around the edge until she found the latch holding it shut. When she finally got it free, the hatch fell inward, hitting her again on the head. Not hard, just enough that she almost lost her balance and nearly toppled Ken.

He grabbed her hard, his hands on her hips, and steadied her. The elevator jerked to a final stop. "Hurry," he whispered. "If the power's off, they'll need to open the door manually, but there's not much time."

Gina scrambled her head and arms through the hatch, clawing for handholds in the dark. Her fingers brushed an empty soda can and it rolled past her, falling into the car. She felt Ken's body tremble with the effort of holding her aloft. Her hand collided with something raised and metal. Its edges were rough, but it felt solid, so she grabbed on.

Ken had to release her long enough to get under her legs with a new grip. She tried to help, but her entire weight was braced against the metal and it was digging into her skin and all she could do was kick, trying to squirm the rest of the way onto the roof.

"Hold still." Ken grabbed hold of her feet and pushed her the rest of the way up and through the opening. She rolled to the side, away from the hatch. The top of the elevator was filthy; it smelled of grease and rotting food. More empty cans crunched and slid beneath her, as did coffee cups and food wrappers.

"Pull the hatch shut," Ken said.

She squirmed around, then reached back down through the opening to grab the hatch.

"Be careful," she told him. He brushed her hand with his fingers and squeezed.

Then he let go. The elevator doors began to grate open, the seals protesting. Gina pulled the hatch closed, and with it went the last of her light. It was pitch dark in the elevator shaft and eerily silent. Her breath echoed like the wind.

She couldn't find a latch on the roof side of the hatch, so she held the hatch shut. Her muscles screamed with the strain of holding it in such an awkward position, lying on her belly, arms outstretched. But if she let it drop . . .

A man's voice came from below. "Out of there! Now!"

Gina couldn't hear Ken's reply. She couldn't hear anything.

FIFTEEN

THE GUNSHOT WAS FOLLOWED BY A WAKE OF stunned silence. The air in the auditorium felt tight and thin, stretched to breaking.

Jim didn't fall; he slumped against the wall, his hand crawling up his chest, searching for injury, a look of horror and disbelief on his face. His hand touched the blood that had seeped through his shirt and came away covered in red. He stared at it in shock, then crumpled to the ground.

And the screaming started.

Nora ran to Jim, ignoring Harris's gun. Footsteps thudded around her as others came to help—she was surprised to see so many, had thought that most people would run the other way. Lord knew that was what every instinct in her body told her to do.

"Get me a trauma kit, O₂, and two lines going," Nora ordered. Using her trauma shears, she sliced Jim's shirt off. The entrance wound was just below his left nipple. Not good, not good at all.

"Was I hit?" Jim asked, his eyes half closed and his voice unsteady. "I think maybe I was shot."

"Just relax," she told him, using her best charge nurse tone. Calm, collected. "You're going to be fine."

Helping hands arrived. Melissa crouched beside her, starting an IV while a nursing tech put Jim on oxygen and hooked him up to a portable monitor. Nora grabbed her stethoscope and listened.

"Lung sounds down on the left and heart sounds muffled," she announced. Signs of a collapsed lung and blood collecting around the heart, strangling it. "He needs a chest tube and pericardiocentesis."

"So who's going to do it?" Melissa asked. "He was the only doctor in here."

Nora looked at her, her mind finally catching up—oh hell. "Mark?" she called out. "Someone get Mark down here."

"I'm coming." His voice came through the crowd of spectators. Two men carried Mark past the others and sat him on the floor beside Jim. "I'll talk you through the chest tube while I needle the heart."

"But—"

"But nothing, you've seen enough of them, you know what to do." It was Jim's only chance, he didn't say. Didn't have to as Jim's eyes slid shut and the monitor alarmed. "Flatline! Let's move, people!"

THE SOUND OF THE GUNSHOT WAS LOUDER OVER the radio than the sound that came through the auditorium wall to reach them in the cafeteria. The screams were loud enough either way—it was heart-wrenching for Amanda to hear them in stereo and not be able to do anything.

At the sound of the shot, Jerry pulled his gun, useless as it was, from his pocket. "Gina!"

Amanda had the same impulse, to run and help the people trapped next door. But Lucas saved them both from their folly. He caught Amanda before she could go two steps. "No. You'll get yourself killed and maybe a lot of innocents as well."

Jerry ignored him, continuing to stumble toward the door.

"Gina's safe," Lucas told him, keeping his voice low so that it wouldn't carry. Not that they'd have to worry about that with the screams and shouts coming from next door. "Jerry. She wasn't in there. We don't know where she is, but she's safe."

Jerry stopped, hesitating, leaning on his cane, his body angled toward the exit, a silhouette of desperation, washed red by the emergency exit light above the door.

"We need more information," Lucas continued. "We can't run in there blind."

Amanda shook free of Lucas and joined Jerry. "He's right. No more running around hoping for good luck and a chance to take these guys out. We need a plan."

It was hard to make out much in the dark of the kitchen, but she felt Jerry nod. "Ask him."

"You mean ask the guard we caught? How can we trust anything he says?" Lucas said.

Amanda thought about it. Jerry wasn't up to playing head games with anyone, and Lucas was much too nice to follow through on any threats. But someone had just gotten shot one wall away from her—probably someone she knew. No more games, no more fairy-tale dress-up, this was real.

Amanda pulled a nine-inch fillet knife from the rack beside her. Much sharper, deadlier than a pair of scissors. "I'll do it."

* * *

ONCE AGAIN, GINA WAS ALONE IN DARKNESS AND silence. She lay against the top of the elevator, her body folded around unknown mechanical equipment that jabbed and jutted into her, but she felt as if she were falling. Gravity seemed to have lost all meaning in the immense and total darkness.

How long had it been? What was happening to LaRose and Ken?

Was it safe?

She tried to count her pulse as an approximation of seconds, but it was racing too fast to be of any use. Every inhalation brought a tickle to her nose and the urge to sneeze, but she didn't dare. She concentrated on breathing slow and steady through her mouth, trying to ignore the various cramps and protests raised by her muscles. Her position—facedown, half crouched, half folded over a metal box, arms outstretched, holding the hatch closed—was precarious at best and definitely not one she could maintain for long.

Finally when she thought her arms would spasm so hard that she'd drop it anyway, she opened the elevator hatch an inch and listened. No one was moving inside the elevator or just outside its open doors. Her arms surrendered their struggle and let the hatch swing free.

No one came, no alarm sounded. She ducked her head down through the opening. The red emergency light was the only illumination; the hallway beyond was in shadows. There was no sign of anyone.

She rearranged herself, sitting upright and adjusting her clothing. She pulled the Maglite out of her pocket and risked turning it on, revealing her surroundings. She was careful to aim it away from the hatch, leaning it upright against the steel box that had kept jabbing her stomach earlier. Her hands were filthy, nails torn, palms abraded. Grease streaked her lab jacket, turning it into from white into a postmodernistic black-and-gray camouflage.

She pulled the hatch closed again. It looked like it was designed to lock on the roof side too, but the latch was broken. She slid her reflex hammer through the eyebolt on the hatch to keep it shut and ensure her privacy.

Her instincts told her to stay on the roof—it was relatively safe and no one would look for her here. She fumbled the radio from her lab jacket and turned it back on.

"Two more," a man's voice came through, echoing against the concrete walls of the shaft despite the volume being set on low. She covered the speaker with her hand until she could barely hear. "One's in a wheelchair. Either send me a few guys to get her up the stairs or I can lock them up down here."

"Got names?" She recognized Harris's voice.

"Yeah. Patient is one LaRose Freeman and the doctor is a Ken Rosen."

They were still alive! Gina bit her lip, fighting tears. Not that anyone would see her crying up here in the void of the elevator shaft, but she needed to concentrate.

"Where are you?"

"Pathology. Outside the morgue."

She raised the radio to her lips but couldn't bring herself to speak. Pretending to be Lydia, stalling for time, was suicide, sheer suicide.

What other choice did she have?

Bracing herself, planting her feet square against the top of the elevator, stray food wrappers crackling beneath her shoes, she hit the squawk button. "This is Lydia Fiore. I understand you're looking for me and a piece of evidence I have?"

Sweat dripped from her forehead and she wiped it away with her sleeve. Gina was used to fear—she'd lived with it all her life. In fact, it felt like her entire life was just a façade, spent waiting for someone to come along and rip her mask away, expose her for who she really was. A coward. Helpless, powerless to face the truth.

That fear was nothing compared to the terror that circled through her gut now, chilling her from the inside out. God, what had she done?

The radio came to life again. "Good to hear from you, Lydia. A mutual friend wants the item you inherited from your mother. Tell me where it is or people are going to start getting hurt."

"It's not here. But let those people go and I'll get it for you."

There was a pause. She could almost hear Harris's irritation over the open radio channel.

"No. I want to see you in person. Five minutes or someone else dies."

Gina stared at the radio. Damn. What the hell was she going to do?

SIXTEEN

THE PITTSBURGH ZOO OFFICIALS HAD BEEN AGHAST at their makeshift penguin restraints but relieved to see the penguins all hopping about, happy and healthy, once they were released from the blanket. Zimmerman puffed up with pride, looking not unlike one of his feathered charges, recounting the story of how he'd single-handedly recaptured the wayward birds.

"Where's Olsen?" he asked one of the officials.

"Still at the hospital. Guess he was hurt worse than they thought."

That took some of the glee from Zimmerman's triumphant return. After he thanked Lydia and Trey, they climbed back into Bessie to drive home.

It was eerie driving through the dark city, no lights anywhere. Even more strange was how they saw no other cars or people during the drive from the zoo—not even anyone out shoveling snow.

"Do you want to talk more about it?" Lydia asked Trey.

The darkness was good for one thing—sharing secrets. And she had one she wanted to tell him. Maybe the time was right.

"About what?" His rigid posture told her he knew what she meant.

"The gun. What happened when you were a kid."

He gave a little shake of his head and blew out his breath. "No. Not now. There's not much to talk about anyway. I'm sure you can fill in the blanks."

Well, hell. Lydia pursed her lips, trying to translate that—learning to figure out what the other person really meant instead of what they actually said was a relationship minefield she was still navigating.

"I want to know. To understand," she tried. "When you're ready."

Trey reached across the seat for her hand. "Right now, all I want is to change into clean, dry clothes and a pair of warm socks."

They pulled onto Merton Street. Their house was isolated at the end of a cul-de-sac, so Lydia was used to returning home in the dark—but never this dark.

Trey parked Bessie at the curb and hopped out. The driveway wasn't shoveled, so he had to stamp down the snow to make a path to the passenger-side door. He opened it and helped her out. Instead of walking directly to the house, though, they stood there enjoying the stillness together.

Lydia reached up to touch Trey's face, then laughed when her glove left behind some errant penguin feathers on his cheek. Trey wrinkled his nose and tried to blow them off, but they were stuck fast.

"You know," he said, nuzzling her nose with his, "I smell pretty bad. Not so sure the guys at the emergency center will appreciate *eau de penguin*."

"You know," she replied, brushing his lips with hers,

"you're also freezing. In cases of mild hypothermia, I would medically prescribe a hot shower."

"Two birds—" He didn't finish the pun, but pulled her closer instead. "Hypothermia treatment, doesn't that also include sharing body heat?"

"In some cases. Do you think you're that far gone?"

He shivered dramatically. "Yes, Doctor."

Holding hands, they shuffled-stamped-slipped through the snow that was as high as Lydia's knees and headed toward the carport. Halfway there, Trey broke away to venture inside the dark carport to open the door to the house.

"Trey, look at this." Lydia stood at the edge of the driveway, looking at the horizon. Her house backed onto the cemetery across from Angels and the medical center typically figured prominently in any view, but not tonight. Tonight there was only a black smudge where the hospital stood.

A black, lightless smudge.

"Looks like the backup power at Angels is out," she called to him. He hadn't come out of the carport—probably couldn't find his key in the dark. "They're in trouble. We should go help."

No answer from Trey.

In fact, no sound from the carport at all.

Lydia peered into the darkness, when a light suddenly blinded her. She raised her hand to block it.

And felt the cold metal of a gun muzzle touch the back of her neck.

GINA STARED AT THE MAGLITE'S BEAM IN THE elevator shaft. The light stabbed through the blackness, at first pure, full of hope and promise, but quickly dissolving into nothing. Just like her gambit to stall Harris. Five minutes? She doubted she could even climb down out of here in five minutes.

Okay, what would the real Lydia do?

Stay calm for one thing. Look at all the angles, see the big picture. Think out of the box. Every cliché in the book—except for Lydia, they weren't clichés. She actually did see the world that way. Too bad Gina wasn't really Lydia.

Still, she had to try.

"In case you didn't notice, these radios have a range of over a mile," Gina said, hoping that her voice didn't sound as quavery on the other end of the radio. She was totally making this up as she went—who knew what the range on a trauma radio was? She sure as hell didn't. "I'm not in the hospital."

Harris's reply was tight with anger. "Where are you?"

"I'm not going to tell you that. But I will retrieve the evidence, and we can meet in a neutral location as soon as the snow stops. You hurt anyone else before then and I'll take it to the police instead."

There, she'd played her trump card. Either he bought it or . . . The memory of the screams that had filled the radio a few minutes ago flooded over her.

There was a long pause, and then the sound of heavy breathing rattled through the radio.

"This is Oliver Tillman," came a new voice. Tillman? What the hell was he doing? He'd ruin everything! Didn't he realize that lives were at stake here?

"Put Harris back on," she commanded. "I'll only negotiate with Harris."

"I don't think so. I think you should listen to me, Gina. Before more people die."

Her heart skidded into her chest wall. *Gina*, he'd called her Gina.

* * *

NORA WAS COVERED IN BLOOD. EXHAUSTION HAD begun to rear its giddy head, and she couldn't imagine how Mark found the energy to continue. But somehow he did—in the darkness of the auditorium it felt like a spotlight shone down on them, the rest of the crowd watching and waiting and holding their breath for a miracle.

No miracles to be found, not tonight. Mark had cracked Jim's chest—right there on the floor, lying beside him and using several flashlights to find his way through the blood as he sliced a window in Jim's pericardium, relieving the pressure that had built around his heart. Mark had pushed fluids, used the internal paddles to defibrillate, done open-heart massage—he'd single-handedly run the entire gamut of the trauma protocol, refusing to let Jim go.

Nora wasn't sure if the light glistening from Mark's cheeks came from sweat or tears. Probably both—plus, she was sure the pain from his broken leg was tremendous and she knew he regarded every member of his ER staff as family. It didn't matter if you were a doctor, nurse, or janitor, if you worked for Mark he'd defend you to the death.

Unfortunately, not even Mark could go past that final limit.

The crowd began to murmur and disperse as people realized the futility of Mark's desperate efforts. People moved away, some sobbing, others glaring at the men with guns, some talking among themselves trying to make sense of the topsy-turvy direction their lives had taken.

Finally, only Nora, Mark, and Jason remained with Jim. Jason glanced at Nora, his expression filled with pain, but nothing compared to the anguish on Mark's face. Nora reached out to stop his hands as they compressed Jim's heart. "It's time to call it."

"No." He kept squeezing the dead muscle between his fingers.

Nora turned off the monitor and removed the oxygen. Mark's body kept bouncing with his movements, and then slowly he slid his hands out of Jim's chest cavity. In the dim light, they were black with blood. He stared at them, uncomprehending.

Then he raised his gaze to meet Nora's. "He was just starting to understand what it meant to be a doctor."

Nora nodded. "Yes, I think he was." She looked at Jason. "Could you help Mark back to his bed? Get him a clean shirt? I'll be up in a minute to give him some morphine."

Jason appeared numb himself. It took him a few seconds to process what Nora was saying. Then he stood, lifted Mark to his feet, and together they hobbled back to the stage where Mark's stretcher lay. Nora sat with Jim, unable to perform any of her usual duties of tending to the dead—all she could do for Jim was to cover him with a sheet.

The South African came over while she knelt beside Jim. He stood where Jim had been when he'd gotten shot and aimed his flashlight on the fabric-covered wall streaked with Jim's blood.

"What are you doing?" Nora asked.

He ignored her, jostling Jim's body with his foot as he stepped to the wall.

"Hey. Be careful."

He aimed the flashlight with one hand, flicked a wicked-looking knife from the sheath on his belt with the other, and grinned with satisfaction as he dug a bullet from the wall.

"Good that it's not in the body," he told Nora as he worked, his tone conversational, one professional to another. "Bullets are evidence."

"What about all those bullets from when you shot up the ceiling?"

"When we're done they won't be looking for bullets in the debris. But they will examine the bodies."

Goose bumps rose on Nora's arms and a chill settled in the pit of the stomach. Her greatest fears confirmed: They weren't planning to let anyone live through this. Jim was just the first casualty.

"So, does that mean you won't be shooting anyone else?" she asked defiantly.

He turned his grin on her—she'd seen cadavers with friendlier smiles. "If we do, we'll just have to dig the bullets out."

His radio sounded. Nora sidled closer, listening to the voice on his radio that was claiming to be Lydia. That wasn't her, though. With the static on the small handset it was difficult to tell who it was, but it sounded like—no, it couldn't be. Gina?

"Sounds like we might be finished here sooner than we thought," the South African said.

Pocketing the bullet, he walked away, leaving Nora alone with Jim's corpse.

She climbed to her feet and headed over to the food cart. Taking a bottle of water, she walked to the rear of the auditorium, the area all the others gave a wide berth to, except the men with guns who stood guard. There were no lights here, so she could stand in the darkness, hidden from sight as she washed Jim's blood from her hands, letting it drip onto the carpet. Tillman would probably bill her for the cleaning.

Harris stood talking with Tillman and the South African. The CEO was shaking his head, not arguing, more like a prisoner pleading his case. She edged through the shadows until she was close enough to hear.

"You have to believe me," Tillman said, "the woman

on the radio is not Lydia Fiore. It was an ER resident, a friend of hers, Gina Freeman."

"Maybe this is another wild-goose chase," the South African said.

Harris tilted his head, assessing Tillman. "He's right, why should I believe you?"

Tillman drew himself up straight, glowering at the idea that anyone would not take the CEO of Angels seriously. "It's my job to protect everyone in this hospital. I don't want Dr. Freeman's poor judgment or half-baked attempt at playing a hero to jeopardize the rest of us."

Harris frowned and raised his radio. "Wendell, what's the name of the lady you found in the elevator?"

"LaRose Freeman. I've got her and the doc cooling their heels down here in the morgue."

"That's her mother," Tillman said excitedly. "Gina Freeman's mother. See, I was telling the truth."

The South African ignored him. "Want me to send a man to finish them all?"

"No," Harris said. "Gina Freeman knew about the evidence before I said anything—she might know something valuable." He looked down at his radio. "Tell Marcus to join Wendell and bring the mother to me as soon as he's finished with the generator. And pass the word on to everyone to switch to channel two for all future communications."

"Will do." The South African vanished through the door.

Nora shook her head, too weary to even feel anger at Tillman for betraying Gina. Clearly, Gina had had a plan, but he'd never given it a chance to work. So typical of the CEO who didn't trust anyone except himself—especially if they had two X chromosomes. The worst thing was that there was nothing Nora could do to help Gina or LaRose or anyone.

She sidled back to the food carts, tossing her empty,

bloody water bottle into the garbage can. Every step seemed to require all her energy and concentration. *Prioritize,* Nora thought as she tried to block out the sounds of people sobbing. She needed to focus, to see this as a mass-casualty response, a disaster drill. Follow the rules of triage.

Red tag: patients with life-threatening conditions. But other than the imminent death facing them all from the men with machine guns, her patients were taken care of.

Okay, yellow tag: less severe injuries with potential to become life-threatening. That would be everyone—how long before someone broke and did something that angered the guards or provoked them into shooting randomly into the crowd? After witnessing Jim's murder, surely most people here realized that there was no way the hostage takers were going to release them. Nora had to find a way to both keep them calm and find a way out.

Emma Grey approached, her great-grandson Deon gripping her hand. "I'm so very sorry about your colleague. What can we do?"

Under different circumstances, Nora would have kissed the woman. "We need to keep everyone calm. How about if you and Deon gather the children and their parents together back in that far corner?" Nora pointed to the safest area in the auditorium, the corner in front of the stage farthest away from the main doors. "Maybe you could tell them a story?"

"I've got my books," Deon chimed in, eager to help.

"You're my hero, Deon." Nora tried to hug him, but he squirmed away—not even the threat of armed men would allow a ten-year-old to be hugged in front of all these strangers.

Emma began to walk between the rows of patients and visitors, earnestly talking to the ones with children. Deon broke away from her and came jogging back to Nora.

"Maybe this can help catch the bad guys," he whispered to her, pulling a small camera from his pocket. "We could sneak up and take their pictures?"

Nora knelt down in front of him. "Great idea, Deon. I want you to keep this handy but don't use it until I tell you to, okay?" Last thing she wanted was for him to try to play cops and robbers.

He nodded gravely, squaring his shoulders under his new responsibility. "Yes, Miss Nora."

"Go on, help your Gram, now." Deon ran back to Emma and helped her herd a group of kids and their parents over to the far corner. One of the nursing techs set up a battery-run work light for them. Slowly, even the adults who didn't have kids drifted over to join them.

Nora watched Harris. He had shifted position to watch the group but only smiled and nodded when Deon pulled out one of his books. Two other men remained at the doors but didn't seem on alert. In fact, they appeared bored, chatting together.

Obviously a bunch of patients and their caretakers didn't pose a significant threat to the armed men. Good, that was exactly how Nora wanted them to feel.

Because as Deon began reading, a glimmer of an escape plan had started to form in her mind. Tricky, but it might work.

She trudged up the steps to the stage and drew up a dose of morphine for Mark. He was slumped against the mattress, head turned away from the rest of the auditorium. Melissa had given him a sponge bath, washing away most of the blood, and had found a clean scrub top for him.

"It's my fault," he muttered. "I should have done something—"

She gave him the morphine. "Nonsense. What could you have done?"

"Something. Anything. It's my ER, my people, my

responsibility . . ." His voice slurred into silence as he fell asleep.

She handed Melissa the syringe. "Make sure he stays comfortable."

Melissa nodded, eyes downcast, too frightened or tired to even look up. She'd given up.

Nora wanted to give up as well. It would be so easy, so effortless. But she couldn't. Not when everyone else depended on her. Not while Seth was waiting for her to come home to him. She was glad he wasn't here—at least she didn't have to worry about him. But she couldn't help but see the warped karma in this happening now, on New Year's Eve—three years ago on another New Year's Eve, she'd been kidnapped and raped, almost killed. Now here she was again, facing more killers.

She didn't know whether to laugh or cry. Felt most like crying, especially at the image of Seth's face as she imagined them telling him she was dead. She cursed every wasted second that they could have been together and hadn't. It wasn't fair. It just wasn't fair.

Laughter came from the area where Deon was reading to the kids. God, she would have loved to have kids of her own one day. Seth would have made a wonderful father. Sucking in her breath, she gave herself a mental shake. She'd seen it too many times in the ER—give up too soon on a patient and they were as good as dead.

And she sure as hell wasn't dead yet. There had to be a way out of this. Seth's face filled her mind. There just had to be.

She thought hard. She had an idea; it was risky, but better than nothing.

"Do we have any ketamine?"

"I think so, why?"

"Draw me up as much ketamine and Versed as you can find into a syringe. Try to look casual."

Melissa hesitated, glancing past Nora toward the front of the auditorium where the guards paced.

"I'll cover you," Nora assured her. She stood and moved to grab an IV pump and bag of fluid to set up, hooking it up to Mark's IV. While Nora drew the guards' attention, Melissa filled a syringe at the medication cart. "Got that Ancef ready yet?" Nora called to her, as if impatient. "You know he should have gotten it an hour ago."

"I'm coming." Melissa almost dropped the syringe as she recapped it, but thankfully her back was to the guards. "Here you go." More quietly she asked, "What are you going to do with it?"

"I figured our friends might be thirsty, so I thought maybe I'd fix them a little Special K–Vitamin V cocktail." Nora pretended to inject the syringe into Mark's IV bag. "How much is there?"

"Enough to put a horse to sleep. Should be more than enough for two guards. But be careful," Melissa urged.

Nora pocketed the syringe and climbed back down the steps. At the base of the stage, gathered in front of the black velvet curtains, the children were whining, fussy with exhaustion and fear, and their families weren't much better.

She had to keep them safe. If she'd only kept Jim away from Harris—

No room for guilt, not now. Not now that she was the one in charge, eighty-six—no, now it was down to eighty-five—lives depending on her.

SEVENTEEN

"JOIN US IN THE AUDITORIUM, DR. FREEMAN," Harris's voice replaced Tillman's. "Or I'll bring your mother here instead and have an extremely unpleasant conversation with her." The radio went dead before she had a chance to answer.

Not that Gina had an answer.

Fear froze her in place. She squeezed her eyes shut, reverting to a childhood habit of making a wish and hoping the world would be changed by the time she opened them.

She opened them. Shit out of luck. As always.

The only question was, should she give herself up to Harris in the auditorium or try to help LaRose and Ken down here? Could she negotiate for LaRose's treatment in exchange?

Shaking herself—she was wasting precious time—she opened the hatch again. No matter what, she couldn't stay up here hiding. She had to do something.

She turned the Maglite off, pocketed it and the radio,

and began to climb down through the hatch. There wasn't really anything to hang on to for leverage, not without risking catching her fingers in the housing surrounding the cables, so she lay down on her belly and hung her legs through the opening, letting gravity do the work. She tried her best to control her fall but ended up flailing for a handhold, then hurtling through the hatch, landing on her butt and back.

The landing made a thud but it wasn't very loud. Hurt like hell though. It took her a second to catch her breath—it felt like she'd left it somewhere up in the elevator shaft— before she could roll over and climb up to her knees.

"I'm waiting." Harris's voice came over the radio in a singsong tone that made Gina want to stick out her tongue. She grabbed hold of the elevator's railing and hauled herself to her feet. There was no way she'd make it to the auditorium in time.

She raised the radio, wondering what to say that could stall him. She'd already played all her cards. So she settled on silence. Let him be the one watching and waiting and wondering.

She staggered out of the elevator. The basement level was a labyrinth of tunnels containing the hospital's infrastructure. Even in the best of times they were dark and dingy, cement-block walls echoing, low ceilings making anyone lost in them feel like a lab rat trapped in a maze. But she knew her way around, despite the dark—that might be her one advantage.

Which way? All she'd accomplish by going to the auditorium would be to get herself killed, and maybe the others as well if Harris was angry at her deception. Who was she kidding; he was livid. A furious sociopath armed with machine guns in a crowd of people? Recipe for disaster.

And what if Harris made good on his threat to burn the hospital down? The thought brought Gina up short. She pressed one palm against the wall. It felt cold to the touch. Helped clear her muddled thoughts. A cigarette would have done the job better.

No, the best thing she could do was try to save LaRose and Ken. They could escape through the tunnels to the research tower, find a place to hide, maybe figure out a way to find Jerry.

She turned toward the morgue, where the man on the radio had said he was holding LaRose and Ken. It felt good to have a plan, however vague it might be. She slowly moved a few steps, pressing her body against the wall so she wouldn't get disoriented and could count the intersections. She couldn't risk using the light.

One thing at a time. She had no clue what Harris was planning or how to stop him; her fiasco pretending to be Lydia had proved that. *Stick to what you're good at,* she decided. *Running and hiding.*

ONCE THEY HAD THE GUARD TIED UP AND LOCKED inside the pantry, Amanda had waited with Jerry while Lucas used his portable otoscope as illumination while he searched for another light source. The high-intensity beam danced around the kitchen, accompanied by the muffled sounds of cabinets and drawers opening and closing.

Jerry sat on the floor, hugging his knees to his chest, body sagged forward. He looked haggard, eyes hollowed out, but his gaze never wavered, drilling through the wall to the auditorium. After hearing Gina's attempt to impersonate Lydia and Tillman's betrayal of her, he was convinced she was in there with the others.

"Gina," he said when Amanda joined him, mirroring his posture—it was the best way to stay warm on the cold linoleum. "All my fault."

"No, Jerry. You can't think like that."

The more exhausted he was, the more muddled his thoughts and speech became. "Yes. My fault. Shooter was after me. And now." Finally his gaze dropped. Defeated. He slid the Beretta from his pocket. "Useless. Worse than useless."

Amanda gripped his arm. "Never. Gina would have died then if it weren't for you. Think of all the lives you've saved."

He dropped the gun to the floor. Amanda jumped in alarm at the clatter. She smacked her hand down over the gun and returned it to Jerry's hand, folding it in his palm. "You keep this."

"Not a cop." He rubbed his eyes with the heel of his free hand. "Not anymore." Jerry's voice was ragged, torn with misery. "Head hurts. Everything hurts."

"Hang on, Jerry. We'll get Gina back, just you hang on, okay?" Tears closed in on Amanda, stinging her eyes. If Jerry, the strongest man she knew, couldn't handle this, how the hell was she going to?

She knew he'd changed—a bullet rattling around your frontal cortex would do that; he'd never be the same again—but he'd showed such strength the last few weeks, such passion for life, as if sheer determination could help him recover . . . "Don't give up on me, not now."

Her words were so low she barely heard them herself—less than a whisper, a breath of prayer.

Jerry heard her, though, raising his head from where he'd laid it on his knees and turning to look at her. "I'll try."

What more could she ask of any of them?

"Any advice?" she asked, nodding at the pantry door behind which the guard waited. "On how to get him talking?"

Jerry rested his chin on his knees, thinking. "Stay off balance."

Off balance? Yeah, that shouldn't be hard—just look at her. Raggedy Ann in a ball gown; the man would laugh so hard, he'd never be able to tell them anything. Then Amanda remembered the look on their prisoner's face when she'd tackled him and held him at knifepoint—startled, stunned, but more than surprised, he'd been scared. Of her. Of what she'd done. Of what she was capable of.

She nodded. "Good advice. I can do that."

"Got it," Lucas called out from the corner. He returned to them and squatted down. "Cans of fuel for chafing dishes." He pulled the top off one of the cans, used an electric match to light it, and a blue flame crinkled across the surface of the gel.

"Perfect." Amanda handed her gun to Jerry. No sense risking the prisoner taking it. She stood, holding her fillet knife in one hand. "Lucas, you go in, remove the tape from his mouth, and set the Sterno down on the floor. Then I'll make my entrance."

"Are you sure about this?" Lucas asked. "Maybe I should—"

The thought of gentle Lucas intimidating anyone made Amanda smile. She couldn't help herself. The man literally wouldn't hurt a fly—he'd sit and freeze in the cold, leaving a window open until a stray fly or moth made its escape.

"No," she said. "I'll be fine."

The blue glow from the Sterno edged his scowl, turning it murderous. Without a word, Lucas wrenched open the door to the pantry and stalked inside. Amanda watched from the doorway. He set the light down near the door, the shadows dancing around the large room, reflecting from the rows of stainless steel shelves. Then he took two steps over to where the man sat, bound with tape to one of the vertical shelf supports.

Lucas stood there for a long moment, staring down at the man, whose eyes grew wide. Lucas abruptly scissored a hand down, ripping off the tape around the man's mouth. The man made a small sound of pain.

"Quiet!" Lucas commanded in a low and deadly voice that made the hairs on the back of Amanda's neck rise in alarm. She'd never seen him like this. "You will answer her questions. If not—" His pause hung in the air like a guillotine. "I can't be held responsible for what she does."

He pivoted on his heel and walked away, giving Amanda a wink as he passed. It took everything she had to swallow her laughter—which played in her favor since the effort twisted her face into a grimace that made the man on the floor flinch. She stood above him, light at her side, just close enough that he could easily read her expression. And see the blue flames reflected in the oh-so-shiny-and-sharp blade of her fillet knife.

"We need to talk," she said in a low, conversational tone. "I'll go first."

He nodded, his Adam's apple bobbing up and down as he swallowed again and again.

"You might have figured it out already," she began, amping up her Lowcountry accent, "but I'm not from around these parts. See, I come from a little town on the coast of South Carolina. And you know how my family makes their living?"

He shook his head, his eyes never leaving her knife hand. She began to idly twirl the knife, without looking, letting its weight and balance pirouette it between her fingers. Her father had taught her the trick.

"My family lives off the water. I was using a knife, shucking oysters faster than a blink when I was four. And fish?"

Amanda paused the knife, the firelight streaming off its

blade like water. With a quick flick of her wrist, she sliced the guard's collar button off. He gagged, staring at it as it bounced down his body and fell to the floor.

"I can take a fish, gut it, and with just a—" She flashed the knife, letting its motion speak for her. "Just that fast, I could have its backbone out, the whole thing, just fall into my hands. If you know where to cut, that is." She lowered the knife so that it touched the back of his neck. "And I do."

His muscles bunched as he fought not to move against the scalpel-sharp blade. "We were just hired to do a job, that's all," he pleaded. "No one was meant to get hurt."

"Who hired you?"

"Harris. He hired four of us, said we just had to watch over some folks while his men made the score. Ten grand each for a few hours of work—easy money. But he's working for someone else, someone I've never met."

"What are they looking for?"

"Never said. I figured it was drugs, ripping off the pharmacy here. But then they started talking about finding this Lydia person, and things started getting freaky-deaky, but what could we do? Accomplice to a felony is still a felony." His words sped up, jumping into a self-pitying whine.

"How many are there?"

"The four of us, plus Harris and his guys: some South African dude who is serious trouble, you do not want to cross him; a guy named Marcus who seems in charge of all the tech stuff, and two more, I didn't get their names."

"Where are they?"

"Me and my guys, we were guarding the hostages with the South African, rotating between inside the auditorium, watching the lobby, and patrolling."

"How many hostages, where are they in the auditorium?" She crouched down to his level, not needing the knife any longer—the guard was eager to please her now.

"There's about a hundred hostages," he said. "They're on the stage and in front of it. We're in the back by the doors. Two inside the auditorium, one outside the doors, one watching the lobby."

"And you on patrol?"

"Yeah. Look, you gotta put in a good word for me. Tell them I helped you, get me a deal."

"No problem." What did he think this was? An episode of *Law & Order*? Couldn't he see she was making it up as she went?

Of course, Lydia always said that was the secret to emergency medicine. Improvisation.

Amanda stood, accidentally kicking the can of Sterno. It skidded past the man's feet and landed at the base of the wall between them and the auditorium. She walked over to retrieve it. There were no shelves here; the wall was bare. Instead, two gray plastic junction boxes jutted out from the wall.

That wall was the shared wall with the auditorium's stage. And those wires—they weren't electrical, too thick for phone lines . . .

She rushed past the man, eager to ask Lucas about her discovery.

"Hey, you're going to help me, right?" he pleaded, sounding like a dog left out in the cold without his dinner.

"No worries," she said. "I've got a plan to help everyone."

LYDIA'S FIRST THOUGHT WAS: HAD TREY BEEN HURT? In that split second, terror that he might be hurt and need her combined with rage that anyone would harm him, and she almost reacted without worrying about consequences, without thinking, and with violence.

Before she met Trey, that was exactly what she would

have done. She even knew the moves she'd need to take down the man with the gun: a quick pivot, use her cast as a club to the man's head or face, followed by a lightning strike to his throat. She could do it. She would have done it, except the worry that Trey was at the mercy of someone else paralyzed her.

"Is Trey okay?" Somehow she managed to grit out the words between jaws clamped tight with anger and fear. He had to be okay; he was a big man, she would have heard something if he had fallen.

"He is for now," a voice from inside the carport called out.

"What do you want?" Lydia asked.

The man behind her hadn't moved or spoken. His gun gouged her skin but she didn't protest—barely noticed it, her senses too focused on what was going on in the carport behind the light that blinded her.

"You have something of mine. It's time to collect."

EIGHTEEN

As she crept through the dark tunnels, Gina was glad for her layers of clothing. Despite the turtleneck, cardigan, and lab coat, she was shivering, and the air was growing colder by the moment.

Other than the moans of overhead pipes cooling, she saw and heard nothing. Not to say that she still didn't jerk to a stop to listen every few steps. Her pulse was pounding so fast, it sounded like running footsteps trying to catch up with the rest of her body. But there was never anyone there.

She'd turned the radio off—couldn't risk exposing her position—and held the Maglite in her hand pressed against the wall, her finger on the switch, ready to turn it back on if she needed it. The scalpel was in her other fist, handle hidden by her sleeve.

One last intersection to cross. The areas of open space unnerved Gina the most—dark bottomless chasms. Every direction harbored the threat of someone waiting to pounce.

She stood with her back to the cold concrete wall, trying to muster the courage for that first step into the black void. Her mouth was so dry her tongue grated against her teeth like sandpaper. And she couldn't shake the feeling that someone was watching her, toying with her, like Jodie Foster in *Silence of the Lambs*. After all, Harris could have night-vision goggles. Maybe that was why they'd turned the power off? The question kept niggling at her. Even with night vision, it couldn't make their hunt for Lydia any easier, although the darkness did put everyone else at a disadvantage.

But still . . . all those patients dependent on electricity— she tried not to imagine what it must be like in the ICUs, everyone scrambling to manually ventilate and care for patients. Thank goodness they had plenty of staff up there. It was harder not to think what would have happened if the power had gone off weeks ago when Jerry had been in a coma, or worse, while the neurosurgeons were operating, removing the blood clot and bullet from his brain.

Anger at Harris and his men, who were playing with lives so carelessly, fueled Gina's courage. She stepped into the intersection. This was the underground corridor leading to the research tower, so it was wider than most of the tunnels. As she shuffled across, her arms outstretched in case she veered off course and hit a wall, wind whistled against the side of her face, coming from the tower.

That was their best way out. She could get LaRose, wheel her through the tunnel, get her to the far side of the tower, then wait for Janet and the SWAT team to arrive. The SWAT team that Gina hoped dearly didn't exist only in her imagination. Everything depended on Janet tearing herself away from her duties long enough to check her voice mail. What kind of lousy plan was that?

It was the only one she had left. Another small problem:

the whole get-LaRose part. Her mother and Ken were being watched over by at least one armed guard, maybe more.

Her foot brushed against something. A linen cart? Rows of metal shelves stacked as high as her head and covered by a drape. The morgue wasn't far—the next door would be the pathology offices, followed by the lab, and then the morgue. But if she went through the labs, she could get access to the morgue from the back door, maybe get a better idea of where Ken and LaRose were being held and how many men she was up against.

She felt her way around the cart and found the first door, followed the wall to the next door—the lab—and felt for the handle. *Please let it be open*, she prayed as she pressed down on the lever. It opened with a soft click. *Amen.*

This was the public area of the lab, cluttered with desks and office equipment, so she had to risk using a light. Swapping the Maglite for the more discreet penlight, she looked around. No signs that anyone had been in here. Good.

Gina navigated around the desks to the rear door, the one that led into the actual laboratory areas. This one had an electronic key lock; would it work with the power off? She turned the doorknob, and it opened easily.

Maybe that was why they'd shut the power off, to open locks? Gina wondered as she began down the corridor, passing hematology on one side, chemistry on the other. No, that didn't make sense, not if all Harris was after was Lydia—unless the evidence he thought she had was hidden here at the hospital?

No more time to think about it; she'd reached the door to the tissue lab that connected to the morgue. She entered, cautiously shielding her penlight so that it wouldn't be visible through the window in the morgue's door. The fumes of antiseptic and tissue preservatives made her nose twitch.

The lab was pretty basic: three rows of benches with microscopes, microtomes, and bottles of stains arrayed alongside them. The larger equipment and storage cabinets lined the walls.

Once she got her bearings and was started on a path to the morgue's door, she turned her penlight off and made her way by feel. Just as she estimated that she was close to the door, she stumbled into a metal container, about the size of a fire extinguisher, almost toppling it from its rack. The clang of metal against metal was louder than church bells.

Damn! She bent down and used both hands to steady the can and silence the noise. The can was cold, freezing in fact. Probably liquid nitrogen, used to transport specimens. She crouched beside the rack, listening hard. There was no sound coming from the morgue, no response to the clatter she'd unleashed.

Gathering her strength, she peered through the window in the door to the morgue. It was a wide-open space designed for flexibility. Storage refrigerator, decomp room, and a freezer were accessed on the wall to her left; the wall to the right was equipment storage and the staff locker rooms, which exited back into the main tunnel; and straight ahead were double doors leading out to the garage where bodies were transferred to mortuary vehicles.

The place seemed deserted. Had she misheard? The guard had said he'd be bringing LaRose and Ken here, hadn't he?

Horror struck her as she realized that he could have easily locked them into one of the body storage areas. Would the guard have abandoned them to die?

Gina opened the door and crossed into the morgue, intent on checking the freezer and refrigerator, when she spotted light. Crossing the empty room, she peered through the double doors into the morgue's garage. To her left, up three steps, sat the small, glass-walled cubicle that security used while waiting for body transfers.

One of Harris's men sat there, his back to the door, feet up on the desk, drinking from a thermos flask—some poor guard's dinner, no doubt. He had his jacket off; his breath wasn't steaming the windows at all. A glow filled the tiny guard shack, probably from a kerosene heater.

It took her a minute to spot LaRose and Ken in the dim light. Ken stood beside LaRose's wheelchair. Silver strips of duct tape circled their bodies, securing them—and the wheelchair—to a metal pole to the left of the cubicle's window—directly in the guard's sight line. Wisps of snow that had blown beneath the garage door swirled around their feet.

While the guard sat safe and snug in his office, they were freezing to death.

FIRST OFF, SHE HAD TO FIND SOMETHING TO MASK the taste, Nora thought. Water wouldn't do—ah, the cafeteria workers had brought some single-serving plastic bottles of orange juice. Perfect.

Next, slip the drugs into the bottles. She slid down behind the stainless steel cafeteria cart so that she was hidden from the guards' sight. Straining to see in the dim light, she carefully worked the needle under the rim of each bottle's cap, aiming it up through the plastic below the seal. She injected half of the ketamine/Versed mix into each bottle, then inspected her work. Even knowing it was there, she couldn't find the puncture—hopefully it would be just as difficult to see once the caps were removed and the bottles opened.

Now she needed a diversion. She looked over at the

floor in front of the stage where Emma Grey was reading Deon's books to the kids.

Harris and the South African were both gone; Tillman as well. Good. She couldn't trust Tillman, and the other two were the ones with the no-nonsense trigger fingers. In their place were two men dressed in hospital security guard uniforms, leaning against the wall between the two sets of doors and talking quietly to each other, barely glancing in the direction of the hostages. They looked bored, not deadly.

There might never be a better time.

"Deon," she called quietly to the boy sitting Indian-style on the carpet, listening to his grandmother's story. He jerked his head over his shoulder and pointed a thumb at himself as if he were unsure who she wanted. "Yes, come here."

Smart kid that he was, he craned his head to see over the seats and look for the guards. Then he scooted on his behind backward to where Nora sat.

"I need you to do something for me," she said. He nodded eagerly. "Do you still have your camera?"

"Yes." He pulled it out of his pants pocket, some rubber bands, a few coins, a pencil stub, and a rock cascading out along with it. "Right here."

"Do you know how to work the flash on it?"

"Oh yes—it has a flash, and a zoom lens, and the book says the flash is the fastest—"

"Here's what I need you to do."

"ARE YOU OKAY?" LUCAS ASKED AS AMANDA RAN out of the pantry and into the kitchen. "Did he hurt you?"

"No. I'm fine, I'm great!" She clasped his arms and stood on tiptoe to kiss him. "I think I know how we can save them."

"How?"

"First, we need to make sure that he"—she indicated their prisoner with a jerk of her head—"can't give us away. Can you put the tape back over his mouth and move him somewhere else? Somewhere we can lock him in and not worry about him."

Jerry spoke up, his voice holding a trace of his old spark. The few minutes sitting alone in quiet seemed to have revitalized him. "Fridge."

"No, we don't want him to freeze."

"There's room in the storage closet where they keep the catering supplies," Lucas said. "That's where I found the Sterno. And there's a lock on the door."

"Perfect."

Lucas went to sort out their prisoner's accommodations and move him. Jerry touched Amanda's arm, hesitantly as if he weren't sure he really wanted to hear what she had to say.

She didn't have the heart to remind him that they had no idea where Gina was, so she tried her best to reassure him. "If Gina's in there, we'll get her out. Don't worry, Jerry."

He nodded gratefully. Lucas returned, out of breath, his face exhilarated. "What's the plan?"

"Do you remember two years ago when the hospital renovated the auditorium? Added all that computer equipment and the new projector and all that?"

"Sure. Why?"

"They had to gain access for all that wiring, right?"

He nodded. Jerry was watching Lucas and nodded as well.

She carried the Sterno into the pantry. "This is where they did it. The stage is right behind that wall. And under the stage—"

"Is access to the rest of the auditorium," Lucas finished

for her. "The drapes on the front of the stage will hide any movement."

"And the dark will help as well."

Jerry left while they were talking and returned with a chef's knife and a wooden mallet. He squatted in front of the drywall and plunged the knife into the wall. He swung the mallet, missed the knife but still made a nice hole in the wall and began tugging at the edges with his fingers. It didn't make as much noise as Amanda feared it would, just a dull thud. "Gina, I'm coming!"

Lucas and Amanda ran back out to the kitchen to get supplies. By the time they returned, Jerry had made a fist-sized hole by tearing the drywall back with his hands.

"Wait," Lucas said as he pulled on a pair of dishwashing gloves. "Don't go higher than the stage floor; we don't want to risk them seeing our light."

Jerry pulled back while Lucas drew a horizontal line about thirty inches off the floor. "The stage is three feet high, so that should be low enough."

He and Amanda joined Jerry in widening the hole. Soon they had all the drywall off, exposing the studs. A metal conduit ran horizontally across the studs about eighteen inches off the floor.

"It's small." Lucas measured the space between the studs with his hands. "Maybe fourteen inches."

"Tight fit," Jerry said, lying on the floor and trying to squirm through the gap. He couldn't twist his body through it, not with the metal conduit blocking the way. He came up coughing, drywall dust flying from his body. "Cut this?"

"No." Lucas examined the conduit. "It's carrying electrical wires, if the power comes back on—"

"Saw through one of the studs," Amanda said. "We can use serrated knives, they're pretty much like saw blades."

"That's going to take a while."

"I'll go on ahead; you guys enlarge the opening."

Lucas shook his head, frowning. "No." He pushed at the two-by-four, his muscles bulging with the strain. "No, I'm not risking you. I'll go."

"Lucas, I'll be fine." Amanda loved that her fiancé was protective of her; he knew he couldn't budge the block of wood by hand, never would have done something so illogical if emotion hadn't blinded him to reality. He also knew she had a little thing about confined spaces, ever since her brothers had locked her in a trunk in the attic when she was a kid. It was nothing as bad as his own phobias about dirt and germs, so even the fact that he was willing to offer to go in her stead was proof of how much he cared for her—not that she needed proof. "I'll scout the path, get everyone ready. I promise, I won't even get anywhere near the bad guys."

Still Lucas hesitated. Jerry started sawing the base of the two-by-four, using a large bread knife grasped in both of his hands.

Finally, Lucas kicked at a piece of drywall lying on the floor and gave a grudging nod. He handed her the Smith & Wesson. "Here. You'd better take this. Just in case."

She secured the gun in her sash and took his otoscope for light.

"Be careful." He punctuated his words with a kiss that made her toes tingle.

"I will." Amanda knelt and shone the light through the opening. Dust and grime and darkness greeted her. Getting on her belly, she had to shift so that she was on her side, crawling between the studs, Lucas helping to propel her until her body was the entire way through. She craned her head up and waved at him that she was okay, then rolled onto her belly and continued into the darkness.

GINA DUCKED INSIDE THE MORGUE AND SAT, BACK to the door, thinking hard and fast. She had to get Ken and

LaRose out of there, but no way could she do it without the guard seeing. Okay, so she had to take care of the guard first. How?

Club him over the head? That would mean climbing up into the guard shack, getting close enough to strike, and taking him out with one blow, all before he could reach for his gun and shoot her. Even though the guard seemed relaxed, she didn't think he'd ignore someone climbing up three steps and coming into the shack with him.

Drugs? Maybe nitrous or an anesthesia gas—she would only have to open the door a crack, enough to slip some tubing into, close it, and wait. But the guard shack looked to be around eight feet on each side, which was . . . damn, she couldn't do the math, her brain was fried . . . sixty-four times eight, call it four-eighty, five hundred cubic feet. How long would it take to work? Shit, there was also the smell— no way to get around that. Plus the fact that if he was running a kerosene heater there might be an open flame, and a few whiffs of anesthesia could turn the shack into a firebomb before she had a chance to free LaRose and Ken.

Think, think! Gina shoved her hands into her cardigan pockets, trying to stay warm, and found the half cigarette that she'd smoked earlier. Her matches were long gone, but she rolled the cancer stick beneath her nose, inhaling its fragrance. Ahhh . . . as always, anxiety churned up cravings, urges to indulge in both pleasure and punishment. Not tonight.

Tonight there was no time for her to fight (and lose to) her personal demons. She needed to save lives. God, she wished Jerry were here. Dropping the cigarette, Gina reached for the ring she wore on a chain around her neck instead. Old Jerry, New Jerry, she honestly didn't care. He'd find some way to cheer her up, motivate her, keep her going. He'd never let her surrender or fail.

She rocked her head back against the door, eyes squeezed shut, conjuring up Jerry's face, his goofy smile that made him look like a pushover although he was one of the smartest men she knew—maybe not book-smart, not genius-smart like Ken, but people-smart, street-smart.

No wonder Jerry and Lydia got along so well; she was like that too. Gina had been jealous of Lydia, the time she and Jerry spent together, but now she realized that it was her own fault for taking Jerry for granted, forcing the relationship—as she did every relationship—to revolve around *her* instead of *them*.

Shit, shit, shit . . . this wasn't time for a Dr. Phil guilt fest, complete with tears; she had to get moving, before Ken and LaRose froze . . . before they could freeze . . . That was it!

Gina sprang to her feet, sneaked a peek back out to the garage—nothing had changed—and rushed through the morgue back to the tissue lab. Amanda was starting her dermatology rotation in a few days and had been blathering on about the dangers of the liquid nitrogen used to freeze warts. What had she said? Gina halted inside the lab entrance, straining to remember.

Amanda had been visiting Jerry, tickling him with some stupid stuffed animal, her pocket guide to dermatology open on the bedside table as she prepared for her next rotation. Gina had just come back from getting coffee and had handed Amanda a cup, when she'd said . . . what . . . wait, yes, she'd said, "It says here you should never carry liquid nitrogen onto an elevator. If the nitrogen gas escapes, it can expand to seven hundred times the volume of the liquid, displace all the oxygen, and asphyxiate everyone inside. Wow, sounds like something out of a murder mystery, doesn't it?"

God bless her roommate and her enchantment with the

most arcane and useless trivia! If Amanda were here right now, Gina would kiss her.

All she had to do was take one of the containers of liquid nitrogen, slip it into the guard shack with the cap off, and let physics work its magic.

NINETEEN

NORA FILLED HER ARMS WITH BOTTLES OF ORANGE juice, making sure that the two drugged bottles were on top. She turned away from the food cart and started down the aisle toward the front of the auditorium, where Deon had arranged a game of laser tag with the other kids, using penlights and his camera flash.

As soon as he caught her signal, he and Nicky, the little boy she and Jim had treated earlier in the ER, began yelling and horsing around, the lights strobing through the dimly lit theater as they hurtled toward Nora, blindsiding her and knocking her into the wall.

"Hey now!" one of the guards yelled. He left his post, brandishing his gun, and approached.

"Sorry," Nicky said, scampering back to his mom.

"Sorry, sir." Deon stayed near Nora.

"They're just bored," Nora explained to the guard. "You know kids."

He almost smiled at her, then blanketed it with a show of machismo. "What's that, a camera?" He took the small camera from Deon. "You taking pictures of me?"

"No, sir."

"He was just playing with the flash. I don't think there's even a memory card in it."

The guard examined the camera, opening the bottom. "You're right, there isn't." He pushed a few buttons on it, pushing his gun aside as he tried the zoom. "Still, it's a nice camera." He glowered down at Deon. "Too nice for a little boy to play games with."

"But—" Deon's face crinkled with sorrow as the guard pocketed the camera.

"I'm hanging on to this for safekeeping. All of you kids, settle down. Now!"

Deon skittered away, joining the others at the open area below the front of the stage where Emma was handing out blankets. Nora turned to walk away, moving slowly, letting the bottles in her arms rattle as she jostled them.

The guard got the subliminal message—just as she'd also known he would be interested in the camera and stop to chat. Just like Seth would have been. Men and their toys. So predictable.

"How about a drink?" he asked.

She turned back. "Okay."

Nora leaned forward a little, enough so that the drugged bottle was the one easiest for him to reach. He grabbed it along with the other one on top. "For my buddy."

With a nod, he turned and walked back to the front of the auditorium, handing the second bottle to the other guard. Nora kept going, her back to them so they couldn't see her smile.

Mission accomplished.

* * *

THE MAN BEHIND HER MARCHED LYDIA THROUGH the snow and into the carport, his gun never moving a millimeter from the base of her skull. Trey was in the carport, where a man holding another gun and the high-beam flashlight also waited. The scowl on Trey's face, the way his muscles bulged, betrayed the cost of his restraint. Lydia had never seen him look so murderous.

"He said he'd have you shot," Trey said. "I couldn't take the chance."

"Let's take this lovefest inside," the man with the flashlight said. He was shorter than Trey, dressed in a wool overcoat complete with scarf. She couldn't make out his features behind the light. His voice was flat, devoid of any accent, as if he came from nowhere—or at least nowhere that he wanted to acknowledge. He nudged Trey with the gun.

Trey opened the door into the house and stepped inside. A streak of brown followed him, skillfully avoiding his feet. Ginger Cat.

She and Trey had been in bad spots before, Lydia reminded herself. And they had come out alive. They would this time as well, she vowed as they proceeded inside the dark and chilly house. This time she had even more reason to fight, and she had more to fight with: She had Sandy's gun.

But by the time they reached the living room and the second man, obviously the leader, shoved Trey down into the corner of the couch and then bent to turn the gas fireplace on, acting as if he were the one who lived there, she'd decided that maybe counting on one gun and a bum arm wasn't their best line of defense.

Because as the fire illuminated the features of the leader, Lydia realized just how much trouble they were in. His eyes were dark, flat, devoid of any emotion. The eyes of a killer.

"Who are you?" she asked.

He smiled, but just like his eyes it was all show and no emotion. "Call me Mr. Black. I think you already know my colleague, Mr. Smith."

The man behind her gave her a shove forward into the center of the room. Lydia stumbled, twisting to catch herself before she fell, and as she turned she saw his face for the first time.

It was the face that had stalked her nightmares for eighteen years. The face etched into not just her memories but the very fabric of her DNA. The face that had forever changed her life.

The face of the man who had killed her mother.

AS SOON AS SHE WAS A FEW FEET INSIDE THE LOW-ceilinged space beneath the stage, Amanda regretted not taking time to find an apron to wear over the top of the remnants of the ball gown. A jacket or janitor's jumpsuit would have been even better.

Stray bits of copper wire, discarded nails, staples, and paper all combined with the dust to abrade her skin, her sweat cementing the mixture so that it clung to her body as she belly-crawled along the floor.

Not to mention the splinters and the dust bunnies—forget dust bunnies, these were molting silverback gorillas. Cobwebs tickled her face as she broke through them and she itched all over, imagining spiders sprinting down her back, gleefully sliding between the dress and her skin to take up residence.

Sorry, Gina, but this dress is gonna be burned as soon as we're out of this mess, Amanda thought.

Sawdust, plaster dust, drywall dust—every kind of dust there was—stung her nose and eyes. At one point she thought for sure she was going to sneeze and ruin everything. Her eyes watered with the effort of containing the sneeze. Amanda rubbed her nose against her shoulder—her hands were filthy with grime and would only make things worse—until the urge passed. She tried not to shine the light straight ahead for fear it might be seen through the drapes at the end of the stage, so all she could see was the space to the next footer as she wove her way through them.

She could hear Lucas and Jerry working behind her— they weren't very noisy, but it was so quiet beneath the stage that even the slightest noise was amplified. Like the rush of her breathing or the sound of her body sliding over the rough floorboards.

She moved on, ignoring the pain in her arms as yet another splinter gouged her skin. It was harder work than she imagined. Every time she raised her head to check her progress, her hair got tangled in protruding cable ties from above. Finally her finger touched cloth. She had reached the curtain that draped the bottom of the stage floor.

She turned the penlight off and hauled her body forward, folding her knees under so she could duck her head forward and peek below the curtain. Just a few inches to her right, a pair of legs dangled over the stage above her. Jeans and purple high tops—had to be Jason.

She tugged on the back of his jeans, hiding her hand with the drape. His leg jerked to a stop. She tugged again. Urgently this time.

The leg pulled away from her grasp. A few moments later there was a thud as he leaped down from the stage and sat with his back to her.

"Who's there?" Jason whispered. Bingo.

"It's Amanda. You guys ready to blow this pop stand?"

GINA CAREFULLY PREPARED A ONE-LITER CONTAINER of liquid nitrogen, transferring the smaller volume from the main container into a vacuum flask. She screwed the cap on but didn't fasten the safety seal, so that all she'd have to do when she was ready to allow the gas to escape was remove the cap.

She shuffled through the morgue, feeling each step before committing to it—if she tripped and spilled the liquid nitrogen, she was risking frostbite as well as her own asphyxiation—until she reached the doors to the garage.

Peering over the rim of the window in the door, she watched the guard. He still sat with his back to the guard shack door, watching his prisoners. Beyond the shack, duct-taped to a support beam, LaRose had slumped forward in her wheelchair, motionless. Gina couldn't see her face. Ken Rosen was stomping his feet in an effort to stay warm. The rest of the garage was in darkness except for the emergency exit light over the door beside the closed overhead doors. The guard was talking on his radio, but Gina didn't dare risk turning hers back on to hear what he was saying.

No better time than now while he was distracted. But if anything went wrong . . . Her insides suddenly felt as cold as if she'd swallowed the freezing nitrogen. Something had already gone wrong, and someone had paid the price with her earlier plan. Who was to say this one would be any better?

She could still safely hide, or escape through the tower. But her mother obviously didn't have much time. If she was even still alive.

Gina squeezed her eyes as tight as she could, fighting to banish the naysaying voices that filled her mind—always her worst enemy. Forcing the hamster wheel of doubt and recrimination to slow and stop, she took a deep breath in from her belly and blew it back out, opening her eyes.

Now or never.

She pushed the door open and crept to the shack, staying below the guard's eye level. Slowly, she climbed the metal steps, placing her weight carefully, ball of her foot first, then the heel, then her entire weight. She knelt on the metal landing outside the door. Reached up and slowly, not even risking an exhalation, turned the doorknob.

Part of her waited for the guard's exclamation and the bullet that would quickly follow. The rest of her was primed for action, her nerves stretched so taut that they sent vibrations singing below her skin.

The knob turned silently. She pulled the door open, just a crack, far enough to spring it free from the latch. Bracing the door against her body so that it wouldn't continue to open until she was ready, she removed the cap from the liquid nitrogen. A gush of white vapor emerged but quickly dissipated. Wiping her palms against her pants—couldn't risk slippery palms, not now—she held the container in one hand and let the door fall open a few inches. She slid the container inside, setting it on the floor, and closed the door, turning the knob as it settled into the jamb so that there would be no click. Then she allowed the knob to turn back, the lock catching with the barest sigh.

Gina held her breath and waited. No noise, no cry of alarm from inside.

Scuttling back down the steps, she dared a look from the shadows. The guard was still talking. Then he lowered the radio and took another drink from the thermos. He settled into his chair, eyes drooping. The thermos slipped from his hand and fell to the ground. He jerked, started to sit up, but then slumped back, eyes closed.

Gina waited another few seconds. The guard wasn't moving, although she saw his chest rising, so he wasn't dead. Should she risk opening the door, taking his gun and trying to restrain him before he woke? But maybe he'd wake too fast, shoot her, and everything would be for nothing?

No, she needed to free LaRose and Ken first. Then she'd deal with the guard, hopefully before he asphyxiated. He had maybe three, four minutes, she estimated.

She ran to Ken and used her scalpel to free him first. The duct tape around his wrists was so tight it had cut into his skin. His hands were white, swollen from the cold and lack of circulation. His teeth were chattering and he could barely stand, but he didn't waste time with words; instead he immediately helped her with LaRose. Gina sliced the bands of duct tape that held LaRose and her chair against the pole. As soon as she was free, Ken took one handle and Gina took the other, pushing LaRose across the garage and into the morgue, where it was somewhat warmer.

She knelt and felt for her mother's pulse. It was there and her breathing was strong. Suddenly Gina's own pulse and breathing seemed stronger as well.

"I've got to get the guard," she told Ken.

"Can I help?"

He could barely walk, much less use his frozen hands for much. "No, stay here with her; I'll be right back."

She pushed back through the doors to the garage and headed toward the shack. The guard might be a bad guy, but Gina didn't want another death on her conscience. Besides, he might have knowledge—and weapons—that they could use. She wrenched the door open and closed the nitrogen container. Then she hauled the guard, chair and all, out onto the landing.

His machine gun was lying across his lap, and his pistol was in his holster. She retrieved the pistol first, shoving it into the pocket of her lab coat. Just as she had the machine gun in her hands, the garage's outside door opened. Two men stomped inside, shining their flashlights about.

Abandoning the guard, Gina leaped down the stairs, the

machine gun clattering against the railing. Suddenly she was impaled by two beams of light.

Followed quickly by the targeting lasers of two guns—centered on her chest.

TWENTY

LYDIA COULDN'T HELP IT. WHEN SHE SAW THE man who had murdered her mother, she froze—just as she had when she was twelve. Fear chilled her veins, she couldn't move her feet, her mouth opened, but she couldn't force any sound out. She wanted to scream, wanted to run, wanted to hit, maim, shoot, kill . . . but all she could do was look.

That was all she could do back then, too.

Memories flooded over her, bursting through a dam built by eighteen years of willpower and desperation. Now they all came hurtling back: the man's face, twisted in anger, as he clubbed her mother with a riot baton; Maria's terror as she tried to scramble away; her pain as he'd grab her hair and haul her back, hitting her again and again.

His voice asking her two questions over and over: "Where is it?" and "Where is the child?"

That was when Maria had surrendered, stopped trying to run. She'd looked once in the direction where she knew Lydia hid, her expression one of sorrow too deep for her daughter to comprehend, and she'd never looked at Lydia again. Had instead given up, not made another sound.

She'd died so that Lydia could live.

And eighteen years later, the monster had returned. Maria's sacrifice had been in vain.

Lydia didn't think about the gun in Smith's hand, couldn't think about the other man and his gun or Trey. If she could have gotten to her own weapon, buried beneath the layers of her parka and sweater, she would have shot Smith without blinking. But she couldn't reach Sandy's gun.

Instead, Lydia lunged forward, startling Smith, bringing her left palm up and under his chin in a blitz strike. He stumbled back, off balance. She swept his legs out from under him, landing on top. His gun went off, the bullet striking the wall between the windows.

Lydia ignored the threat of the guns. They wanted her alive or else they would have already killed her and Trey. More than that, the weapon barely registered in her vision, she was so filled with hatred. She'd never understood the term *bloodlust* before. Not until now, as her pulse pounded in her temples and her vision darkened. The only thing that filled her mind, the only thing strong enough to displace the fear, was rage. The rage wasn't red or hot—it burned cold, crystallizing her vision and the killer standing at the center of it, blurring everything else.

The other man behind her, the leader, was shouting something but she couldn't hear it through the blood pounding in her ears. She pinned Smith's left arm against his body with her knees as she leaned her weight on his right thumb, twisting until it popped out of its socket. The gun slid from his hand. She reached for it, but it skidded across the hardwood floor. He twisted his left arm free, almost bucking her off him as he clawed for his weapon.

Her fury wouldn't be denied. She clubbed him with her

cast, ignoring the pain that stampeded through her arm. Kneeling with one knee pressed against his windpipe, choking him, she hit him again, breaking his nose, releasing a spray of blood. But that wasn't enough to satisfy her primal rage.

This man had killed her mother, stolen her life, wanted to kill her and everything she loved . . .

"Lydia!" Trey's voice finally sliced through the roar in her brain. His arms were around her, hauling her off Smith before she finished what she'd started. "Stop! You'll kill him."

"Do as he says, Dr. Fiore," the second man, Black, instructed, his voice as calm as a computerized GPS navigator giving directions. "Unless you want your friend here to die."

She glanced back, saw that Black held his gun to Trey's head. Trey! How could she have put him in danger like that with her brash attack? She could have gotten him killed.

She relented, sagging in Trey's arms, allowing him to drag her back to the couch. Her anger receded—not totally, never totally—but enough that her vision widened and she began to feel the pain drumming along her arm. Her parka and face had been sprayed with Smith's blood. She licked her lips and tasted copper. Swallowed it without regret.

"Don't move," Black said, turning to keep Trey and Lydia in sight on the couch as he backed up. Smith was on the floor groaning, climbing back to his feet. Black kicked the gun across the floor to him. Smith took it, wiping his bloody nose on his sleeve and aiming a look of pure venom at Lydia.

Black laughed. "You're getting old," he told Smith.

"I ought to kill her right now," Smith said, his gait unsteady as he took up a position across the room in front of

Lydia and Trey. "We might need *you* alive, but your boyfriend here is another story."

"Hey!" one of the men shouted at Gina. The red beams of the lasers angled up as they both fired over her head. "Stop!"

Gina had no idea what she was doing or if she was aiming anywhere near them, but she raised the machine gun and pulled the trigger. Bullets flew out in a rush, the recoil pushing her back through the door to the morgue. She released the trigger, stumbling across the floor. Bullets pinged against the steel behind her, their impact louder than the actual shots.

Ken was already pushing LaRose toward the locker rooms, the fastest exit to the main tunnel. He stumbled and tripped. LaRose and the wheelchair careened off the door jamb. Gina scrambled to her feet and took over, navigating the wheelchair through the door.

Behind her, the morgue doors slammed open. Bullets flew past, thudding into the wall beside her.

"Hurry, Ken!"

Gunfire drowned out her words. Ken fell through the door, barely keeping to his feet. Gina pushed it shut behind him and locked it. Not that it would last for long against machine-gun fire. Already bullets splintered the door. She figured that the only thing that had saved them this far was that Harris had obviously told his men to take her alive.

She hauled Ken along, both of them hunched over LaRose and the wheelchair as they hurtled down the short corridor dividing the men's and women's locker rooms. They flew out the door to the tunnel and made a sharp right-hand turn.

"Are you okay?" Gina asked. She couldn't see in the dark, but Ken was obviously having trouble keeping up.

"Fine." The lone syllable emerged with a gasp that was less than reassuring.

They passed the laundry cart. Gina took a moment to topple it onto its side, hoping to slow their pursuers. As they rushed through the intersection with the tunnel to the research tower, she heard the men emerge into the tunnel behind them.

Between Ken's wheezing, the rumble of the wheelchair, and Gina's footsteps, they weren't exactly in stealth mode, but the men behind them were making even more noise as they collided with the linen cart. Gina took that as her cue and turned to fire the gun at them again, this time bracing herself before pulling the trigger.

Ken's grasp on the wheelchair slipped as they turned down a side corridor, and he was almost lost in the dark. Gina grabbed him, leaning his weight against her as she pushed LaRose forward. She wrapped her arm around his waist, and her worst fears were confirmed.

Ken's side was slick with blood.

NORA MADE SURE THE KIDS HAD ALL THE BLANkets they could spare—over the last hour the temperature had plummeted in the auditorium. The cold quieted everyone, leaving them huddled together in groups. Mark Cohen was on his stretcher on the stage, still out from the morphine, and being watched over by Melissa, who seemed relieved to have something to occupy her attention. Jim's body lay on the far side of the room and no one wanted to be anywhere close to it, leaving them all to congregate in one quadrant. Someone had produced a Bible, and a group of staff and patient families prayed together.

Jason sat on the edge of the stage, feet dangling, body rocking as he played one of his incessant video games. As she made her rounds, Nora sneaked a peek at the guards.

Fifteen minutes and they were still wide awake—she'd thought the ketamine-and-Versed combo would have worked by now. Could she have gotten the bottles mixed up?

Patience. Versed took at least fifteen to twenty minutes to work when they used it for sedation, and who knew how long it took ketamine to be absorbed orally. Plus, neither guard had finished his juice yet.

She shivered, hugging herself against the cold and the fear that they didn't have much time. If Harris or the South African returned too soon . . .

Then she realized Jason was gone.

Nora whirled on her heel, doing another mental head count. There he was. He'd been sitting on the edge of the stage near Mark all night, but suddenly now he was sitting on the floor, his back to the stage, still playing his game. Jason caught her eye and beckoned with one finger.

Trying to look nonchalant, she meandered over to him. "How's the game?"

"Great. Want to learn? I think you'd like it."

He knew damn well she despised the damn things. If he hadn't been the best clerk in the hospital, she would have forbidden him from bringing it to work. She smiled in case anyone was watching and lowered herself to sit beside him. "Sure."

He handed her the game and leaned over as if teaching her to play. He whispered, "Amanda's here."

Nora jerked, then covered it by cursing at the game. "Where?"

"Here," came a disembodied voice behind her as a finger jabbed her through the drapes lining the foot of the stage. "I found a way out."

"Under the stage?" Nora asked, ducking and bobbing, pretending that the game had her mesmerized. But she really was calculating the number of people she could get under the stage—even though most of the patients were ambulatory, she didn't think many of them could crawl. Certainly Mark couldn't. Also, the space under the stage didn't seem to be very big, which would eliminate any larger adults.

"We made a hole in the wall through to the kitchen. It's small—I can only take the children at first—but Lucas and Jerry are making it larger."

"I drugged the guards," Nora whispered back, ignoring Jason's look of surprise and admiration. "As soon as it takes effect, we can all walk out the front door."

"No. There are more guards out in the lobby. You'd be mowed down."

"Not all of my people can crawl under the stage, though. Plus, it'd take too long."

Jason put his arm around her shoulders, pointing out something especially exciting on the game. "Amanda, can you make the hole higher? Above the stage?"

"Won't the guards see?"

Nora smiled at Jason. *Good idea.* "Give me a few minutes, I can take care of that." She looked at her watch, pretended to be surprised, and handed the game back to Jason.

"Melissa," she called to the nurse on stage. "We're late doing Mark's dressing change. Could you pull the right-hand stage curtain so he can have some privacy?" The guards would never allow her to pull both stage curtains shut. She waved to them as Jason helped her climb up to the stage. "That's okay, isn't it?"

The guards nodded, their response sluggish. One of them was actually sitting on the floor now, cradling his machine gun as if it were a baby, talking to it. The other was still alert enough to be standing, although he was leaning heavily against the wall. Jason joined her on the stage, helping to move Mark and position the curtain partway closed so that it would screen the wall to the kitchen from the guards.

Nora made a show of him helping her and Melissa position Mark's stretcher. "Let Amanda know we're ready and then spread the word for people not to move even if they see the guards go down. We can't risk someone trying something too soon and getting hurt."

Jason nodded and jumped back down to the main floor, pausing near the curtain below the stage to retrieve his video game and then moving slowly through the crowd as if he were taking drink orders.

"Melissa, you pretend to do a dressing change," Nora instructed. She unwrapped Mark's splint, being as gentle as possible but glad that he wasn't awake to feel any pain. Then she dropped the fresh Ace bandage, kicking it behind the curtain toward the wall. "Whoops."

The guards didn't even seem to notice. Nora followed the bandage roll farther behind the drapes, scooped it up, and went to the wall. Softly knocking on it using the Morse code for SOS, she waited for a response.

There was a small flaw in their plan, she realized as a muffled knocking returned. They'd need to cut through two layers of drywall up here, not just the single layer that was probably below the stage. It would take too long unless they worked at it from both sides.

Nora went back out onto the stage where she'd be visible. The one guard looked asleep; the other was still standing, but his hands had dropped to his sides, away from his gun, and his head had rolled to one side. She wheeled one of the IV stands to just beside the drapes, pretended to be adjusting it, then pushed it behind the drapes, pulling Mark's IV over to take its place.

Melissa watched her with wide eyes, performing the longest mock dressing change in the history of nursing.

Nora put a finger to her lips before quickly dissembling the IV pole, reversing the top of it so that the two-foot steel pole jutted forward like a pike. That ought to go through drywall without too much noise.

She hoped. She stole one last glance at the others. Everyone except the guards was alert, watching her—they'd give it away if the guards noticed.

"Melissa, tell everyone to start singing a song or something," she whispered. "Anything to create a little noise and keep them occupied."

Melissa nodded and left Mark to pass the message to Emma Grey, who sat on the edge of the stage, tirelessly entertaining the children who refused to sleep. A few moments later "The Twelve Days of Christmas" rang through the auditorium.

Nora moved back behind the curtain to the wall. She listened and could hear drywall being torn apart. Hoping that she wouldn't hit Lucas or Jerry, she plunged the sharp end of the IV stand into the drywall and began jerking it back and forth, making a nice-sized hole.

She pulled the pole free and put her eye to the hole.

Jerry grinned at her from a few inches away. "Hey beautiful, where've ya been?"

EVEN IN THE DARK, GINA KNEW IT WAS BAD. THE way Ken's breathing sounded louder than the gunshots that had come before, the coppery smell of blood filling the air. Ken somehow stayed on his feet, periodically nudging her penlight to direct their route. He steered them around a corner and down a side tunnel she didn't recognize. They came to an imposing solid metal door, one she'd never noticed before. Ken slumped against it.

"Take LaRose someplace safe and meet me back here."

"No. Come on, Ken. You can do it." She wanted to pretend that there was nothing wrong, that she hadn't just gotten him shot, that she wasn't responsible for yet another death. "We just need to make it to the tower and everything will be all right."

His face was ghastly white in the glow of her light. "Final stop."

He slid to one side, and the light splashed red with the blood he'd left behind.

"We'll take you upstairs. To the ER. I can help you."

He shook his head, his expression a half-smile but his eyes sad. "Open the door."

No sounds from their pursuers. She handed him the penlight and pulled the door open. It was heavy, as thick as her fist, but once she got it started, it swung silently on well-balanced hinges. The room beyond stank of burned matches, reminding her of her college chem lab. "What is this place?"

"Chemical storage room. It's built to withstand an explosion." He lurched into the room, the penlight swinging madly as he held both hands against his right side. "Hurry back. I can't do this alone."

"Ken—"

"Hurry." His voice snapped at her like a mad dog, pain and fury adding claws and teeth.

For once she didn't argue. Instead she hustled LaRose down the hall and around the corner to the laundry. LaRose had woken from her stupor sometime during their headlong flight through the tunnels, and now she raised a quavery hand, pointing to some sorting baskets that stood at least four feet high. "There."

Gina pushed her behind the baskets and camouflaged her with a sheet. Resisting the urge to huddle with LaRose and wait out whatever terrible thing was coming next, she kissed LaRose on the forehead. "I'll be right back. Promise."

"Go."

She ran back to Ken. He was sitting on the floor, his back to one of the room's many storage cabinets. "I need you to find me a container of sodium metal. It will be a plastic tub, probably filed under *N* for natrium."

Sodium? She scurried around the room, shining her light into the many glass-fronted cabinets. She found the sodium, but the cabinet was locked.

"Hurry," Ken said, his voice tight and sounding miles away even though the room was only ten feet across. "I heard them talking," he continued in that awful beyond-the-grave voice that made her shiver. "They've rigged the generator. Harris controls it—I think through his radio."

She reversed the Maglite and used it butt first to smash the glass, then grabbed the tub of sodium.

"Water." Ken nodded to the sink in the corner. "Get me a glass of water—a paper cup would be best."

"There are plastic specimen jars."

"That will do. Bring everything here."

She gathered the water and the sodium and returned to kneel by his side. "When I was a kid, I remember a high school science teacher who tried to impress us by throwing a tiny piece of sodium into water—made for a nice bang and a splash."

"I'm going to do the opposite. Add the water to the sodium."

"And what's that gonna do?"

He leaned his head back against the cabinet, his eyes vacant. "Room this size? This much sodium? About four seconds after I drop the water in there's going to be one helluva explosion and a huge ball of fire."

"Thought we were trying to stop a fire, keep them from burning down the hospital."

"This room is blastproof. But the door needs to be secured."

"You lost me."

Ken's hands were trembling. His entire body lurched with each inhalation as he raised the cup of water and braced it against his thigh. "Find something to barricade the door with. It won't lock with the power out." He heaved in a gasp after every word. "Then bring them here. I'll be ready."

She gagged in horror as she faced the truth behind his words. He was going to kill himself and take out Harris's men with him. "Ken, no. There has to be another way."

"There's no time." Gina knelt beside him, reached for his wrist. His pulse was fast—too fast. His skin was cold and clammy. "I can feel the pressure building," he said as calmly as if he were giving an anatomy lesson. "Retro-peritoneal bleed. Probably nicked my kidney."

An injury that had a high mortality rate even if she could get him to an OR and trauma surgeon right away. Which she couldn't. "Maybe you're wrong."

He finally met her eyes. "I'm not."

"Ken, you don't have to do this." Gina heard the tears in her voice even though her eyes were still dry.

He squeezed her arm to quiet her. "You need to listen. Everything happens for a reason. Everything. Remember that."

"What are you talking about?"

"I don't know why my family had to die the way they did, but if they hadn't I wouldn't have been out on that street last summer to save those kids and you wouldn't have been there to save me and I wouldn't be able to save—" The words emerged in a breathless rush. He grimaced in pain as sweat beaded across his lips. "I wouldn't have been able to save you."

"You wouldn't have been able to save everyone." She kissed him on the forehead.

"You need to go. Now." She stood. He looked so much

smaller than before, huddled on the floor. And yet . . . He raised his face to meet her gaze. "Promise me. You'll remember."

"I'll remember."

Tears choked her vision and strangled her words. All she could do was nod and blindly rush out the door.

TWENTY-ONE

LYDIA MOVED IN FRONT OF TREY, PUTTING HER-self between him and the gun.

"Shut up and do as you're told," Black snapped at his partner. "I'll tell you when it's time to start shooting people."

Smith grinned, then aimed his glare at Lydia again as more blood dripped from his nose.

"You really don't know who I am, do you?" Black asked Lydia.

She didn't bother to answer. Instead, she let Trey hold her against him on the couch, trying to block out the pain in her arm. She hadn't broken her cast, but the bones inside had been rattled enough that pain twanged through her entire body.

Black wandered around her living room, examining the artifacts of their daily lives with an interest that surprised her. Then he ended up at the mantel, fingering Lydia's two most precious possessions: the only surviving photos of Maria.

"Leave those alone." She couldn't help herself. She'd fought for eighteen years, particularly all those years in foster care, to hang on to those two photos and the only other legacy she had left from Maria: a charm bracelet that circled her wrist, hidden from sight by her sleeve.

Black arched an eyebrow at her outburst. "She never told you, did she? Did she tell you anything?"

Trey pulled Lydia closer, trying to restrain her temper, one arm around her back, one across her lap, holding her free hand and squeezing it tight. As he moved, the afghan that his mother had knitted them slid from the back of the couch, bunching between their bodies.

"Do you even know your own name?" Black continued, relentless.

Anger straightened her posture and she slid to the edge of the couch, glaring at him. "I know enough."

He chuckled. "I don't think you know anything."

Lydia leaned forward, hiking her parka up over her hips. She hoped Trey would get the message. She squirmed closer to him as if seeking comfort, pressing her back—and Sandy's gun—against his arm that encircled her waist. He stiffened, and she knew he understood.

"Tell me," she said, breaking the staring match with the stranger. "Tell me who my mother was."

"First you tell me," he commanded. "Who am I?"

He stood in the full light of the fire, the yellow glow flickering over his features. High cheekbones, dark almond-shaped eyes, hair blacker than midnight.

Beside her, Trey started, a small noise escaping him as he hugged her tighter.

"Who am I?" the stranger repeated, the firelight making his eyes spark.

"You're my father," Lydia said.

She'd intended to speak the words in a clear, unrepentant tone, the tone of someone not frightened, a tone of calm confidence. But nearly thirty years of imagining her father as the most dangerous monster any nightmare could conjure betrayed her. Instead her voice emerged as a hushed whisper, a child trying hard not to attract the bogeyman's wrath.

His laughter filled the room to bursting.

"That's right, little girl." Mr. Black's voice was booming. "That's exactly right."

BY THE TIME AMANDA REACHED THE KITCHEN again, she had so much dust trapped in her eyelashes that every blink brought with it a light show of rainbows along with a cascade of itching. Her eyes felt gritty, her skin grimy, and she didn't even want to try to imagine an adjective for how bad she smelled.

The flicker of the Sterno flame illuminating Jerry's and Lucas's legs warmed her, drawing her close as if she were coming home. She'd reached for the final stud, hauling herself through to the pantry, when Lucas's hands clasped hers and she flew out of the dark, through the broken wall, and landed with her feet back on solid ground.

"You're okay," Lucas said, pulling her against his body, ignoring the dirt and cobwebs and sweat-caked grime.

Once Amanda caught her breath and pushed his arms away enough so that she could breathe, she shook her hair and invisible bits of construction fodder rained down against the floor in a sprinkle of sound.

"I'm fine." She looked past Lucas to where Jerry stood on a step stool, wobbling as he kept his balance with one hand against a shelf while he tore drywall with the other. Nora waved at Amanda through the hole she and Jerry had created. It was already more than twice the size of the hole below, large enough for most of the adults to be able to slide through sideways, if they ducked below the horizontal two-by-four.

A few feet on the other side of the hole sat a chair where another hole was begun—Lucas's contribution to the rescue efforts. He still wore his dishwashing gloves, now covered in dust and threads of gray wallboard.

"Two holes, twice the people," he said, waving a hand at his work like a proud father.

"I'm going to get the children," Nora whispered through her side of the wall.

"What about the guards?" Amanda asked.

"One's asleep. I think the other one's having a reaction to the ketamine—he's awake but pretty out of it, talking and gesturing to people not there."

"Sounds like a dissociative episode," Lucas said as he climbed back onto his chair. "Be careful. Some people get violent during those."

"I've told everyone to stay away from them. I don't want to risk taking their guns and having something happen."

"Can you lock yourselves in? In case the other guards come back?"

Nora shook her head. "No, not from this side of the doors. That's why we need to hurry."

She disappeared from sight. Lucas and Jerry kept working on expanding the escape passages. The light from the Sterno can began to flicker out, so Amanda went back out into the kitchen to get a new can. By the time she returned, Jerry had gotten down off the ladder and had formed a bucket brigade of sorts, catching the children Lucas helped to squirm through the hole from the stage.

"That's right," Lucas told them. "Get down on your bellies, feet first, and just come on through; we won't let anyone fall."

Deon was already safe in the pantry, and his great-grandmother was trying her best to keep her skirt from flying up as she climbed through the hole on the opposite side.

"Don't worry about it, Emma," Amanda told her as she helped guide her through it. "Look at how bad I look—can't get worse than that."

She steadied the footstool so that Emma could plant her feet on it and hop down. Another woman immediately took her place, squirming through the hole backward on her belly, not needing the stool for the short drop.

"Everyone gather right outside the door," Amanda directed them. Lucas and Jerry finished with the last child, and now adults were scrambling through both openings.

Amanda took a moment to seek out Emma, pulling her away from the children for a private word. "We heard a shot earlier."

Emma patted her shoulder, not making eye contact. "I'm sorry, sweetie. It was Jim Lazarov."

Jim? A thrill of relief, immediately followed by a stab of guilt, swept through Amanda. She'd never liked Jim—no one had—but still, he shouldn't have died. She'd been so worried that it was someone she cared about, like Nora or Mark Cohen or even Jason. She'd never dreamed it would be Jim . . .

"Okay. Thanks for telling me. Okay." The surrealism of the day disoriented her. Amanda wandered back to the pantry and huddled with the two men. "Someone needs to lead them through the atrium to the tower, where we can get them as far away as possible."

"You do it," Lucas said. "Wait there in the stairwell with them. Jerry and I can finish here."

"No. We still have the lobby guards to contend with. Someone has to be able to provide cover fire if they're seen."

"A group this big, you *will* be seen."

Jerry said nothing, frowning as more and more people crowded past them from the auditorium. Already at least twenty people were gathered in the kitchen.

"We need a diversion," Lucas said. "Something to keep the guards away from both the auditorium and the atrium."

"Me," Jerry said.

"No," Amanda argued. "You can't move fast enough. You lead the way to the tower. I'll stand guard with the gun at this end of the atrium and cover your flank. Maybe we can start another fire, draw their attention?"

Jerry shook his head.

"They'll never fall for it again. If you and Jerry are taking them to safety, that leaves me as a diversion." Lucas stripped the long black gloves from his arms and brushed off his lab coat. "How about my absentminded professor routine?"

Amanda didn't like that, not one bit. Lucas was no actor. He couldn't lie to save his soul. But absentminded? It was a natural fit. "They'll catch you—"

"No, they won't. I'll act a bit crazy, wander across the lobby, grab their attention, then disappear into radiology. That place is a maze, there are thousands of places to hide. As long as they don't think I'm a threat, they won't shoot."

"I don't know. It's too risky."

"Like you crawling into that auditorium wasn't?" Anger threaded his tone. Lucas never got angry. Irritated, oblivious, pigheaded, yes, but not angry.

"Wow, we've set a record," she said, throwing him off balance. "Two arguments in one day."

Jason came in from the kitchen, interrupting. "I don't see any guards out there right now. I'm taking this bunch to the tower before they come back. Even if we can't leave because of the weather, we can put some distance between ourselves and them."

"Wait." Amanda rushed after him, Jerry following. She pulled the gun from her sash. "Let me cover you. Just in case."

She and Jerry pushed through the rear cafeteria doors and peered around the corner to the auditorium entrance. Jason was right. No guards in sight. None in the lobby either.

"Okay," she told him and the group of women and children waiting behind him. "Move as fast and quiet as you can."

All the children were being carried by adults except Deon, because he was the oldest. Jerry held the door open for them while Amanda kept watch. Their footsteps rang out on the slate floor of the atrium but were quickly muffled by the snow insulating the windows.

It was easier for them than it had been for Amanda, Jerry, and Lucas earlier. All of the lights were out now, leaving them the shelter of darkness as they crossed the atrium.

Once they were sure the first group was safely inside the tower, Amanda and Jerry returned to inside the cafeteria, where Lucas had another group, this time all adults, waiting for them. Amanda lined them up and gave them their instructions to follow Jerry to the tower and move to the farthest stairwell. "Okay, let's go."

Again they made it safely through to the tower. Amanda was just beginning to relax, to think that this would all be over soon, when she heard Jerry's footsteps returning across the atrium.

Two lights appeared in the lobby. One of them arced through the air, as if the person carrying it had pivoted abruptly, and then it spiked through the darkness, dancing through the atrium.

"Who's there?" a heavily accented voice called. The light found Jerry, hopelessly exposed, still a dozen feet to go before reaching the cafeteria entrance. He froze, holding his hands up in the universal sign of surrender.

But that didn't stop the man from shooting.

GINA KNEW THAT KEN'S PLAN WASN'T PERFECT, especially the part about him dying with the bad guys. But in order for him to do that, there was still the little feat of finding the bad guys, not getting shot and killed herself, leading them back to Ken, then putting up some kind of barricade—what could she use to keep the guards locked in long enough for Ken to . . . Gina's mind stuttered, unwilling to visualize exactly what Ken was about to do.

She didn't have time to prowl through every door, so she ran back to the laundry where she'd left LaRose, searching for something to use as a barricade. Not a linen cart; they were too difficult to maneuver quickly. She needed something heavy but easily moved into position once she shut the door behind the gunmen.

Her light beam hit upon a low-slung trolley, the kind she'd seen at home improvement stores, piled high with bags of soiled linens. Disengaging the hand brake, she gave it an experimental tug. It glided readily despite its weight. Perfect.

Gina steered the trolley back to the chemical storage room, positioning it at the far side of the door. She'd lead the gunmen here, pull the door open so they'd think she'd gone into the room, and hide behind the trolley; then, once they followed her trail into the room, she'd push the trolley into place.

And then Ken could . . . finish his plan.

Gina couldn't resist one last good-bye. After parking the trolley, she pulled the door open. Ken was where she left him, his eyes closed, chest heaving in and out with each breath.

"I'm ready," she said. "I'm going to get them now."

He opened his eyes to a slit, waggled one finger in acknowledgment, and tightened his grip on the cup of water. The open jar of natrium was ready and waiting.

"Hurry." His voice was like sand, dispersing in the air between them, only a few harsh grains left by the time it reached her.

"I—" Gina stopped. There were no words. And they were out of time.

She ran back out into the hallway and headed toward the tunnel where they'd last seen the gunmen. She didn't try to be stealthy. Instead she turned on the Maglite, not worrying about being seen—that was the idea—and hoisted the machine gun. She had no idea how many bullets, if any, were left in it.

She felt silly running through the tunnels, trying to get caught. Surely Harris's men would see right through her, not take the bait. But, as she rounded a corner and saw the two men a mere twenty feet ahead, facing her, it didn't feel silly anymore. Not with their guns aimed at her.

She turned and ran. Something must have changed; Harris no longer seemed to want Gina alive, because their aim seemed to be right at her instead of over her head like before. She careened through the tunnels, only taking the time to stop and fire back at them when she feared they would go the wrong way.

Then the machine gun died. She threw it away, letting it clatter across the cement floor. Stopped twice to fire the pistol at the men until she emptied that as well. She shoved it into her coat pocket and ran faster—past the laundry where LaRose hid, past the door to the lab where Ken was, pausing only to wrench it open and then crouch down behind her trolley laden with its load of dirty sheets, and waited in the dark. She tortured herself with a thousand alternative scenarios: staying with Ken, hauling him out of there, throwing the water inside just as soon as the bad guys arrived. . . .

She knew it was hopeless. It had to be done this way. And she hated that. Hated that she hadn't been able to return Ken's love, that it sometimes felt like maybe she couldn't love anyone, hated even more that he was able to perform this act of courage and self-sacrifice for her . . . and she had no idea what to do to make it right, to earn it.

Because she didn't deserve it. Ken was a much better person than she was or would ever be. If there was any justice in the world, he should live through this night.

Justice. Her lawyer father would scoff at the idea, say that concepts like justice, truth, and right and wrong were meaningless fantasies. Moses embraced the certainty of the law. His law. The law was about winning arguments, persuasion, being the last man standing.

Moses would see Ken's sacrifice as weakness—just as he didn't consider the consequences of his actions, the lawsuit that led to the death of Ken's family, as having had anything to do with him. Moses was like a duck: He quacked loud, got the attention he craved, and anything he didn't want to acknowledge or that was inconvenient simply slid out of his life like water.

But Gina was here. A witness to one man's courage. And she couldn't deny it. Couldn't ignore it. All she could hope to do was to someday deserve it.

Now her tears came, shaking her body. She braced herself against the trolley's handle, was about to forget about all their plans and lead the men away, let them take her, shoot her, when they pounded down the hall, just as the door to the storage room was swinging shut.

Two lights immediately targeted the door and before Gina could do anything, the men had yanked it open, bran-

dishing their guns. She shoved her trolley into place, blocking the door from opening again. In her mind, she was
counting. Four, three, two . . . She ran, heart tugging as if
she might leave it behind . . .

One.

TWENTY-TWO

"WHAT DO YOU WANT?" LYDIA ASKED THE stranger—her father, but no less strange to her.

"Your mother stole something from me. Something I need to protect my future." Black leveled his gun at Trey. "And I'm not leaving without it."

Lydia frowned. How the hell was she supposed to give him something she didn't have, something she'd never known existed? "I don't know what you're talking about. Maria didn't have anything. We lived off the streets. She never had anything worth killing for."

"Maria?" He rolled the name on his tongue, tasting it. "Is that what she was calling herself? You know that's not her real name. Maria." He chuckled. "So exotic—she always dreamed of being someone else. A gypsy princess, a lost descendant of Anastasia and the czars, a ballerina chosen by a prince to become his queen."

Lydia tried hard not to let him know how close to home he'd hit. Maria had often posed as a gypsy while running her fake-psychic scams, and she'd claimed to have once studied ballet in San Francisco. Even had a pair of battered toe shoes for a while, until they'd gotten lost during one of their many evictions. They'd spent a lot of time sheltering in public libraries, and Maria would pore over books about the San Francisco ballet. Used to show Lydia pictures of famous ballerinas, tell her the stories behind the ballets. In fact, one of the charms on Lydia's bracelet was a pair of toe shoes.

"Who was she, really?" Lydia dared to ask, not at all certain that she wanted the answer. As far as she knew, her mother had been only seventeen when she'd gotten pregnant and run away from this man, who looked like he had to have been at least a decade older.

"Martha," Black said, stressing the name, "was a silly girl from a dirt-poor Indian reservation, not even pureblood Indian. Only her paternal grandmother was Plumas. But she was pretty—when she didn't hit the needle too hard—and she did what I told her to do, which made her useful."

"You never loved her."

He scoffed at that. "Don't be ridiculous. Of course not. Is that what she told you? That I was some obsessed Don Juan chasing his lost love to the end of the world? Sounds like the kind of fantasy Martha would spin. Anything to hide from her reality."

"What was the reality? What was she hiding from?"

"How about the fact that she got her own father killed?"

Trey's inhalation was audible as he pulled closer to her. Lydia felt his fingers slide the gun from the holster at the small of her back while his hand across her lap gripped hers and squeezed encouragement.

"What happened?" Lydia asked, her voice small, childlike. The man—she couldn't bring herself to think of him as her father—seemed to enjoy instructing her, correcting her idea of her family history, so she indulged him. The longer he talked, the longer they might live.

"The only reason I hooked up with Martha was her dad. He was head of security at the Plumas casino."

"You killed her father to rob a casino?"

"I encouraged him to give me the security codes and safe combo. Went a little too far with my knife—we'd snorted some meth to rev up for the evening." His voice lost its cultured quality, revealing a Mexican accent. "Wasn't counting on sweet Martha double-crossing me."

"If you think Maria—Martha—took your money, you're wrong." All this, nearly thirty years of pain and fear, and it all boiled down to money?

"No. I'd never trust her with the cash. But she was smarter than I gave her credit for."

"What did she take?"

"She stole my future." Black paused for effect, the fire making his teeth gleam as he bared them. He wasn't smiling. "Bitch took the security video that showed me and my guys torturing and killing her father. I didn't even know she had it until we were long gone and she realized I was going to cut her loose, then she sang me a sob story about how she was pregnant and loved me and trusted me but after seeing what I did to her old man, she was leaving me and keeping the tape for protection. All she wanted from me was to leave her and her child alone, she whined, so she tried to blackmail me—after everything I'd done for her!"

"She kept her end of the bargain. She never said a word about you to anyone. There was no need to send him"— she jerked her chin at Smith, who was still staring at her with venom in his eyes—"to kill her."

"You think I'd trust my future on the word of a junkie whore who sold out her own father?" he scoffed. "No way in hell am I going to risk that tape surfacing and destroying everything I've worked for. You have no idea how much I stand to lose."

He leveled his gun at her, then swung it to aim squarely at Trey. "So, I'm asking one last time. Where is it?"

NORA WAS HELPING LUCAS SQUEEZE A RATHER STOUT cafeteria worker feet first through the opening between the two-by-fours when the sound of gunfire interrupted them.

The worker, a Polish woman in her late fifties, began to scream and squirm, wedging herself tight. "Get me out! I don't want to die!"

Lucas, who had her feet, was being kicked mercilessly. Nora squatted down beside the woman's head and took her face between her palms, forcing the woman to meet her eyes.

"Calm down, just stay calm," Nora said, at first loudly, matching the woman's volume, then sliding down to a whisper. "It's okay, we're all going to be okay." As Nora spoke, mesmerizing the woman into ending her struggles, Lucas tugged the woman's legs and hips through the wall. "See, now, all you need to do is duck under and you're through."

The woman blew her breath out, pulled her tummy in, twisted her torso, and made it through.

Nora left her to see what was going on back in the auditorium. People too big to get through the wall—bigger even than the cafeteria worker—had hit the ground, hiding between rows of seats as the sound of gunfire grew closer. That wasn't what frightened her, though.

The agitated guard had his machine gun at the ready and was spinning around in a circle, searching for a target.

Nora was used to dealing with emotionally disturbed people in the ER as well as intoxicated ones, but never with a machine gun in the mix. She slowly walked down the steps at the edge of the stage, getting away from the work lights that framed her as a target, and approached the guard.

"Those shots are coming from outside," she said in a calm, level voice. "We're not going to hurt you—you're here to guard us, protect us, remember? We're not your enemies, we're unarmed . . ." She basically said anything that came to her mind, trying to get him to point the gun away from her and the others—or better yet, to surrender it.

"Your buddy looks like he needs help." She nodded to the sleeping guard curled up on the floor. "Why don't you give me your gun while you check him? Or I can check him for you."

She heard the others behind her dousing lights, using the darkness to cover them as they moved behind the stage curtain. Even though most of the people left couldn't fit through the hole in the wall, she understood why they'd feel that "out of sight, out of mind" was the safest course of action.

The guard slanted a wary look at her. Another round of gunfire sounded from beyond the doors. He jumped, aiming his gun in their direction, away from her and the others.

Crack! The sound of wood breaking came from the stage. The gun whirled around, firing his gun into the air.

"Who's there?" he shouted, his voice edged with drug-induced hysteria. "Show yourself or I'll start shooting people!"

GINA HADN'T GONE THREE STEPS WHEN THE FLOOR shook. The explosion roared through the narrow confines of the corridor, and she fell to her knees, covering her head with her arms, waiting for the ceiling to collapse.

Instead all that happened was silence. She ran back to the chemical room. The barricade had toppled over but the door held. She tried to open it but it had buckled enough to jam it into the steel frame. She shone her light through the small space between the frame and the door. No sounds. No signs of life.

The only thing moving beyond the door was smoke.

Coughing, holding her sleeve over her nose and mouth at the acrid fumes and the stench of burned flesh, Gina turned away, retching. The need to purge, to run and hide in a dark corner and let all of her pain and sins and failures claw their way up her throat and out of her, was overpowering. *Come with us,* her demons whispered. *Leave this horror behind, save yourself.*

Her knees buckled and she almost surrendered. No. LaRose. She had to save her mother. And stop Harris before he incinerated the hospital.

She stumbled forward, hitting the wall in her blind rush. The voice in her head scoffed, *You can't do it, not alone.*

Alone. No Jerry or Ken to guide her. No Lydia or Nora to tell her the right thing to do. Not even Amanda to make her smile.

She was no hero.

She doubled over, clutching her belly, her strength consumed by her doubt and fear.

But she was their only hope.

Laughter ripped through her. Sharp and brittle and painful. If she was their only hope, they were doomed.

Ken. Someone had to remember, bear witness to what had happened here today. She had to do it. For Ken.

Gina straightened and pulled in the deepest breath she could, as if she could inhale Ken's courage along with it. She reached for Jerry's ring, rubbing it as if she were making a wish.

It wasn't enough, not near enough, but it was all she had. Then she ran toward LaRose. What the hell—if they were already doomed, might as well die trying instead of standing here feeling sorry for herself.

As her footsteps reverberated through the empty tunnel, she had the fleeting suspicion that the thought was the most mature one she'd ever had. Wouldn't that be ironic? Finally figure out what she wanted from life, have something worth living for, and the world ended in a big bang?

"Hell of a way to ring in the New Year."

The splintered echoes cheering her on from the darkness agreed.

AMANDA WATCHED IN HORROR AS JERRY THREW himself to the ground, skidding across the atrium's slate tiles. Keeping behind the corner as much as possible, she let off two shots, aiming at the lights of their attackers. A man cursed in a foreign language and the flashlights went out as the men returned fire.

She huddled against the wall, cringing as bullets crashed against glass windows and pinged against rocks. A few thudded into the wall perpendicular to her, but none came close. She felt more than heard Jerry's movements as he crawled to safety under the barrage of bullets.

Then there was a sudden silence that made her ears pop. Jerry grabbed her ankle, letting her know he was okay. She fired off two more rounds to keep the bad guys on their toes before helping him to his feet. They stumbled through the doors, finding half a dozen panicked escapees waiting for them.

"Quiet," Jerry ordered. His voice sounded strong, in control. As if coming under fire had triggered his policeman reflexes, something so ingrained in him that no head injury could erase it.

Amanda left him to race into the pantry and warn Lucas that company was coming. He'd crawled up onto the stage, where he and another man who had his leg in a brace and was on crutches were battering a two-by-four that was preventing the larger-built hostages from escaping.

"Lucas, they're coming!" she whispered. "Get down from there."

"Almost got it," he muttered, straining at the wall stud. It was the one they'd cut the bottom of earlier, so all he needed was to wrench the top part aside. It cracked, the sound cleaving the silence, echoing into the auditorium.

An obese man who'd been standing behind Lucas and the man on crutches, watching for his opportunity, pushed them aside to squirm through the gap. The man crutches went sprawling, and Lucas stopped to help him up.

Gunfire sounded from within the auditorium. The fat man yelped, finally got through the hole, and fled.

"Show yourself or I'll start shooting people!" a man's voice shouted.

Amanda lunged, reaching for Lucas to yank him through the wall, back to her. He gave her a look filled with sorrow and yearning.

"Told you I'd make a good decoy," he whispered. Then he blew her a kiss, turned his back on her, and marched to the center of the stage, silhouetted perfectly by the work lights near the patient cots, his white lab coat making him an impossible-to-miss target.

A cry of panic escaped Amanda. She grabbed the step stool, ready to follow him, when Jerry's arms pulled her back. "No!"

Bullets screamed through the air. Lucas fell to the ground.

"Hide," Jerry told the man with the crutches, who was still caught on the stage.

Melissa came running in, grabbing at Amanda's other arm. "We need to get out of here."

"No. Lucas—we have to get him," she protested, her

gaze fixated on the scarlet streams that shone bright against Lucas's white lab coat. Blood.

Her breath escaped so fast it was as if her body had suddenly been turned inside out and then shuffled right side in again, leaving her disoriented, feeling as though she were in a dream and none of this were real.

Then she heard Lucas groan.

She twisted in Jerry's grip, fighting to get to Lucas. He and Melissa hauled her out of the pantry back to where the others waited in the cafeteria.

Jerry said nothing, just pointed at the hostages gathered in front of them, six of them focused on her, hope in their faces. The fat man wasn't among them, she saw, and was glad because she wasn't sure she could have reined in her anger.

"Where do we go?" Melissa asked in a small voice.

They trusted her; they thought she could save them. *Fools*, Amanda wanted to scream. But she didn't. Instead she adjusted her grip on the Smith & Wesson, pulled Lucas's otoscope from her sash, and stood up straight, bare feet already numb from standing still in the cold cafeteria.

"Follow me."

TWENTY-THREE

GINA'S TEARS HAD DRIED BEFORE SHE REACHED LaRose's hiding place. She didn't have time or energy to mourn for Ken now. She had to save her mother, try to save the others.

Knowing what to do was one thing—having any idea how to do it was another. She couldn't simply evacuate LaRose and the others out of the hospital; they'd die in the blizzard. She needed a place to send them to, someplace with shelter from the storm and out of Harris's range.

Out of range of any danger if the hospital did go up in flames would be nice as well. Which brought her right back to her original idea of hiding out in the tower, as far as she could get from the hospital.

Gina glanced at her watch. Eleven twenty-seven. Almost four hours since LaRose presented with her stroke symptoms. Okay, first things first. She had to get her mother's TPA begun. Then she'd figure out an evacuation plan.

Followed by a rescue plan. Followed by a stopping-the-hospital-from-burning-down plan.

Breaking it down into tiny steps didn't help as much as she'd hoped.

"You okay?" she asked LaRose as she unlocked the wheelchair's brakes.

LaRose nodded, her mouth moving but only guttural sounds emerging. Gina felt her pulse—too fast, but strong. She didn't want to guess what LaRose's blood pressure was doing with all this exertion and excitement.

Excitement? Hah—there wasn't a word for what they'd been through.

"Ken's gone." The words tasted of bile, more rancid than anything Gina had ever purged. "But he bought us time. I'm going to get you to the ER and we'll start your treatment."

LaRose's good hand fumbled for Gina's.

"Don't worry, Mom. I know what I'm doing. Trust me." Gina wished she felt half as confident as she pretended to be. She steered the wheelchair through the dark tunnels to the staircase leading to the ER. Now came the hard part: carrying LaRose up the steps.

Pulling her up in the wheelchair was too dangerous. One slip and LaRose would fall. Not to mention too noisy. Even though Harris's men had already cleared the ER, she couldn't take the risk that he might have left someone behind to patrol it. "I hope you didn't overindulge at all those holiday parties."

She reached under LaRose's arms and hefted her into a poor imitation of a fireman's carry. Nothing like having your mom's ass block your vision. She staggered against the handrail, using it to guide her up the steps, trying hard not to bounce her mother too much. Maybe hanging upside down would break up the blood clot that had caused her stroke? Or the strain might cause a new bleed, make things worse.

Each step brought with it new and more dire imaginings. Her father would kill her if anything happened to LaRose. He was bound to find some way to blame her for this mess, no matter how it turned out.

"Let's not tell Moses about this part," Gina huffed as she reached the final landing.

She was desperate to take a break, her back screaming in pain, but she knew it would be next to impossible for her to lift LaRose again once she put her down. She pulled the door open, peered into the darkness. No signs of Harris or any of his men. A frigid breeze whistled through the open waiting room wall, rustling the debris left behind by LaRose's car crash. God, that seemed ages ago.

She was on the other side of the triage desk, which meant that there should be a wheelchair nearby. She took the chance and flicked her penlight on. Nothing. Of course, they'd used them all to evacuate the patients. Shit. Then she saw Jason's wheeled desk chair sitting among the rubble of the nurses' station. Good enough.

LaRose almost slipped out of the chair, but Gina caught her in time, pushing her around and over the debris until they reached the back hallway. It was quiet there, quieter than the morgue. Just as freezing, though. LaRose shook with cold.

"Not much longer. I'll get you some blankets and we'll get your medicine started." Gina flicked her penlight down the hallway. No debris here. Gina wheeled LaRose through the dark into the OB-GYN room. Located at the end of a corridor in the back of the ER, it was a small room, easily overlooked. And it was the only patient care room with a privacy lock on it—plus the door was solid, no windows, and it would block any noise. "Here we go. Home sweet home."

LaRose tried to chuckle, but it sounded more like a death rattle.

"I DON'T KNOW WHERE ANY VIDEOTAPE IS," LYDIA said, edging herself closer to Trey, trying to get between him and Black's gun. As she moved, she pulled the afghan with her, covering his right hand—the one that held her gun. "Maria never told me any of this. Those two pictures are the only things she left behind after you had her killed."

Black frowned at her, obviously not believing. "No. Maria wouldn't have left you without protection. She knew I'd never stop until I had that tape."

He paused, scrutinizing Lydia, exploring her weaknesses. "Maybe *he's* not enough to get you to talk." He pushed his jacket aside with his free hand and pulled a small radio from his waistband. "How about an entire hospital full of people, Doctor? What are their lives worth to you?"

"What are you talking about?" She was afraid she already knew.

"My men control Angels of Mercy. They're holding everyone there hostage. One word from me and they'll kill them all." He raised the radio to his lips.

Lydia jumped to her feet, took one step toward him— and away from Trey, freeing his line of fire to the second man, Smith. "No! Please, no. Don't."

He lowered the radio, his smile sliding across his face like a knife's edge. "You have three seconds. Tell me where the video is."

Lydia didn't dare risk a glance at Trey. But somehow, despite the distance between them, she knew he was ready, knew he knew which way she would go. It was as if their bodies needed no words to guide them, just like when they made love. At least she hoped so, because she was risking more than only their two lives on her next move.

"I don't need three seconds," she said, sidling a little more to the right. "I'll give it to you right now."

Black relaxed the tiniest bit, seemed reassured to learn that Lydia had been lying to him, that she had what he wanted all along. As if in his world, a lie was more certain than the truth. Lydia was glad she'd never grown up in that world—for all her faults, everything Maria had done, even sacrificing her life, had been for the love of her daughter.

Lydia hoped she could one day be a tenth the mother Maria had been.

She reached toward the bookcase on the other side of the man, the one that held not only stacks of her books but also Trey's shoot-'em-up videos and DVDs. Both men followed her motion, their guns tracking away from Trey for one critical moment.

As Trey stood, bringing his right arm up from under the afghan, Lydia feinted, drawing Black's attention. He pivoted to face her, but she charged, pushing his gun arm—he was a lefty, like her—up as they crashed into the mantel.

A shot rang out, followed by another. Behind Lydia, Trey and Smith grappled, overturning the bookcase, and falling into the ground.

She wanted to turn to look to see if Trey was okay, but couldn't. Lydia kneed Black in his groin, putting nearly thirty years' worth of fury and fear into the blow. He doubled over, his gun falling to the floor.

She scrambled for his gun, retrieving it just as Trey separated himself from the second man and swung to aim at Black.

"Drop the gun!" Trey shouted, sounding just like a

Hollywood cop before he saw that she'd already taken care of business.

"I got him, Trey." She heaved in a breath, then backed up so she could cover both men. "Get the radios and check them for more weapons."

Trey didn't even look in Lydia's direction but stayed focused as he retrieved the guns and radios, placing them out of reach on the end table. Smith was crumpled on the floor, blood streaming from a bullet wound in his leg, right around his kneecap. Another bullet had shattered a planter beside him.

"Nice shooting," she told Trey.

"Said I didn't like guns. Never said I couldn't shoot them." He went into the kitchen and returned with the first-aid kit, making quick work of binding the man's wound.

"My climbing rope and knives are in the hall closet." Lydia kept guard over the men while Trey went back out to the hall to retrieve them.

Once his pain subsided, her father sat up, staring at her. "You're just like your mother," he said. "An untrustworthy bitch."

Laughter bubbled out of Lydia as the irony of the situation became too much to bear. "No. It seems I'm just like you."

Black glared at her, even as Trey returned carrying the rope, knives, and two sturdy dining room chairs. He hauled the men into the chairs and quickly secured them.

"They're not going anywhere." Trey handed her Sandy's gun, which she returned to her holster. Lydia took her knife—her favorite, a Ken Onion—and examined it in the firelight.

"Shouldn't we get to Angels?" Trey asked, a hint of anxiety that only Lydia would be able to detect in his voice.

She ignored him. She held the blunt edge of the knife

to her father's jugular and pressed hard enough to collapse the vein. "Do you know that I killed a man?" She didn't wait for his answer. "You need to know that. You need to understand that I want to kill you—that I could kill you."

She slid the knife a centimeter away, allowing him room to swallow and breathe. His eyes had a new light in them, something she felt ashamed for inspiring. Fear. She *was* more like him than Maria. The knowledge scared her, but she didn't relent. She couldn't—he threatened everything she had fought for. "Do you understand that?"

Black nodded.

"Do you want me to kill you?"

He seemed surprised she was giving him a choice. He glared at her—just as stubborn as she was—for a long moment before his face revealed his surrender. Lydia felt no joy or triumph. Just disgust.

"No."

"I didn't think so. Call your men off."

He shook his head, a sly smile playing across his lips. "I can't. No one can."

Lydia and Trey exchanged glances. Trey jerked the chair violently, almost crashing it to the floor. "Call them off now!"

"After my first man failed, I called in a more motivated crew. Highly skilled and relentless. They all have felony convictions, all have current felony warrants. They know the price for failure is the death penalty. Now that they have control of the hospital, they'd rather burn it down and kill everyone in it to cover their tracks than leave potential witnesses behind. Especially Harris—he's with me on the video of your grandfather's murder. He has nothing to lose—if we don't walk away clean, he's a dead man."

Lydia stared out the French doors at the black void in the skyline—the void where the lights of Angels normally shone. "We have to stop them."

"You can't." Her father laughed, amused that they were just as helpless and powerless as he was. "Nobody can. Those people are as good as dead already. But you can save yourselves. Let us go. You keep my secret and I'll never tell anyone that you let a hospital full of people die in order to save your own lives."

THE GUARD KEPT PULLING THE TRIGGER ON HIS machine gun long after he ran out of bullets. Finally, he threw the gun to the ground in frustration.

"Everyone just calm down," Nora yelled, trying to engage the guard's attention.

Thank God his partner still slept, curled up with his own machine gun, oblivious. The wonders of a little Versed. She just wished this one had reacted the same way.

"Just stay calm." She looked the guard in the eye, nodding her head slowly as if they shared a common goal. "That man is a doctor. He's here to help. He won't hurt you. I'm going to go help him. See if he's hurt."

As she spoke, her voice calm and level as if singing a lullaby to a colicky newborn, she backed down the aisle toward the stage, toward where Lucas lay, and where Mark Cohen and his stretcher still blocked the hole in the wall. The guard stayed where he was, a blank expression on his face. She was tempted to go back and take his partner's weapons, but Lucas needed her.

She'd just reached the stage when the auditorium door burst open. Harris and the South African ran inside, guns drawn, scanning the almost-empty auditorium.

"What the hell?" Harris shouted, sounding like a petulant child whose toys had been taken from him. "Where is everyone?"

Nora ignored him, checking Lucas's wound—it didn't look serious—and ensuring that Mark was okay. The ER department head was still sleeping from the hefty dose of morphine Melissa had given him. Nice that someone wouldn't have nightmares about this, at least. She chided herself immediately, remembering the anguish Mark had felt when he lost Jim.

She looked around the stage. Only one more patient remained on the floor behind the curtain, crutches beside him as he squirmed through the opening in the wall. Mr. Olsen from the zoo. The penguin man.

There were more people hidden in the seating area. If they were smart, they'd keep their heads down and stay quiet until Nora figured out a way to calm Harris down.

She caught sight of the expression on Harris's face as he kicked the sleeping guard, unable to stir him, and wished Seth were here. No, not here, she didn't want Seth any-where near—she just wished she had a chance to talk to him one last time. About something more important than the Nittany Lions. Wished she'd told him what he meant to her.

Harris bent over and took the sleeping guard's pistol. Then he shot him point-blank in the face. When the other guard, who was now waltzing with his machine gun, turned at the sound, Harris shot him as well.

"Want me to collect the evidence?" the South African asked, drawing his knife.

"No. Don't bother."

The South African looked puzzled. "But Mr. Black said—"

"Screw Mr. Black. Mr. Almighty Black isn't answering his radio. Either Mr. Black has left town, leaving us to hold the bag, or he's dead."

"So, you want me to just kill them all now?" The South African made it sound as easy as deciding on cream or sugar for his coffee.

"Yes."

The South African raised his machine gun.

Nora glanced up wearily. She was so damn tired of guns pointed at her that she almost didn't care. She was tired of being a pawn to these men. Something of no value.

"You don't want to do that," she called out from her position on the stage.

She stood up, making herself a target but also towering above them, forcing the men to look up at her. Finally, for the first time since Tillman had tried to usurp her power earlier today, she felt like a charge nurse.

"Wait." Harris gestured for the South African to lower his weapon. "Let's hear what she has to say."

AMANDA LED HER NOT-SO-MERRY BAND THROUGH the dark cafeteria and out into the blackened hallways leading to the ER. Jerry trailed at the rear of the group, pushing the stragglers to move faster and ensuring that no one got left behind. It would have been a good system if she had any idea where in hell she was going.

Her one thought was to get the others to someplace where they could wait safely and get back to Lucas. She kept seeing him fall, seeing the blood, over and over again and couldn't turn the image off.

They turned down the rear hallway of the ER, headed toward the intersection with the corridor containing the locker rooms, OR 13, and the OB-GYN room. The tunnels, that was their best bet, she decided. All she could hope was that Harris didn't know about them or have enough men to cover them and she could use them to get to the research tower and the others.

Then she could return for Lucas.

*   *   *

GINA PARKED LAROSE BESIDE THE EXAM TABLE, banging her hip on the stirrups. The one thing the OB-GYN room didn't have was TPA. The ER's stash would be locked up in the computerized drug dispenser or down in the auditorium with Nora, but Gina knew where there was one unsecured source: the transport team's medical bags. She set her Maglite on the counter so LaRose wouldn't be left alone in the dark.

"I'll be right back," she said. To her surprise, LaRose grabbed her arm with her good hand, tugging hard, bringing her daughter's ear to her mouth.

"Careful." Gina could barely make out the word, it was so slurred. "Love. You."

Gina was glad for the darkness; it hid her furious blinking, fighting tears.

"It's going to be all right," she whispered back, hugging LaRose—the first time she could remember embracing her mother in decades. What an idiot she'd been, playing along with her parents' power games and warped reality instead of just loving them the way she wanted to.

She slipped back out into the hall, down to the transport nurses' office, and quickly retrieved the med bag. Her penlight finally died as she made her way back to LaRose, but she knew these halls well enough to navigate them in the darkness.

As she was passing the door to the men's locker room, the door opened and a hand grabbed her, jerking her off balance.

Before she could scream, another hand clamped over her mouth and she was hauled inside.

TWENTY-FOUR

"IT'S ME," CAME AMANDA'S VOICE.

Gina's pounding pulse choked her words. Damn, she hadn't thought she had any adrenaline left, but suddenly she was spilling over with it, gut twisting, fingers trembling, toes tingling.

Two flashlights clicked on, revealing Amanda and Jerry.

"Gina," Jerry said, rushing to hug her. "You're here."

He tasted of plaster, smelled of sweat, but he was warm and whole and there, really there, she wasn't imagining it.

Gina's mind couldn't comprehend the reality, and for a moment she froze until her brain could reboot. She buried her head in his neck, kissing and inhaling and absorbing the facts her senses told her were true.

Jerry *was* here, alive. Joy surged through her, drowning out any doubts or fears. He was here, right here in her arms again.

She could have stayed there kissing him until the next New Year's. Finally, she remembered LaRose and reluctantly pushed him away—not too far, just far enough that she could breathe.

"LaRose had a stroke." Gina gave them the PowerPoint version of their odyssey. "I need to get her this TPA. She's in the OB-GYN room."

"I can do that." A woman's voice came from the shadows between the rows of lockers. Melissa, one of the ER nurses, came forward.

Gina handed her the transport bag. "Everything you need should be in there."

Amanda stood watch by the door, holding her gun at the ready like a James Bond girl. She cracked the door, checked the hall, then held it open far enough for Melissa to pass.

Jerry's light hit her, and Gina barely contained her laughter. Amanda's blond hair was streaked with dirt and cobwebs, her pale skin was smeared with gray powder and black grime, her dress—Gina's dress—was in tatters, and she was barefoot. "What the hell happened to my Manolo Blahniks?"

Gina didn't really care about the shoes, just wanted to see a smile—Amanda was always smiling—replace the look of desperate anger her friend now wore.

"They got Lucas." Amanda's voice had no tears; instead it was resolute.

Then the light caught her eyes. Gina was wrong. She didn't look like a James Bond glamour girl. She looked like Rambo. Ready to kill to avenge the man she loved.

"They're in the auditorium, but I think there's only two or three guards now." Amanda quickly filled Gina in on their hostage rescue and how it ended.

"So Jim's dead?" A heavy blow hit Gina midchest at the thought. Now she knew who she had killed with her stupid attempt at bluffing Harris. It seemed like a lifetime ago, a murky distant memory, but she knew she'd never be able to totally forget or forgive herself.

"We can't just run," she told them. "Harris rigged the backup generator to blow. If it goes, the entire hospital will go up in flames. We have to stop him."

"How? I have six bullets left. How many do you have?" Amanda nodded to the gun in Gina's pocket. Gina had forgotten about the damn thing.

"None. It's empty."

"Not a big help."

"We need to split up. Take out Harris and his men. And get Harris away from his radio, the detonator."

"Sure, sounds easy—in theory," Amanda said, sounding more like cynical Gina than Gina herself did. Since when did Gina become the optimistic one?

"We take the fight to them."

"Best defense," Jerry said, taking Gina's hand and swinging it back and forth as if they were in the schoolyard planning a bout of capture the flag.

"Exactly. If there's only two or three of them left, they can't cover both doors *and* the hole in the wall you guys created. Who has the greater firepower?"

"The South African," Amanda said. "He has both a machine gun and a pistol."

"So you two go in the main doors, one to each entrance. Amanda, you act as a decoy, get the South African's attention. Jerry can take him from behind."

"No," Jerry said.

"He's right. He's still pretty unsteady," Amanda said.

Gina knew that, but if he was too unsteady to threaten a man at a distance, how could she possibly let Jerry get close enough to be a decoy? He'd never move fast enough to get out of the line of fire.

"I can do it." Jerry grabbed her hand, squeezing. He knew what she was thinking. Just like he used to.

A faint hope flickered to life in Gina's heart, and she squeezed back. "You sure?"

He nodded.

"Amanda, you okay taking down the South African?"

"No problem. But how do we keep Harris from detonating the generator?"

"That's my job. You threaten him, get him running. I'll be waiting."

Jerry reached for Gina again. "No. Stay here. Stay safe."

Gina swallowed her laughter. They wouldn't understand. But safety wasn't an option. Not anymore. Not if she could take out Harris and finish this now.

IT BECAME CLEAR VERY FAST THAT LYDIA'S FATHER—the thought of those two words together when face-to-face with this killer made her gag—wouldn't tell them how to stop Harris from burning down Angels. If he even knew.

Instead he insisted on playing mind games with them, alternating between threatening them with dire consequences and trying to bribe them, saying he had access to vast amounts of wealth and power. Lydia tuned him out, which only infuriated him more.

"Do you have any idea who I am?" he demanded.

"Yeah. You're the guy who gets to sit in the dark with his buddy until the cops get here."

After making sure that he and the other shooter were securely restrained, Lydia and Trey ran back out to Bessie. Lydia tried to call Angels while Trey drove. No luck. She used the radio to call the emergency response center and learned that Janet Kwon had just requested a SWAT team to Angels, but they were still en route. She asked the operator to dispatch police to her address to pick up her father and Smith.

"Looks like we're the cavalry," she told Trey as he turned off Penn Avenue.

The snow had slowed, as had the wind. In the distance

they could see the lights of the first plow trucks slowly making their way down Penn Avenue. The street in front of the hospital was piled deep with drifts—probably from the wind having had little to slow it as it scoured through the cemetery, Lydia guessed. Even with the snowplow on Bessie, Trey couldn't get them any closer than the far end of the ER drive.

"Guess we walk from here. You up to it?" He nodded to Lydia's arm with its broken cast. She'd wrapped it in duct tape to give it some stability; it still hurt like a son of a bitch, but not half as bad as knowing that her friends were in danger because of her. No way in hell was she waiting on the sidelines.

"Let's go." She opened her door and climbed down onto a snowdrift, settling her weight slowly to make sure it wouldn't collapse. She didn't slam the door shut, worried about how far the noise would carry now that the wind had died down. Only the faint scrape and diesel grind of the snowplow in the distance interrupted the silence.

Trey climbed around to meet her, and together they slid down the side of the drift and into the shelter of the ambulance bay.

"Who the hell are you?" A man's voice came from an Excursion parked to Lydia's right. He came around the SUV, aiming a machine gun at them.

"We're here to help," Lydia said in a bright tone as she edged her left hand into her pocket. She had the Taurus holstered on her belt and the nine-millimeter she'd taken from Black in her pocket. She'd forced Trey to take the other semiautomatic, although she suspected he wouldn't use it.

"That's nice," the man said. "I need some help. Starting with the keys to your snowplow."

"It's not really a snowplow," Trey said, reaching into his pocket. He didn't make eye contact with Lydia, but he didn't have to. She knew exactly what he was planning. She stomped her feet as if she were cold and eased over a little more to her right so they could catch the man in a crossfire. "It's a rescue vehicle."

"Whatever. Just give me the keys."

Trey and Lydia drew their guns simultaneously. The man jerked his own gun, but his gloved finger caught in the trigger guard before he could fire. Trey moved with the grace and speed that always made Lydia catch her breath—they were what had attracted her to him in the first place—easily snatching the gun away. Then he patted the man down and took a pistol and a knife from him as well. They soon had him restrained with some Flex-Cuffs they found in the Excursion.

"How many inside?" Lydia asked as Trey examined the machine gun. For a man who hated guns, he suddenly seemed very interested in them.

"I want a lawyer." The man pinched his lips tight together, his eyes slitting into a sullen stare into oblivion.

Lydia ignored him as she rummaged through the rear of the vehicle. She pulled out a roll of building plans. "Look, pictures."

Trey joined her and they scrutinized the plans. "Looks like they were containing everyone ambulatory in the auditorium. And blocking the fire doors to all the floors so no one would be able to leave from the other patient floors."

"Makes sense—once they locked the elevators down, they could search the hospital at will." Lydia tried not to think about how the men with guns had been searching for *her*, wandering the halls of the hospital, taking her friends hostage. "Probably at least half a dozen men."

"More like eight or nine," Trey said. He flipped the page

of schematics to one showing the utilities and wiring. "They were making notes on the wiring for the backup generator and its fuel intake."

Lydia drew back and stared at him. "Black said these guys were going to burn the hospital down."

"That'd be the place to do it." Trey craned his head up at the dark towers above them. "And it would explain why they needed to turn the power off."

"Does it say what they did?" To her the blueprints were a squiggle of lines—but Trey had experience reading building plans; they obviously made sense to him.

"No, but there aren't many ways they could. Easiest would be to rig the wires to send a live current through the fuel when the generator is started. Maybe add a long-distance current source as an igniter so they could remotely control it."

"Can you fix it?"

He squinted, his features solemn in the map light. "I think so."

"Okay, you go after the generator, I'll go after the hostages."

"Wait, alone?"

Lydia loved it when Trey wrinkled his eyes in dismay like that and his eyebrows collided in an inverted V—it was so nice that someone cared. Even if he didn't have a chance in hell of winning this argument. "Yes, alone."

NORA HAD NO IDEA WHAT THE HELL SHE WAS doing—it was a very uneasy, yet liberating feeling. She could understand now why Gina had been tempted to impersonate Lydia. She felt like she was impersonating someone else herself, anyone but a by-the-book charge nurse.

"Just because you didn't get what you came for is no reason to leave empty-handed." She leaped down from the stage and ambled down the aisle toward the men, her stride confident, cocky even.

"She's stalling," Harris said. He waved the South African onto the stage. "See what's going on behind that curtain."

Harris kept his gun trained on Nora as the South African bounded past her and leaped onto the stage, ignoring the stairs. He yanked back the heavy velvet curtain, revealing the escape route. "Looks like this is how the others got out."

"Okay, come on back." Harris raised his voice. "The rest of you—yeah, I know you all are down there—just stay where you are."

"I don't trust you," Harris told Nora as the South African rejoined them.

"You don't have to trust me," she told them. "This is a hospital. We have a vault full of drugs. Not to mention cash—you'd be surprised how much cash a place like this has on hand, especially for a holiday weekend."

"She's right," the South African said, his eyes glinting. "We should walk away with something for our trouble. They'd need more cash on hand for the holiday weekend," he reasoned. "You know, for the cafeteria and pharmacy and all."

One down, one to go.

Harris was still unconvinced, shaking his head at Nora. "What's in it for you?"

"Simple. We get to live. You get the money and leave."

"How do we access the vaults with the power off?"

Ah, now he was hooked too. Greed, it never failed. "You didn't kill Tillman, did you?"

"No, we've got him stashed outside. Couldn't put up with his whining any longer."

"Good. He has the override key in his office." She couldn't believe the words coming out of her mouth—she was creating a vault and overrides and keys, spinning them from thin air. And from Seth's addiction to caper movies. Which was why she gave them Tillman. Every good caper needed a fall guy.

A light went on in Harris's eyes, and she saw him calculating how long it would take them to get to Tillman's office, ransack the vault, and get out before triggering the explosion that would burn down the hospital and kill everyone—which, of course, was why he didn't seem to really care about the hostages escaping the auditorium. He knew their fate was sealed.

"Okay," he said finally. "But you come with us. Anything goes wrong—"

The South African laughed, finishing the sentence for Nora by hoisting his machine gun.

AMANDA STILL THOUGHT THE PLAN WAS A SUICIDE mission. But if it gave Lucas a chance to get out alive, she was willing to go along with Gina's crazy ideas. She and Jerry helped Gina gather the equipment she needed and carry it down to the auditorium. They set up in the lobby right in front of the doors, using the darkness as cover.

"Okay, I'm ready," Gina whispered to them, pocketing Lucas's otoscope to use as a light source when she was ready. "Remember, send Harris out the far door."

"Maybe I'll just shoot them both, save you the trouble," Amanda muttered, surprising herself by being more than half serious. It was one thing to have your fairy-tale New Year's Eve dream date ruined, quite another to have the man you love placed in danger. She wondered if she could actually kill someone—not that Harris and the South African didn't deserve it.

"Don't take any unnecessary chances," Gina reminded

her, seemingly following Amanda's thoughts. "Remember, Jerry only has one shot."

Amanda had offered to split the ammo she had left, but they decided all Jerry needed was one shot to get the South African's attention. Better that Amanda keep the rest since she might actually hit what she was aiming at.

"Be careful," Jerry told Gina. Despite the fact that he had whispered the two words, he'd made them sound loud and urgent. "Maybe I should—"

"No." Gina said. "We stick to the plan. And don't forget, stay inside. I can't risk anything happening to you if things go wrong."

Amanda tugged at Jerry's arm. She wanted to get this over with before something could go wrong, like everything else that had gone wrong today.

TWENTY-FIVE

LYDIA AND TREY CROSSED THROUGH THE AMBU-
lance bay. The ER doors were locked—the first time Lydia
had ever seen that happen. But a short distance away, they
saw a tarp billowing through a broken window.

"What the hell?" Lydia held the tarp to one side while
Trey shone his light inside. He'd grabbed a satchel of
tools from the Excursion and had it slung over one shoulder, the machine gun over the other.

"Told you, someone drove a car through the waiting
room. But the door to triage is open; we can get through
there."

He helped her climb through the debris until they reached
the hallway on the other side of the triage desk.

"Sure you don't want to come with?" he asked when
they arrived at the stairwell door. "I'll let you carry my machine gun." It would have been funnier if they both hadn't
known that the only reason he'd taken the machine gun was

because it would make for a better diversion if he needed to use it.

"Just be careful." Lydia stood on her tiptoes to give Trey a quick kiss. Wished it were longer, wished they had all the time in the world.

"Me, I'm just playing with a little electricity—you're the one who'd better be careful."

She walked away before she could think twice about it. The ER was a shambles: the nurses' station destroyed, snowdrifts swirling around her feet, wind whistling down the long, deserted corridors. It was like being in a spook house on Halloween. Except the spooks she was looking for carried guns.

Keeping her gun hand free, she held her flashlight between the fingers left exposed by her cast. It meant she had to move her entire arm to aim the light, and every movement brought a new wave of pain from her arm, but it was better than holding the light in her teeth.

She'd made it almost to the intersection with the corridor leading to the auditorium when she heard a small scraping sound. Whirling, Lydia spun the light high and low, her gun following its aim.

"I know that smell." The man's voice came from behind a laundry hamper. "You're not one of them."

"Come out," she ordered, not lowering her guard.

The man leaned on the hamper to climb to his feet, and she saw that one of his ankles was swathed in a brace. "You're not from the zoo. What were you doing with my penguins?"

NORA HAD NO CHOICE. IT WAS THE PRICE SHE PAID for coloring outside the lines, but if it gave everyone else time to escape, it was worth it. And with Jerry, Gina, and

Amanda running loose around Angels, she still had hope. They had all pulled together before for tough saves in the ER—"minor miracles," Amanda called them—so why not tonight?

Nora might have even believed her inner pep rally if the South African hadn't yanked her forward and tugged her wrists into plastic riot cuffs that pinched so hard she thought they were about to slice through her skin.

"Let's go," he said, pushing her in front of him toward the door.

"Hold it!" Jerry's voice called from the second doorway behind them.

The South African wheeled, pulling Nora close as a shield. The action momentarily blocked his access to his machine gun, though, so he drew his pistol instead.

Jerry stood, silhouetted in the scattered lights from the stage and aisle, aiming a gun at the South African, needing both hands to keep it steady. Nora's stomach sank into her toes—Jerry's gun had no bullets; it was more a security blanket than a weapon.

Then he fired off a shot. She jerked in surprise.

"Drop your weapon!" another voice—could that be Amanda?—came from behind them.

The South African tried to whirl around again, aiming to put his back to the wall so that he could face both adversaries—and keeping Nora in the crossfire as he did.

Nora wasn't about to let that happen. As he pivoted his weight, she elbowed him in the groin with the combined force of both her arms and threw her weight forward.

He released her, grabbing his machine gun. Shots rang out above her. Then a body crumpled beside her.

The South African. His machine gun had fallen to one side. Nora grabbed the pistol from his limp hand. He wasn't dead, just writhing in pain from twin wounds in his thighs and another in his belly.

"Jerry, you did that?" she asked, amazed that Jerry's co-ordination had allowed him to make such precision shots.

He shook his head.

"It was me," Amanda said, shoving a pistol into the sash of her ball gown, which now looked like someone had sent it through a paper shredder. "Where's Lucas?"

"Where's Harris?" Jerry asked, looking around.

"He left right before you came in. Went to get Tillman."

Jerry did a stutter step, and then his eyes went wide at her words and he raced back out again.

GINA COULDN'T BELIEVE HER BAD LUCK—ALL THEIR planning and Harris had waltzed out of the auditorium while Jerry was checking around the corner for guards. She'd left her position to tell Jerry, but he'd been too far away.

So instead she grabbed the bare essentials and tracked Harris. It wasn't hard; he had a flashlight and wasn't looking over his shoulder or trying to hide. Guys like him never did—like her dad, always assuming he could get away with anything, never thinking to cover it up. If Moses Freeman did something and you didn't like it, tough luck because he wasn't going to back down.

Harris crossed the lobby to the information desk, usually staffed by volunteers. There was a small closet behind it, just large enough for a few coats and some office supplies.

He pushed through the swinging half-door into the area behind the desk. Gina took the opportunity to empty a liter bottle of saline, creating a puddle a few feet in front of the swinging door. She made no noise until the very end when the bottle made one tiny gurgle.

Harris's light swept over the air above her. Gina froze, flattening herself against the slate floor. Then he went back to jangling the closet door—obviously trying to unlock it, cursing as he went through keys on a ring.

She placed an electrode pad on each side of the half-door. She only had ten feet of wire to work with, but she inched her way backward until she'd used it all, hoping the shadows would hide most of her work.

When she looked back she couldn't see anything except a black void—hopefully Harris wouldn't shine his flashlight down at the floor. The LifePaks were already charged and ready to go—all she'd need to do was hit a button on each. When the time was right.

Harris had the door open and was hauling a man from the closet. As the flashlight angled over him, she saw it was Tillman—gagged with a length of gauze and his hands bound in front of him. His toupee hung by a few strands, looking like he'd grown a second head—one bald and the other an orangutan pelt with a cheap bleach job.

Damn, that changed everything. She tried to work the physics problem in her mind, but there were too many variables. She had no choice but to play it out. The fate of the entire hospital rested on it.

Harris pushed Tillman through the swinging half-door. The CEO went sprawling, stumbling into the wall, then sliding down it to sit on the floor, looking stunned.

Good, that got him out of the way. Hopefully far enough. She had to stop Harris before he grabbed Tillman again. Which hadn't been part of her plan—of course, it wasn't like anything she planned seemed to go right. What was Lydia always telling her was the key to life in the ER? Improvisation—Gina had had more than her fill of it today.

She stood and turned the otoscope on. "Hold it, Harris."

His light hit her square in the face. She squinted but could still see enough to play her part. "You. The secretary. Or actually—Dr. Freeman, I presume?"

Gina raised her gun. "Drop the radio and your gun."

He regarded her. Then laughed. "Tillman told me all about you, Dr. Regina Freeman. Poor little rich girl working here, hoping to win Mommy and Daddy's approval. You hid like a coward when your boyfriend was shot. You're not going to shoot me."

Every fiber, every nerve and cell in her body screamed for her to run and hide, but Gina held her ground, the hand holding the gun shaking uncontrollably. No need to pretend to be scared, she was terrified.

"You have no idea what I'm capable of." Even more frightening—*she* had no idea what she was capable of.

"Put the gun down." He took another step forward. One foot in the saline puddle. Just one more step . . .

The auditorium doors crashed open. Jerry ran out, coming from Gina's right side. "Drop it!"

He held a gun. His Beretta. His *empty* Beretta.

Damn it, he was going to ruin everything and get himself killed in the process. "Get out of here, Jerry!" Gina shouted.

Harris stepped sideways, into the center of the saline, as he turned to cover them both. Then he laughed and resolutely turned his back to Jerry and aimed at Gina. "Put the gun down, Detective Boyle. Unless you want to watch your girlfriend die."

Jerry took another step into the lobby, coming perilously close to the puddle.

"Stop, Jerry. Go. Now!"

Harris laughed. "There's nowhere for him to go. Nowhere to run. Nowhere to hide."

Jerry, confused, stared at Gina. She couldn't try to warn him, not while Harris was watching. To her relief, he lowered his gun and took a step backward. Hopefully far enough—not like Gina had ever tried this particular experiment before.

"Drop the gun, Gina," Harris said.

She held the gun out in front of her, moving in slow motion as she squatted and placed it on the floor, skidding it away from them both. As Harris's gaze flicked to follow the movement of the gun, she pressed the buttons on both LifePaks hidden at her feet, releasing all the current at once.

Sparks flew from the defibrillator pads. Harris screamed and jerked, his body jackknifing into a bizarre salute. Smoke billowed from his feet and hands. His gun careened across the floor into the dark. Then he fell forward, landing with a thud in the saline.

The stench of ozone, burned flesh, and blood filled the air, mingling with the crackling noises coming from the puddle.

"Don't move," Gina called out to Jerry, trying to find him with the otoscope, which now flickered as weakly as a firefly. "Don't go near the water—it will still be charged."

Jerry had backed up against the wall. "Is he dead?"

"No way of checking until the current dissipates. What were you thinking, waving that gun around? You knew you had no bullets."

Jerry shook his head as if bullets were meaningless. "You okay?"

Gina skirted around the puddle and collapsed in his arms.

Lydia came sprinting around the corner from the ER, holding an industrial-sized flashlight, feathers flying from one arm, her body caked with snow, and smelling, Gina wrinkled her nose, like dead fish.

"Gina, Jerry, are you okay?" Lydia shone her light around, taking in Harris's body. "I take it that's one of the bad guys? Any idea how many more there are?" She held her gun at the ready.

"Amanda and Nora are in the auditorium with the other hostages."

"South African's down," Jerry put in.

"I think that's everyone," Gina said. "Unless there are still men searching upstairs."

"The police will be here soon; they can take care of them." Lydia nodded to Harris. "You sure he's beyond helping?"

"If you're gonna help anyone, help Lucas," Amanda said, hauling Lucas into the circle of light. She had her gun in her free hand, slipping it into the sash of her dress when she saw only friendlies waiting for her. Lucas had blood dripping from his arm and was leaning heavily against her. "He's hurt."

"What happened?" Lydia asked as she rushed to help.

"I think—I think I was shot," Lucas said in a stunned voice. "I didn't feel anything—not until I looked down and saw all the blood." His voice trailed off and he slumped against Amanda who propped him up against the auditorium door, scattered light streaming through it.

"Maybe I shouldn't have moved him. He doesn't do well with blood. Keeps fainting." Amanda told them, glaring at them as if daring them to scoff. She and Lydia helped Lucas down to the floor, and his eyes fluttered open once more. "He was a hero, saved a lot of people."

Lydia made quick work of stripping Lucas's lab coat off and tearing his shirtsleeve to assess the damage. "Hate to say it, Lucas, but it's only a flesh wound."

"Really?" He seemed embarrassed. "Hurts like hell."

"You'll be fine," Amanda said. "I'll take good care of you." She handed Lydia a radio. "I called upstairs. No one has heard or seen any bad guys since they came through looking for you, so I think the coast is clear."

Gina turned to look inside the auditorium. Nora was

rousing people and herding them toward the doors, despite the fact that hanging from her wrists were two cut plastic handcuffs.

"All right, everyone, let's get to work," Gina said to the hospital workers streaming through the doors. "We need to unblock the exits to the floors upstairs, check on all the patient wards, triage anyone who needs immediate attention."

Lydia smiled at her and Gina stopped. "What?"

"Nothing. Just that was exactly what I was about to say. Good work, Gina."

Gina smiled back. It was the nicest thing Lydia had ever said to her.

"You guys look like hell," Lydia continued. "Why don't you find a warm corner and some blankets?"

Jerry held his arm out to Gina like an old-fashioned courtier inviting her to dance. She hooked her arm through his and turned to leave the auditorium and the chaos behind.

"You're not going anywhere!"

Harris, one hand blackened and burned, his hair standing straight up, smoke still steaming from his clothing, had climbed to his feet, holding his radio in his hand.

Jerry raised his Beretta—and then his eyes went wide as he realized that it was empty. He lunged in front of Gina, placing his body between her and Harris.

From the corner of her eye, Gina saw Lydia reach with her left hand, reaching for her gun. "No, don't," she yelled. "That radio is a detonator."

"That's right," Harris said, wobbling a bit. One eye was milky white, and he seemed to have a hard time focusing. But he didn't need to see in order to incinerate them all. "I go, you go, we all go. Happy New Year's!"

They stared in numb disbelief as Harris pressed a button on the radio.

Nothing happened. No explosion, no fireworks, no smoke alarms, no *whoosh* of a fireball.

Harris frowned, glanced down at the radio. Jerry used that flicker of distraction to make his move. He rushed Harris, his unbalanced gait sending him tumbling into the other man. Amanda and Lydia quickly joined in, prying Harris's hand from the radio. Gina scooped it up and backed away from the melee.

"It should've worked, it should've worked," Harris kept muttering.

"Check him for any other weapons," Lydia told Amanda.

The lights came on.

Everyone hushed for a moment, holding their breath, waiting to see if a wall of fire accompanied the return of power.

"Ladies and gentlemen," Trey's voice boomed over the intercom, "I give you the miracle of electricity. And since the time is now one minute past midnight, Happy New Year's."

But that wasn't the most surprising miracle of the evening. When Gina turned around, she spotted a large black man dressed in a snowmobile suit and flanked by two other men storming down the corridor toward them.

"Regina Freeman!" he bellowed. "Why did I learn of your mother's accident from a damned onboard computer instead of my own flesh and blood? And would someone tell me where the hell my wife is?"

TWENTY-SIX

Monday, January 3

LAROSE WAS MAKING GOOD PROGRESS—SHE'D EX-
pect no less of herself, of course. In fact, as Gina watched
her mother maneuver through the parallel bars, listening
intently to the physical therapist's instructions, she had to
admit that if LaRose set unreasonably high standards for
everyone else in the world, she sure as hell didn't cut herself any slack.

"Good work." Gina praised her mother once the therapist released LaRose and returned her to her wheelchair.

"Really?"

Gina was taken aback to see that her mother appeared
surprised by her praise. Maybe it was a two-way street.

"They told me you were up here," Moses boomed as
he pushed through the doors, regal in his John Phillips of
London suit. The room seemed to shrink with him in it,
as if he used up all the oxygen and needed all the space.
"Are you done already?" he asked LaRose, favoring her
with a kiss on the cheek. "Sure you don't need more?

We want you out of this place"—he dismissed the Angels staff and facility with a one-shouldered shrug—"as soon as possible."

"She's doing fine, Moses. Believe me, she's pushing herself as hard as she should. We don't want her blood pressure to go sky-high."

Moses barely glanced at Gina, ignoring her as if his only child didn't exist, taking her place behind LaRose's chair and pushing it toward the door.

Gina watched him go, no longer angry—the years had wrung that out of her—but suddenly sad, thinking about the potential father-daughter relationship that both she and Moses had lost out on. As they moved toward the door, she expected LaRose to smile, basking in the glow of his attention.

LaRose surprised her, yanking on the wheelchair brake and stopping before they could reach the door.

Gina jogged over. "Are you okay?"

"Tell her, Moses."

Moses remained silent, his gaze hovering somewhere between Venus and Mars on the horizon, far away from Angels and the concerns of mere mortals.

"We're going to establish a scholarship in the name of your two friends, Ken Rosen and Jim Lazarov," LaRose said, barely slurring her words at all. "We—I—want to thank them for saving my life."

Gina was stunned. No press conference to make the announcement? No media event complete with Moses's favored politicians and celebrities?

"That's great," she finally said. "Thank you, LaRose." LaRose nodded toward Moses and Gina relented. "Thanks to both of you. Ken would have liked that."

She had to blink back tears at the mention of Ken's name—too many emotions still swirling around that open wound. LaRose patted her hand, her own eyes glistening.

"They aren't the only ones I should thank," she said. "You belong here, Gina."

"She does not," Moses thundered, startling the physical therapist and her next patient, the room's other occupants. He lowered his voice, still not talking to Gina but rather directing his comments to LaRose. "No child of mine is going to work in this, this cesspool—"

LaRose snapped her head up, stealing her husband's thunder with her glare. And then she said something Gina never dreamed she'd ever hear. "Shut up, Moses."

NORA GLANCED UP AS THE SURGICAL RESIDENT dropped the first patient's chart on the clinic nurses' desk. "Can I help you, Dr. Cochran?"

"Nora." Seth did a double take, his eyes growing wide as he took in her outfit, making Nora especially glad that she'd dug out her old nursing uniform, complete with tight-fitting skirt and white pantyhose. "What are you doing here?"

She grinned, loving his surprise. He'd been dreading today, returning to work only to drudge away in the surgical follow-up clinic. Especially since, with the city still digging out from the New Year's storm, the clinic was certain to be slower than normal.

She lowered her chin and batted her eyelashes demurely. "Don't you think I can handle suture removals and dressing changes?"

"But you hate the clinic."

Nora slipped out from behind the desk, glanced around to make sure no one could see them, and then grabbed him by the lapels of his lab coat and pulled him to her. "Depends on which doctor is working. You know those surgical residents can be so bossy and so—"

He kissed her, his hands squeezing her hips as their bodies rocked together. "So . . . what? Intelligent, handsome—?"

"Hmmm . . . not sure about that."

He tickled her belly. She twisted away only to have him snag her by her waistband and pull her back. He kissed her again, making sure to take the time to do a thorough job. Her cheeks heated—she never had done anything like this, not at work. Tillman would have had her fired if he knew. Too bad the obnoxious CEO had been fired himself after the board heard of his gross mishandling of the New Year's crisis.

Besides, after the events of the past few weeks, she'd finally learned not to waste a single second worrying about the rules. People came before silly rules and regulations—and, of all the people in her life, Seth came first.

"How about sexy?" he asked, his breath brushing against the small hairs on her neck as he tasted her. "Do you think surgical residents are sexy?"

A soft sound caught in her throat. "Oh yeah. Definitely sexy."

"That's good. Now, let's go lance a boil."

She pushed him away, laughing. "Ooh, right. Because there's nothing sexier than draining pus with the man you love."

"Hey, say that again, I like the sound of that."

"Draining pus?"

"No. The other part."

She pursed her lips as if she couldn't remember the words, turning to grab an instrument tray and packing gauze. "Oh, you mean the part about the man I love?"

He took her hand as they walked down the empty corridor. "Yeah, that part. That's my favorite part."

"Mine too."

IT TURNED OUT THAT "MR. BLACK" WAS ACTUALLY Felix Moreno, a high-powered mover and shaker in

California politics who had maneuvered a number of men into office. Along with them had come power and influence—all of which stood to be lost if a certain thirty-year-old video ever came to light.

Finding the video hadn't been hard, once Lydia remembered to think like her mother. Maria with her fairy tales, spinning gold from the stars as they slept on the beach, making each charm on Lydia's bracelet—the only thing Maria had ever given her daughter—come to life in her bedtime stories.

In the end, the charms were the key, literally. The bracelet had a pair of ballet toe shoes, a cathedral, a heart, the Golden Gate Bridge, and a brass key.

The Golden Gate Bridge, for San Francisco. Toe shoes, for the ballet, though Lydia doubted that Maria had ever really danced. But across the street from the building where the San Francisco Ballet performed, the Metropolitan Opera, was City Hall. Which looked exactly like the charm Lydia had always thought was a church cathedral. Except that on the bottom of the charm was carved the number 308, which wasn't the address for either City Hall or the Ballet.

"But you said she talked about taking lessons," Trey said. "Maybe she meant the ballet school. It's here on the map."

Lydia looked where he pointed. The January wind here in San Francisco had the same knife-edged chill as it did in Pittsburgh, but to Lydia the Pacific air felt cleaner, more refreshing. As if it were trying to scour her clean rather than chill her to the bone and steal her warmth.

From where they were at City Hall, the school was only a block away, so they walked to the school. Now you could see only the dome of City Hall.

"The address here is four fifty-five," Lydia said. They walked down Franklin Street to the end of the block. The school stood on the corner behind them, and if they looked to their right there was an open plaza that revealed a frontal view of City Hall.

And directly across from them, at 308 Fulton Street, was Hart Bank and Trust. Could the heart charm stand for the Hart Bank? A long shot, but totally in keeping with the way Maria's mind had worked. And besides, there was still the small brass key unaccounted for.

At least, it seemed like a long shot, until Lydia went inside the bank and spoke to the manager. It appeared that Hart Bank and Trust specialized in what the manager termed *legacy preservation*. As he verified Lydia's credentials—which turned out to require the charm bracelet that matched faded Polaroid photos he had in a file that bore no names—he explained that people from all over the world stored their valuables with Hart's because they could prepay for up to one hundred years and access to the safe-deposit boxes could be controlled by a variety of unconventional means, such as the use of a child's charm bracelet.

"We're the only company I know of that continues to allow its patrons such flexibility," he said with pride. "As long as your key fits the box, of course."

Which it did.

So, less than an hour later, Lydia was delivering the thirty-year-old video to an FBI agent that Janet Kwon had contacted. The FBI had already expressed a great deal of interest in Felix and his accomplices, and the Pittsburgh police were cooperating with them fully.

"I feel like she's finally been allowed to rest," she told Trey as they drove from San Francisco to Plumas, the Indian reservation just outside Reno where Maria—Martha—had grown up. No one there would remember her—she had no relatives left—but Lydia felt an urge to walk the same streets as Maria, to see the place that had made her who and what she was.

They arrived late and checked into a motel on the outskirts of Reno—quieter than the ones near the casinos. Most of the long drive had been spent in silence, but it had felt like a good silence. One full of promise and understanding rather than the angry silences that had punctuated the past few weeks.

Lydia thought she might finally be ready to share her final secret with Trey. She'd been selfish to wait, she knew, but she needed time to think everything through to be certain that she knew exactly what she wanted—which had been silly, because everything she wanted was right in front of her.

She changed for bed and stood in the open bathroom door as Trey washed his face and brushed his teeth.

"I have two questions for you."

He kept brushing, spit, then said, "Sure."

Tugging in her breath as if it were a lifeline, Lydia plunged right to the heart of the matter. "Knowing who I really am, where I came from, do you want to marry me?"

He gagged and spun around to her, toothbrush hanging in the air, toothpaste drool slipping down his chin. "Don't kid about that."

"I'm not kidding."

Trey's whoop filled the air as he grabbed her and spun her around, not even jarring her cast. "Yes! Of course, God yes!"

Finally he set her back on her feet, then frowned, scrutinizing her. "We can do it now, tonight, today, right here!"

She laughed. "Guess that depends on the answer to the second question. Do you want a boy or girl?"

He stumbled, off balance, knocking his elbow into the counter top, toppling his shaving kit into the sink and not noticing. "For real? You're pregnant?"

He crumbled to his knees, cradling her belly, laying his

head against it, listening for the heartbeat. Tears shone in his eyes, stained her shirt, rolled freely without embarrassment down his cheeks.

Lydia ran her fingers through his hair, clutching him, loving his warmth against her body. She wasn't crying. For the first time in her life she had no reason to: She felt safe, secure, stable. She had a family, friends, a man who loved her, a home.

And no one could ever take it away from her. This was Maria's legacy.

"Thank you," she mouthed into the air, not knowing who was listening but for the first time in her life confident that someone, somewhere was.

"AMANDA, WHAT ARE YOU DOING HERE SO EARLY?" the dermatology nurse practitioner asked as she joined Amanda in the otherwise empty clinic. "We don't start until nine. Then we'll do consults on the ward, have lunch here—don't worry about bringing your own, there's always some drug company sending food—and then clinic in the afternoon. Really, you need to relax. This is dermatology, we don't believe in emergencies."

Amanda stared. She'd thought that she wasn't cut out for the life of an ER doc, but after her month in the PICU she'd discovered that she liked being able to change the course of events when the worst thing possible was happening. A nine-to-five life in a clinic suddenly seemed boring in comparison.

The nurse turned to hold the door as a caterer wheeled in a steaming tray of food. "Yum, pancakes from Pamela's. Oh, Amanda, you're going to love this rotation."

I don't think so, Amanda thought as her phone chimed with an e-mail message. Lucas with an update on their research project, as well as pictures from her mother of bridesmaid dresses. Amanda forwarded the photos on to Lydia, Nora, and Gina.

A few moments later there was another chime. An e-mail from Lydia. With a picture of her and Trey holding a bouquet of roses under a canopy that read JUST MAR-RIED. What?! Wow!

The text read: *Sorry you couldn't have the first wedding. Dresses look great, but make mine maternity. Having fun, Lydia*

"I COULDN'T BELIEVE IT," GINA TOLD JERRY AS SHE gathered all his stuff, ready to take him home with her once Lucas finished the paperwork. "LaRose actually told him to shut up, and he did. My father, the great Moses Freeman, speechless. Can you imagine?"

"Wish I could've been there," he said, but his voice was distant as he watched her from the bed. She tried to ignore his discomfort, but she couldn't deny that she felt it as well. "It was a miracle, that's what it was," she continued, emptying the contents of his closet into a tote bag. "And she's going to establish a scholarship in Jim and Ken's—" She couldn't finish, had to stop and gulp down sudden tears.

Dropping the bag, she backed away from the closet, one hand covering her face. Jerry snagged her arm and pulled her onto the bed, sitting with her back to him.

"It's not easy," he said, one hand clumsily stroking her arm. "People died for us. Living with that—"

He faltered but it was easy to fill in the blanks. "That sacrifice?"

He nodded. "Never easy."

"You've been through it before?" How had she never asked him this before? She'd always avoided asking the tough questions—afraid of the answers, she guessed. Wanting to protect their perfect fairy-tale romance, with herself at the heart of it, the poor little rich girl who desperately needed to be loved.

Pathetic. Gina swiped her tears away with her fist, then turned to look at him.

Jerry didn't nod, but she knew his answer was yes by the pain that filled his eyes as he looked past her, staring into the dark recesses of his memory.

"There was a hostage taker," he finally said. "Had his ex's kid."

Jerry squeezed his eyes shut. His lips clamped tight and his jaw muscles were working so hard that she knew he was swallowing tears. When he opened his eyes, they spilled down his cheeks. "Sorry. Big baby. Big blubber-baby."

"It's okay, you don't have to tell me." She'd known something awful had happened to make him leave the SWAT team and his position of hostage negotiator, but she'd had no idea it was this painful.

"Want to." He heaved in a breath. "I was cocky. Stupid. Thought I had the guy talked down."

She intertwined her fingers in his, not wanting to break the spell. The distant memory was obviously—if painfully— easier for him to remember clearly than new memories. This was the most lucid she'd seen him since the shooting.

"Went to meet the guy. Promised to give me the kid. Had my team behind me. Guy came out and—" He swallowed hard. "And he threw the kid. Off the porch. Onto cement."

Gina gasped, working hard to blink back her own tears. "What happened?"

"I dove for the kid. But that cleared his line of fire. My team—my guys . . ." He swiped his face along his sleeve. "Sandy got hit, it's why he left SWAT. And Brody, my part—my partner, he didn't—he didn't make it."

"The kid?"

"Didn't make it. I messed up my shoulder. That's okay. I didn't think I could go back to SWAT, not after that. Sandy maybe could have. I dunno. I just couldn't get, stop seeing—" He cleared his throat and wet his lips. "That's when I started—" His forehead furrowed as he searched for the word. He held his fingers up, mimed clicking a picture.

"When you began your photography?" she supplied.

"Yeah. Trying to—" He wiped his palm across the air like cleaning a slate.

"You wanted to erase the memories. Replace them with something new."

He nodded. Squeezed her hand. Nodded again, wanting her to understand this was important. Did he really think taking up a new hobby would make her forget what Ken had done for her? For them?

"Did it work?" she asked, her voice tiny and tentative.

He shook his head. That wasn't the lesson, she realized. He pulled her against his chest, held her tight, his tears warming her cheek. "No. Found something better. You."

Gina nodded, too overwhelmed to attempt words. Finally she understood what he meant. Life was the answer. Living and loving and never forgetting what was really important.

Ken would have approved.

Gina's tears mingled with Jerry's and she never wanted to release him. But she realized that she needed to let him know that she totally understood; she needed to tell him not just in words but in actions.

She removed the ring from the chain around her neck, placed it in his palm, and squeezed his fingers tight around it. "Do you remember this?"

He fingered it like a blind man, shaking his head. For the first time that she could remember she saw true fear in his eyes. "No."

"Ask me, Jerry."

"No."

"Then I'll ask you." She closed both her hands over his, the ring caught between. "Jerry Boyle, will you do me the honor of marrying me?"

His face tightened and he turned his head away. "I can't."

"Why the hell not?" She stood before him, hands on her hips. Old Gina would have pouted, but instead she now waited for his response.

"Gina. How could I? You're so—" His voice was choked. "So smart, so beautiful. You could have any man you wanted. I can't let you, I can't find, can't promise . . ." Pain mixed with frustration as he fought for the elusive words. He ended by simply hanging his head and shaking it.

She sat beside him on the bed, then reached for his hand again. "Jerry, I know there are no guarantees, and yes, that scares me. But I'm more afraid of a life without you. Because if I can have any man I want, then I choose you, Jerry. I choose you." Gina drew in her breath and did the bravest thing she'd ever done in her life. She said the words. "I love you."

Jerry stared into her eyes for a long time, longer than she could hold her breath. Then he smiled—a real smile, just like the old Jerry. His hand trembled, and she had to help him guide the ring onto her finger where it belonged. By the time it was in place they were both crying and giggling and fumbling for words.

They sat together, staring at her outstretched hand. Gina felt like she could do anything with this man at her side, like she could be anyone she wanted to be, and most of all, she felt she'd earned the one thing she'd been searching for all her life: someone to love, cherish, protect, and care for.

"This is forever, you know," Gina said. "I don't believe in divorce. You're not getting out of this until one of us is dead and gone."

Jerry jerked his head up at her words—she didn't mean

for them to sound frivolous, not like Old Gina. She was dead serious. After what they'd been through, she needed a guarantee.

Even better, she wanted him to know that she was giving *him* one. New Gina kept her promises. And her vows.

"Forever is a long, long time. That okay with you?" she asked him.

He laughed again and let out a crazy bellow of a whoop that brought the nurses running. "Forever isn't even a start. Not for me and you."

NOTE TO READERS:

As you know, Critical Condition *is the finale of the Angels of Mercy series, which made it both fun and painful to write.*

The way these four characters have evolved over the course of the series has surprised even me! Like you have, I've fallen in love with all of the behind-the-scenes action going on at Angels.

So, the first people I'd like to thank are you, the readers who have embraced these characters, who searched out my books even when they were difficult to find, and who have written me such wonderful letters telling me about how my books helped you get through tough times or have inspired or empowered you. Surely that is the most gratifying thing any writer can hear from her audience! All I can say is that your notes have inspired me.

There are many others who helped make the Angels series. I'd like to take this opportunity to thank them all, including: Shannon Jamieson Vazquez, my editor; Leslie Gelbman, Susan Allison, and all of the wonderful folks at Berkley/Jove who helped bring these books to life; my agent, Barbara Poelle; and my critique partners who keep me honest: Toni McGee Causey, Kendel Flaum, KJ Howe, Carolyn Males, and Lois Winston. From the bottom of my heart, thanks! I couldn't have done this without you!

My research (don't try any of this at home!) was aided by Laurie Weaver RN, BSN, EMT-P (EMS Coordinator,

Wooster Community Hospital) and the Wooster Division of Fire EMS professionals. Also thanks to Carl Causey, for helping with the penguins, and to Rob Winston, my technical adviser.

Astute readers will notice many movie homages in Critical Condition—*I'm a huge movie buff, and I hope you enjoy finding references, overt and covert, to some of my favorite films. If you want to search them out yourself they include:* Die Hard *(of course!),* Raiders of the Lost Ark, Rear Window, Terminator II, The Birds, Psycho, *and* First Blood. *Enjoy!*

Finally, as always, please let me know your thoughts about Critical Condition *or any of my books by writing to me at cj@cjlyons.net or contacting me through my website: www.cjlyons.net. My new project, cowritten with the great and wonderful Erin Brockovich (I know, how cool is that?!?) should be hitting the stands in early 2011.*

In the meantime, thanks for reading!
CJ

FROM NATIONAL BESTSELLING AUTHOR

CJ Lyons

WARNING SIGNS

On rotation at Pittsburgh's Angels of Mercy Medical Center and struggling to finish medical school, Amanda Mason can't afford to make any mistakes—or to reveal a troubling secret. Mysterious symptoms that defy diagnosis have been affecting her performance, and as she struggles to keep control, the only person who seems to notice is the irritatingly observant— and sexy—Dr. Lucas Stone.

But when two patients who experienced the same strange symptoms die, and another slips into a coma, Amanda realizes the clock is ticking on her own survival...

penguin.com

M496T0609